Acclaim for Books by Kendy Pearson

In Tempest Winds tells a captivating tale of family, war, love, and hope. Kendy Pearson skillfully brings the turbulent days of the US Civil War to life with historical accuracy, poignant description, and a cast of characters whose lives are tossed by the tempest winds many of us can relate to. With everything that matters at stake for Zander and Lola, readers will not want to put the book down until they've read the very last page.

Michelle Shocklee,
Award-winning author of
Appalachian Song and *All We Thought We Knew*

In Tempest Winds is a beautiful story of faith lost and found again, of trauma and redemption, of family pulling together in impossible times. I will be reading more of Kendy Pearson's work!

Shannon McNear,
author of Daughters of the Lost Colony series

Kendy Pearson brings to life the Kanawha Valley's explosive Civil War history in this multi-faceted jewel of a tale inspired by true events. Endurance, faith, and love shine through **When the Mountains Wept**, the first book in what is sure to be a stellar series.

Laura Frantz,
Christy Award-winning
author of *The Rose and the Thistle*

I could not put this book down. I had no idea what I was in for. It was beautiful. It was heart wrenching. It was so perfect! (*When the Mountains Wept*)

Redeeming Lit Podcast

Gifted storyteller Kendy Pearson makes ***When the Mountains Wept*** spring to life with her vivid storytelling, every character so expertly sculpted that I found myself missing them when I closed the cover. Augusta and James stole my heart, and I rooted for them from page one until the very end.

Karen Barnett,
Award winning author of *When Stone Wings Fly* and the Vintage National Park Novels

Kendy Pearson's devotion to history and faith shines through every chapter of this novel. Brimming with heart, ***When Heaven Thunders*** is an emotionally charged journey for characters and readers alike. A must-read for fans of well-researched, immersive Christian historical fiction.

Jocelyn Green,
Christy Award-winning author of *A River Between Us*

When Heaven Thunders is a Civil War romance that beautifully weaves historical detail with deep emotional resonance. The characters are richly drawn, and the narrative unfolds at a deliberate pace, allowing readers to fully immerse themselves in the era and the heart-touching journey of the protagonists. A captivating read!

Lynnette Bonner,
USA Today Bestselling author of

the Wyldhaven series, The Shepherd's Heart series,
the Oregon Promise series, and more

❧

It is refreshing to read a Christian based story line that has the courage to step out of the caricature expectations of faith-based writing and be real about war, human nature, romance, and Christian living.

Ken Pratt,
author of the Bestselling
Matt Bannister series

❧

Even though I researched this era extensively for my own historical novel, I found new insights and information as this story follows the intrigue, dangers, and complications of dedicated people fighting against the injustices toward a disadvantaged population. ***FIRES OF INJUSTICE*** combines beautiful writing with an important part of history that shouldn't ever be forgotten. A real page-turner!

Heather B. Moore,
USA Today bestselling author of
The Paper Daughters of Chinatown

❧

In ***FIRES OF INJUSTICE***, Kendy Pearson brings to life a little-known chapter of American history and tells a compelling story of courage in the face of injustice. This engaging and deeply emotional novel follows brave women and men determined to protect the vulnerable, even amid deep prejudice. I couldn't put it down!

Karen Barnett,
award-winning author of
Through Water and Stone

Also by
Kendy Pearson

April 2026

A story of resilience, redemption, and love, **FIRES OF INJUSTICE** blazes with the courage of those who dared to stand against the darkness of America's Forgotton War.

West Virginia: Born of Rebellion's Storm 3

IN
TEMPEST
WINDS

Heart of History
an imprint of
PEAR BLOSSOM BOOKS

In Tempest Winds

Copyright © 2025 by Kendy Pearson
All rights reserved.
No Scraping

No portion of this book may be reproduced in any form without written permission from the publisher or author, except as permitted by U.S. copyright law. No part of this publication may be stored in a retrieval system or transmitted in any form or by any means—for example, electronic, photocopy, recording—without the prior written permission of the publisher. The only exception is brief quotations in printed reviews. No A.I. scraping.

Published by Pear Blossom Books, Dundee, Oregon, U.S.A.

Scripture taken from the King James Version of the Bible (public domain)

Publisher's Note: This novel is a work of fiction. Names, characters, places, and incidents are either products of the author's imagination or used fictitiously. Because this is a work of historical reconstruction; the appearance of certain historical figures, places, and incidents are therefore inevitable.

ISBN 979-8-9899317-2-9 (paperback)
Library of Congress Control Number (LCCN): 2025914238

Cover Design by Mountain Creek Books, LLC

Subjects: Novel / Historical Fiction / Christian Historical Fiction / American Civil War / West Virginia breaks from Virginia / Christian Historical Fiction inspired by true events / Appalachian Historical Fiction / Military Fiction / U.S. History / West Virginia History

It is not the light that we need, but the fire.
It is not the gentle shower, but the thunder.
We need the storm,
the whirlwind,
and the earthquake.

Frederick Douglass
July 5, 1852

1861–1865

Rebellion's tempest swept the land
and a state was born of a nation torn.
West Virginia: a Child of the Storm

And he said, Come.
And when Peter was come down out of the ship,
he walked on the water, to go to Jesus.
But when he saw the wind boisterous,
he was afraid; and beginning to sink . . .

Matthew 14: 29–30

One

CHARLESTON, WEST VIRGINIA

April 1864

Cantankerous weather or not—that finish line was his!

Zander Dabney laughed as mud pelted his cheek. Leaden skies spat great drops, and a frigid wind showed spring the door—but no matter. He tucked his head lower, squinting as hair whipped across his eyes.

Settling the reins against Rampart's pulsing flesh, he yielded to the roan gelding's instincts. The shouts of rowdy spectators disappeared, replaced by thrumming hooves with a rhythm as smooth and familiar as his own heartbeat. The horse skirted the ancient sugar tree in a graceful list, kicking soggy turf high into the air as he angled back toward the finish.

"Atta boy," Zander crooned. "Patience, old son, patience."

Throwing a quick look over his shoulder, he gauged the trailing challenger's distance. Just a mite closer. Come on, Crowder. Closer . . . that's it. *Now!*

Grit salted his smile as he squeezed his knees and shifted his weight. Rampart's powerful legs stretched and his speckled withers quivered with anticipation. The sheer rush of an all-out sprint—horse and rider as one, skimming across the ground, airborne, yet tethered by the brief touch of hoof to earth.

A raucous crowd of soldiers and civilians amassed near the finish line where Paul Skanks waited. His long beard whipped with a gust as he flailed a yellow kerchief in the air.

As the last few seconds ticked by, Zander paired his breath with the cadence of the gelding's chugs. One hand raised in victory, he slipped past Skanks and tugged twice on the reins to grab Rampart's attention. The gelding shook his head and slowed to trot a wide circle. He knew just what to do. He always knew.

"Dabney wins again!" Bass shouted joyously, swiping dark curls from his face. "Collect your winnings, men. A bout of bad luck for one Private Crowder. Maybe next time. Great courage there—going up against the undefeated Private Zander Dabney of Fayette County!"

The boy could sure handle a crowd, Zander would give him that. Henry Bassoom would've made a better city hawker than a German baker. But here he was, stuck in the Fifth West Virginia Cavalry, right along with everybody else.

Zander threw his leg over the cantle and landed on both feet. With a broad sweep of one arm, he bowed to the audience. Rampart deftly extended one front leg and bowed in tandem to enthusiastic laughter and applause.

When Zander turned his back, the great chestnut head butted his shoulder. He feigned ignorance with a shrug. After a third nudge, he rewarded Rampart with a bit of biscuit, saved in his pocket for the occasion.

"Wish my woman was that well behaved!" blustered a bystander.

"If she was, she'd ne'er tolerate the likes of you." A gruff voice sailed over the merriment of the crowd.

Zander remounted and walked Rampart through the dispersing onlookers. He patted the sleek wet shoulder. "Good boy. I knew you could beat him." The horse responded with a contented whicker.

He complimented the horse on a job well done every which way he could think of. It wasn't the words that mattered, after all. It was more that he needed to talk, and he was pretty sure Rampart needed to hear his master's voice.

A broad-shouldered man in a velvet derby approached, admiration sparking in his eyes. "A race well run, son." He ran a hand along the horse's neck. "Fine piece of horseflesh you got here. Don't suppose you would consider parting with this steed?"

"Rampart's not for sale, sir." How often had he fielded that question?

"Humph. You can't blame a man for asking now, can you?"

"No, sir. Nothin' wrong with asking."

"Dabney, huh? Where have I heard the name?" His brow wrinkled and his grizzled mustache jerked like a dying frog.

Here it comes.

"Ah, yes . . . you related to that guerilla fighter Dabney? What do they call him?"

Again.

"Dragon killer . . . something like that."

"Dragon Slayer, sir. And yes, that would be my older brother, Fin." He swiped his kerchief across his face and dismounted.

The gentleman clapped Zander's shoulder. "Well, you must be proud. Bet you can put those bushwhackers in their place yourself. Probably shoot as well as you ride, too."

"No, sir, I don't."

"And you'll likely be joining up with those Blazer Scouts real soon, too, I expect."

"No, sir. I won't be."

"And—" His chin disappeared like a turkey's. "What's that?"

"I won't be joining Captain Blazer's men, sir. If you'll excuse me, I've got some things I gotta do." Now that was a record. A whole three minutes after winning a race before somebody reminded him—he was just Fin Dabney's little brother.

"Dabney! People are waiting to tell you congratulations." Bass pointed out a gathering of soldiers. "And to say thank you for making them some money."

"You thank them for me, all right? How much did we make?" Zander pulled a hoof pick from his pocket and lifted Rampart's front foot. He dug out a wad of grass. "Mmm?"

"You made thirty dollars." Bass collected a fistful of coins and bills from his hat.

Zander raised an eyebrow and studied the forage cap. "You sure you ain't dipping outta there?"

Bass sputtered. Zander pounded him on the back. "I'm only funnin' with you." He chuckled. "You shoulda seen your face. You don't close that mouth, a wasper's gonna fly in."

His friend frowned. "You are not as funny as you think you are, Dabney."

"Just take your half and put mine in the bag." Zander started for the paddock with Rampart close behind.

He figured Bass was too serious to be the thieving sort, and that's why he trusted his friend with his savings. Some would call it winnings, but that sounded a touch shady. The money was his savings, so he called it such. Four months so far, and the funds for his future were accumulating nicely.

Rampart nibbled at his sleeve. "Not paying enough attention to you, am I, boy?" He hadn't meant to keep his meanderings to himself. Most days, he would ramble on and on to his four-legged confidant. Horses didn't compare you to your brother. They merely nodded their understanding and agreement to your plight. Yes, sir. And their soulful eyes spoke a measure of wisdom that was hard to ignore. Better company than most humans, too, no doubt about it.

Zander turned out Rampart after a thorough brushing and set out for the stables. Tomorrow he would request a furlough. It wouldn't do to be this close to his family and not even share a meal with them. And it wouldn't do for any of them to hear about his racing. Some things a body just knows.

The dark clouds had scooted farther east, settling for the evening over the Alleghenies. Blinking into the clearing sky, he smiled with a keen satisfaction. A day well spent, all in all. As much as he hated making the occasional enemy of a disgruntled loser, his racing was a means to an end. Wide blue skies and all the land he could claim waited for him out West, and he was not about to let anything get in his way.

Let that limelight shine on Fin for now. Zander would make a name for himself, too. Soon as this war was over, he would earn himself a reputation as the best horseman west of the Ohio. Folks would talk about Zander Dabney, the horseman for years after his brother was back to being a nobody farmer, just fighting off critters in the crops instead of Rebel guerillas.

Orders.

Zander dropped onto his cot and stared up at the hut ceiling, hopes of visiting his family trampled to dust. Second day here, and his furlough was denied because of orders. Four long months of garrison duty up at Cumberland, a sudden order to Charleston under General Hayes, and now . . .

"Maybe they will send us to a different garrison." Bass looked up, his hound dog eyes flashing with excitement. "Maybe Gauley Bridge. You would like that, ja?" He dug through his saddlebags, his frustration evident until he finally dumped the contents onto the blanket. He collected a pencil and paper.

"You're writing *another* letter to your family? You're making me look real bad, Bass," Zander teased.

Bass scowled at the jab. "They are surrounded by the enemy, Zander. They are Unionists on Virginia soil. I need to make sure my sister behaves. I worry for Mutter and Vater since I am not there to help. They are not so young now."

Skanks plopped onto one end of Bass's cot, sending the other end to bouncing.

"Ach! What do you think you are doing, Skanks?"

"Same as the Union Army's doing to us. Upsottin' your stuff. I, for one, was thinking on going into town this evening to the Kanawha House for a fine meal and entertainment." He stroked his sparse whiskers right down to the wiry hairs resting on his chest.

Zander grumbled, remembering the family's frantic escape from Charleston and leaving Melinda Jane behind. He'd kicked himself good for following her orders, leaving her stranded to wait out the Rebel occupation. It all worked out in the end, he guessed. But the waiting had been thorny.

He rummaged through his saddlebags for paper—paper he had saved to write all the letters good intentions never quite seemed to get to. "You don't want to go to the Kanawha House, Skanks."

"I don't?"

"It burned to the ground."

"When?"

"Second year of the war, when General Loring took Charleston." Zander touched the stub of a pencil to his tongue. "Anybody got ink?"

"Well, no wonder we got orders. If'n I'd made plans to do something normal, like playing cards, we'd stay put. Just wish I'd known is all."

Bass looked up, his mouth agape. "Skanks, I sometimes wonder how your mind works."

Taps sounded, and Zander shoved the paper and pencil back into his pack. Another loss for good intentions. Hopefully, his family would be more understanding than the Fifth Cavalry.

Two

May, 1864

The whippoorwill's call set Zander's heart to beating a little faster as his senses stirred to the familiar smells and surroundings. Two and a half years seemed another lifetime ago.

Apple blossoms. He grinned and sucked in a long breath. No mistaking it. He scanned the area and spotted the ancient apple tree, bent and mangled with age. And close enough to toss a dirt clod and send the white petals sailing to the ground like snowflakes.

Up ahead, the leaves of a silver maple winked in the sunshine, bidding him to stop and sit a spell. Its thick trunk stood sentinel where his company turned off the pike to march to the supply depot. The farm was only five miles up the road. Why, he could just about make a run for it, sit on his very own bed, and return before the column of troops moved on from Gauley Bridge.

But home wouldn't be the same. According to Fin, bushwhackers took it over right after the family fled to the safety of Charleston. He likely wouldn't see the farm again until after the war. Best get his mind on something else.

Sergeant McNeer trotted alongside the column, hat in hand as he smoothed back thinning salt and pepper hair. "We're spending the night at the garrison and taking on more troops. Everyone to remain in their company. In the morning, our next stop is Fayetteville."

"We never did find out where we are going, Sarge." Bass smiled, his ample cheeks squishing his baggy eyes to look somewhat normal. "Can you tell us *now*?"

"Don't think so, Private Bassoom. You might be a spy." His serious eyes drilled into Bass before moving up the line with a wide grin on his face.

Zander chuckled at the scowl on Bass's face. Patience never did find a comfortable chair to sit where his friend was concerned.

He dismounted and scratched under Rampart's mane. "Feels good, don't it, boy?" Walking would feel good, too, and he aimed to walk himself all the way in to camp.

Twisting his shoulders, Zander pulled at the stiff muscles in his back as Rampart plodded along. Seemed almost cruel to be so close to the home place only to be dragged off in a sea of men heading to Fayetteville.

Early on he learned the best way to thwart the boredom of garrison duty was to steal away to his dreams. He could ruminate for hours about a place all his own, bought with his own money and settled with his own labor. Fin had the farm, and his older sister, Augusta, had married a doctor. Likely, they would stay in Charleston. So, he'd raise horses for the Army. Fine, strong horses from good stock.

"Ach, I know that look," Bass said, shaking his head. "You are dreaming of going west, after the war."

"Beats being frustrated, not knowing where we're heading. Beats feeling like a gear in a big ol' come-along—just a piece of machinery."

"We could be heading into battle, Dabney." Bass leaned closer and lowered his voice. "We could be fighting for our very lives in a matter of hours, and you are daydreaming."

Zander fixed his gaze on the hills to the east, an outline he knew from memory.

Bass wouldn't let up. "There is a chance you will not make it out of this war alive, you know."

"Seems pretty unlikely seein's how I've dedicated four months of my life to fighting this Rebellion and haven't laid eyes on a single Reb. I saw more action back home and in Charleston than I have since I donned this uniform."

He had held those memories of that first year at bay just fine until Bass started flapping his jaw. But Bass had a point. Drilling was one thing, but an actual battle? If Fin could do it, so could he. His brother's shadow was mighty big, but somehow, he would find his way clear of it. Maybe one day real soon.

As the morning wore on, the possibility of battle loomed as real as the Alleghenies themselves. By the time they reached Fayetteville, boys from Ohio, Pennsylvania, and West Virginia had swollen the ranks.

As the long roll sounded through General Crook's camp, Zander stood at attention with thousands of others. A thunderous response from the troops roared in his ears and a wave of pride flooded his chest. Bass's lip kicked up on one side, and he pulled his shoulders back, so sure of himself. Skanks stood rigid as a fishing pole, his face a mask of dedication.

Weeks of discontent bowed to a fierce sense of honor. Honor he had not felt since he enlisted. He would serve in this machinery of General Crook's grand mission—whatever it may be. And he would prove his mettle, he could feel it. And his brother would be proud.

∞

A week of days fell away, trodden beneath thousands of hooves and leather soles as the troops marched south through Beckley, then east to Princeton. Battered by a two-day deluge, they reached Confederate Virginia, soggy and spent.

Nary a Rebel had been spotted since leaving Charleston. Word was that General Crook sent his brother's unit, the Blazer Scouts, to Lewisburg to wreak havoc and draw the Confederates' attention away from this expedition.

An unnatural silence settled in the ranks. He craned his neck, scanning the trees on either side of the road. Something was happening up ahead.

As they marched down the Dublin-Pearisburg Turnpike, a color-bearer passed along the column at a strong lope. Saddle and weaponry rustled in his wake as men quickened. They must be close to Dublin by now. Captain Giles followed several yards behind the color bearer, his face grim. He halted, and the sergeants of Company B flocked to him as the column mashed to a halt like a herd of cows.

Bass jarred Zander's arm. "What do you think that is about?"

He shook his head, sitting a little taller in the saddle to ease the growing pressure in his chest.

Sergeant McNeer trotted over. "Ready your arms, boys. We've run into Confederates—General Jenkins. We outnumber them, but they're seasoned. Best we can hope, they're a mite weary. You're fresh, now. We'll fight dismounted, so be on your toes and remember your training. Follow me."

Zander stroked Rampart's mane and silently called on the Almighty for protection—and to pry off the fingers of dread squeezing his windpipe.

Three

CLOYD'S FARM, DUBLIN, VIRGINIA

May 9, 1864

What are they waiting for? Zander eyed his sergeant, aching for the command to move out, open fire—something. Anything. For hours, his unmounted Federal unit had held their position this side of the creek. All the while, artillery bantered from both sides like two schoolboys flexing their muscles.

Earth erupted to his right, spurring his heartbeat to a gallop. A body sprawled on the ground, and a soldier prayed, motionless, his face and knees tucked under him. The next instant, the man tumbled over. Zander gasped as a familiar face, drawn and frozen in agony, dredged the new spring grass.

Another shell exploded, pitching Zander to the ground to cover his head against the rain of dirt. His breath skittered and halted like a spooked horse. He hugged the solidness beneath him as it vibrated with another blast. His fingers felt for the knife strapped to his thigh—a gift from Pap for his twelfth birthday. Somehow, it comforted him.

"Fire at will!"

The command sounded from somewhere far away. He glanced at Sergeant McNeer as the man lifted his carbine and fired. Skanks huddled behind a fallen tree, gripping his rifle, his eyes squeezed tight, stammering a panicked prayer. He was not alone.

Those butternut uniforms had huddled behind breastworks and flattened behind rises for hours. Now in the open, Confederate infantry extended across a third of the battlefield which was nothing more than a farmer's pasture. A pasture not so different from the one back home, where one shaded corner watched over the bodies of Federal and Rebel alike.

"Fire!" Sarge glared at him.

Zander raised his carbine, reluctant to eyeball his first human target. Finally, he squeezed the trigger—just like he was hunting with his brother.

Only this was not hunting.

Another shell hit—the ground its only victim. For long minutes, a barrage of fire between the opposing batteries rent the lines, raising smoky plumes. The foreboding silence that followed hung heavier in the air than the acrid fog of gunpowder.

A handful of bodies lay on the ground several yards out. Surely that wasn't his doing. He had been trying to pick off some Rebs poking their heads up behind a rise. He couldn't swallow. Had he reloaded after the last shot? His hands shook as he checked the musket's breech. Flashing a look in every direction for Bass, concern kicked in. *He was just here.*

Zander rose to his knees, then dropped again. *Was that an order?* He hadn't been paying attention. Gripping the cold steel tighter, he closed his eyes against the salty sting. What was he supposed to do?

He startled to a hand on his shoulder.

"I could hold it no longer." Bass fell to his elbows and resumed his position. Zander hissed out his relief. The fool was gonna get himself killed.

"Get ready, men!" Captain Giles jogged along behind the Federal line with his saber drawn. "Get ready to meet their line! Get ready to meet their line!" He continued on, as the command echoed behind him.

An iron cannon ball must've found its way into Zander's belly, anchoring him in place. *Attack.* They were going to *attack.* He should pray, which he hadn't done nearly enough since leaving home. Pap would've been disappointed in him. But, pray he did—an anxious cry for help and a penitent plea for forgiveness.

A deafening yell split the air as valor ignited hundreds of voices. Zealous men plunged into the swollen creek with muskets held high. Swept up in the melee, Zander lurched into the creek, struggling to keep his carbine and pistol dry. Carried by the surge of impassioned troops, he clawed at the muddy bank and scrambled up the other side.

An endless line of Confederates stretched across the battlefield as the Federals narrowed the distance between them. Both sides blazed away. Heart pounding against his throat, Zander fired at the enemy line. He reloaded with trembling fingers and fired again, propelling himself forward, tugging his boot from the saturated ground with each step.

A rhythm of sorts stole his concentration—load, shoot, load, shoot. He stumbled over a branch and pitched headlong. Zander recoiled with the realization—the *branch* was an infantryman's arm. He scrabbled backward. Bile seared his gullet. He rose to his knees, but a boot caught his shoulder, jolting him back to the ground.

Where was Bass? Skanks? Where was his sergeant? His captain? Panic strangled his wind. He scoured the field, horrified to see men falling in grave numbers. A flood of Federals converged on the Rebel line, breaking around him as he huddled motionless, a useless hunk of rock in a river of fighting men.

Off to the right, the Pennsylvania color guard stumbled, then plummeted headfirst into a briar patch. "Retreat! Pennsylvania, retreat!" An officer snagged the unit's ensign from his fallen comrade, ordering retreat again. The Pennsylvania unit fell back, their numbers shrinking by half as men dropped mere steps from the refuge of trees.

Zander climbed to his feet, stumbling like a drunk. He considered simply forging ahead as he would in blinding snow, one foot in front of the other, chin to his chest. But, no—he was a soldier, wasn't he? He raised his carbine. Had he loaded it? Shoot, reload, shoot. A Rebel fell to his bullet—he was sure of it.

Smoke billowed from the grove to his left, and flames shot into the air. Ohio Infantry poured from the blazing woods, some with weapons still trained on the enemy, others screaming in agony as they staggered, eyes glistening white and red against their soot-coated faces. One man spun in a circle, arms flailing as flames consumed his jacket.

Zander bounded over a body and sprinted to the burning soldier, knocking him to the ground. He rolled him back and forth—flames biting into his own fingers. Frantically scraping up mud, he smeared it on the sizzling fabric and flesh. Within seconds, the man's cries melted into whimpers. He mumbled his thanks to Zander and curled on the grass like a newborn.

The rush of a bullet returned him to the battle. To his horror, Confederate forces began flanking. They drove forward, pressing in on two of the Federal regiments without mercy, dropping them like crows. When the Federals fell back, the enemy followed hard on their heels—a most unhallowed slaughter.

Zander's head swam. *Breathe!* He sucked in a quick breath and aimed, but could not look into the nameless faces. No. He aimed at the bodies working their way toward him. Cold. Numb. He was a machine.

An impassioned rally cry carried over the battle's din as fresh Ohio and West Virginia units bore down on the Rebels. The Johnnies ran like scared rabbits to the feeble sanctuary of their breastworks.

Concentrate, man! Gunpowder fog stung his eyes, and he wiped them on his sleeve.

He tripped again, slamming his chin into a rock. His stomach turned with the pain. He spit blood, half expecting to see part of his tongue hit the ground. Man after man bounded over him. If he was ever going to get up—But what if he didn't? He could feign death.

The thought vanished. He needed to reload. Zander reached for his cartridge box and groaned. There, scattered in the mud, lay his best hope for survival. He scooped up the cartridges and jammed one into the breech. He drew in a desperate breath before scrabbling over the breastworks. The enemy inched backwards to escape the swell of Federals advancing over their only fortification.

Finding his footing, he aimed into the tangle of Confederates. One, only a boy. Another a grandpappy. He squeezed the trigger.

Nothing. The mud-covered cartridges were useless.

He turned his head to a strangled cry as an infantryman pulled his bayonet from a Rebel's gut. A soldier rushed him from the left, and he swung the butt of his carbine into the attacker's face, rewarded with a hollow *CRUNCH* before the man crumpled to the ground.

He grappled for his revolver. Gone—lost somewhere on this field of blood, right along with his humanity. Dread poured over him, suffocating like dirt on a coffin.

Saber in one hand and knife in the other, Zander pressed into the onslaught as the dirge of battle enveloped him. The chink of steel against steel. The slice of blade against flesh. And amid the dirge, a most haunting hymn—the sorrowful groans and laments of men caught fast in suffering.

A knife flashed and a Rebel uniform flew at Zander. His back slammed the ground. Breath whooshed from his lungs. Fire sliced his arm, and a metallic scent assaulted him.

He let loose of the saber and struggled to wrench the knife away with his free hand. Zander heaved for wind and sucked in the stench of sweat as the clamor of battle faded. Only a senseless flurry of might and desperation forestalled his end. Suddenly the man fell limp, a birthday knife pinned beneath him and blood soaking Zander's uniform.

"Dabney." A weak voice begged his attention and when he turned his head, Skank's wide eyes met his own.

"Skanks."

"They. . . they kilt me."

"*Shh. . . Shh . . .* You'll be just fine, now." Zander pried his hand free and reached for his friend, but life had already faded from the familiar eyes.

"Nooo!"

He heaved off the body and crawled to Skanks. A storm surged inside of him as he closed staring eyes with a trembling hand. *I'm so, so sorry.* His chest ached with a silent scream. He wanted to rail at God, to—

On instinct, he turned, thrusting his knife into the soft belly of a Rebel. The soldier staggered back, but tried to rush again, wielding his blade higher. Zander jumped to his feet and tackled the charging soldier, throwing him to the ground. In a frenzied struggle, Pap's knife found its mark.

He wiped the sticky knife on his britches and retrieved his saber. With leaden feet and numbed mind, he shut out the cacophony of battle and stumbled forward, every step taking him further into hell. Had God been here, Zander would've prayed for a merciful deliverance. But the God he had called Lord was nowhere on this field of blood.

At last, victory shouts rang out. He looked up to see the last of the Confederates disappear over the hill.

He collapsed to his knees and sobbed.

Zander rocked on his haunches in the dark, wearing nothing but his clean drawers—and minding his footing in the soapy mud slurry he hadn't meant to cause. Wringing water from his jacket one last time, he managed to splatter a wet glob smack onto his nose. How many times had he dunked the bloody clothes into the creek? He had scoured them on a rock, squeezed out the water, repeating the whole process again and again until his hands ached and grew numb from the cold water.

Too bad his smeller wasn't numb. The stench of death had seared his nostrils. Now it terrified him to think he would never be rid of it.

An owl hooted. He jumped, eyes darting to the shadowy branches above. A shiver coursed down his spine. *Calm yourself. It's just an owl.* Suddenly self-conscious, he combed his surroundings. Straining to see through the darkness—he searched for something that likely wasn't even there. Campfires dotted the field, and somewhere in the distance, a horse whinnied. The moonless night pressed in on him, setting his nerves on edge.

He squinted at the wet jacket, willing the stains gone—and willing yesterday purged from his life entirely.

Bass slept a few yards away, his intermittent snores somehow a comfort. *Sleep.* A foreboding vise squeezed the air from Zander's chest. He gulped in several breaths and shook it off. Sleep had a way of reminding you of things too ugly for the light of day.

Keeping a lookout for any movement, he sidestepped over to the brush where his drawers were drying. It was obvious from the onset of battle that he had not been the only one to wet himself, but it still disgusted him—shamed him. He spread his britches and jacket over a bush, then examined his hands and arms in the darkness, wondering if he had managed to get all the blood off. When he went to take off his saddle earlier, Rampart wouldn't have it—snorting, stomping and wrenching away from his master's touch.

At last, a blush climbed the horizon, and Zander heaved a sigh of relief. He blinked, rubbing away the sting in one eye. Finally, yesterday could work on being just a hideous memory. He tugged on his only other shirt and britches. He would let the jacket dry a spell, then wear it anyway. Better wet than . . . stained.

Invisible fingers held open his eyes, and even weariness evaded his body. Surely it had been the longest night of his life—assisting the medics until they had carted off most of the wounded. He had sat with a man as he breathed his last—a man named Harlan, from Cincinnati. Zander had promised to write to his wife. What could he say? He didn't know the man—didn't even see him go down. After Harlan passed, Zander loaded the dead into wagons. He stacked them like cord-wood, leaving Confederate bodies to be collected by their own.

He slipped his knife from its sheath and frowned as he turned the blade over in his fingers, testing the fine edge. He had scoured it with mud. A lot of mud. And sharpened it the best he could on a rock. Strapping it to his leg, he searched the dull gray canopy above. Had it always been so . . . so endless? And had he ever felt so puny? *Little ol' Zander and a great big God.* A sob caught in his throat and tears stung the backs of his eyes. There was no name for what he felt just now. He was numb. Just numb. Words that should have been directed to his Maker crumbled to dust and scattered in the wind.

"Dabney." Sergeant McNeer appeared in the noiseless dawn, stitches across one cheek and his arm in a sling.

"Sergeant."

He laid a meaty hand on Zander's shoulder. "I have a son a few years younger than you. I'd give my life to protect him from what you went through yesterday."

Yesterday.

"You fought well, Dabney. Plenty of boys couldn't bring themselves to take those breastworks, but you didn't balk."

Zander looked down at his hands. *Sticky. Even after all that washing.*

"The artillery is moving out soon to start taking out the railroad. Get some food in your belly, you'll need it."

"Yes, Sarge."

Food. He didn't care if he ever ate again.

Four

New Creek, West Virginia

"Thirty-two, thirty-four, thirty-six. Mmm . . . four cans short!" Lola Wade spun and crossed the room as the sharp *crack* of her heels on the oak floor echoed through the mercantile. Frowning, she made a note in the open book on the counter and shifted her spectacles farther up her nose. She puffed a stray hair from her eye, then batted it away. Just one more irritation. For the second time in as many weeks, the inventory did not agree with her figures. Her book said one thing, but the stores on the shelf said quite another.

"What are you going on about?" Her father slipped through the striped curtain behind the counter. He paused with a knit brow and a white knuckled hand on the doorjamb. One eye squinted in pain, as it often did.

Lola ached to rush to his aid, but she dare not let on that she noticed. Closing the book, she swung around the end of the counter and beamed. "Nothing important, Papa. How was your rest?" She looped her arm through his, and he shook it off.

"I know what you're doing, honey, but I'm not an invalid."

"Of course you're not!" *Stubborn man.* "Can't a girl show her papa she loves him?"

His face softened, and he pulled her close. "I'm sorry. I'm just getting to be a crotchety old man, I guess. Time will come soon enough when I'll need help. Let's not hurry it along."

She smiled, even as uncertainty pressed on her heart. "Yes, Papa."

"I was resting just fine until those blasted cannons woke me up." He scrubbed his grizzled head, mangling the upper hairs into a peak before smoothing it again.

"It's not so bad. You know they have to fire them every now and then in case . . ." She had said too much.

"Durned Federals. It's not enough they have to go and plant those blasted guns everywhere, but they traipse all over this town like they live here."

"But they do live here, Papa. Most of the officers, anyway. And you know we get a good deal of our business from Fort Fuller."

The door groaned, then slapped shut. Her little brother skidded to a halt, his nine-year-old exuberance brought up short with a look from Papa.

"Now just a minute, boy. That's no way to enter a business establishment." Papa scowled, but waved Felix on over.

"Sorry." Her brother twisted his lips to one side, stepped left, then right. "I was trying to get here before the next cannon sounded so I could see the time."

A miniature of Papa in so many ways, her brother's penchant for logic and all things bookish could always entice a smile from their father.

"Well, now. You mind your manners next time." He ruffled the boy's sooty-dark hair.

Lola plopped a fist on her hip. "Where have you been, any-way?" *And why could he not stand still?*

"Just over to the barber's bench. You can see one of the big guns from there." The words tumbled over themselves in a sputtering repetition as he bounced up and down. In a comical display of gritted teeth and rolling eyes, his face pinched in desperation. "Right now. I gotta go!"

Lola chuckled and threw up her hands. "Go, then!"

Felix darted through the curtains toward the privy. An instant later, the back door slapped shut with a bounce. Papa grinned, shook his head, and hobbled across the freshly swept floor, to the yard goods.

It pained her so, the way that hip of his gave him more grief with each passing year. Had she even noticed it before Mama passed? She had probably been too busy growing up to take note of such things. But she was fully grown now, and she would tend to Papa whether he was agreeable or not. Already he had seen fit to turn over responsibilities to her—the everyday running of the store, inventory, and the bookkeeping. The easier she could make things for him, the happier she would be.

The morning passed at Wade Mercantile in a whirlwind of customers and inventory. When Mrs. Tesley finally showed up in the afternoon, Lola was more than ready for a break.

"Good afternoon, Miss Wade. It is a lovely day, isn't it? The sun is shining and the day is bright with promises enough to lift one's spirit to soar above the heavens." Her sparkling salutations, amusing for the first few months, now fell to the worn floorboards, as tired and ordinary as Lola felt.

The woman floated to the curtain, chased by a pleasant mixture of cinnamon and lavender. She snatched an apron from a nail beside the doorway. "I've come to render your relief, my dear. Please, take your break. You look positively done in."

"Yes, I suppose I am." *Perfect.* Why was the woman's hair always so *perfect*? How did she get it to stay in that big swoop on top of her head? Lola nudged the bridge of her eyeglasses higher and swiped away the traitorous flaxen wisps crowding her face. Rebellious locks so downy-fine they slipped right through her combs and brushes like errant children. Why, every morning she'd fritter away a quarter of an hour trying to tame them into submission. And for what? She always managed to look like the victim of a windstorm by noon, anyway.

Lola sighed, slipped off her apron, and started through the curtain, still puzzling over the ledger numbers. But she could not let it go, not yet. She scrutinized the woman who fairly danced about tapping here and there with the feather dusty.

Swallowing back a puckish accusation, sure to be construed as rude, she inquired, "Are you *sure* you are recording every item sold, Mrs. Tesley? There seems to be some discrepancy in our inventory again." Even if the woman *had* failed to record a sale, the accounts receivable still did not add up.

"I strive most ardently to be as accurate as you are, Miss Wade. Perhaps one of the town's children has availed themselves when your father was not looking. I have oft observed the way he visits excessively with customers—even while ignoring the needs of other patrons." Her words filtered through a toothy smile, and her chin lifted more with each sentence.

The woman was a good worker and the customers adored her, but her comments grated on Lola at times. Surely, she meant well. *"Always look for the best in others."* Isn't that what Mama had taught her? *"Aren't we all sinners?"* she would say. Yes, that much was certainly true. We are all sinners. *Some more than others.* Guilt spanked her conscience, and she was quick to silently ask forgiveness.

She had let her mind wander again—to places and incidents best forgotten. Oh, why didn't her Heavenly Father make it easier for His children to forget once they decided to forgive?

"Thank you, Mrs. Tesley." Lola grabbed the record book off the counter and headed for the back room. There was nothing she could do but recheck her figures. And make another pot of tea.

Five

Zander watched wooden slivers fall to the dust as he whittled a pencil's tip. He thought to write his family. How long had it been since he had written? *Months.*

After Cloyd's Mountain, he had helped burn the New River Bridge. Then his Regiment hightailed it to Lewisburg to evade the Confederates. He had never been so happy to cross those mountains—or so hungry in all his days.

Was the battle only four days ago?

He put the pencil to paper, trying to work up a thought. His hand quivered, so he squeezed the pencil tighter. After a few half-hearted attempts at writing, he chucked it to the floor. He couldn't do it. Not now, anyway.

Zander folded the paper and slipped it back into the Bible he kept in his saddlebags—not a special sort of Bible, just one of those New Testaments the Army hands out. If only he had Pap's Bible, but Fin was the one who ended up with that. He snorted. Wouldn't have made any difference, anyway. Grabbing his hat, he launched off for the corral.

Nodding to another private, he led Rampart out of the rope enclosure. He ran a hand down each of the gelding's legs, checking the feet as Rampart nickered softly. "Let's you and me take a ride, old son." When he scrubbed the star on the sleek forehead, the horse closed his eyes and leaned into his master.

"Yeah. I know what you like." Zander clutched the mane and threw his leg over the speckled back. "Let's get out of here."

The breeze swept a measure of dampness from the warm day and briefly lifted the gloom that had settled on his heart. A buckeye tree waved in the distance from a puddle of lush spring grass. It called to him, and plainly Rampart, too, who whinnied and wiggled his ears in answer.

They loped to the tree, and Zander vaulted to the ground. "You can eat your fill while I rub you down." He found the perfect piece of bark and started working on Rampart's hindquarters. "I need to write home. I don't want to, though. What am I supposed to say, huh?"

Rampart pressed his neck against Zander, and understanding eyes urged his master to bare his soul.

"Boy, I've seen, heard, and smelled things I never wanted to. But what did I expect?" Dust settled from the churned-up fur and he flicked it away. "I ain't no hero like Fin, that's for blame sure." *How did his brother do this—this warring?* "If this is anything like what Fin's been doing the last three years, then I don't even know him anymore."

He scraped the bark across the horse's back, following with his hand. "I can't even cry any more, boy. I'm all cried out. Got no tears." He walked around to face Rampart. The great head stretched skyward and Zander pressed his cheek against the warm coat, feeling the blood pulse through the muscled neck. It smelled like home, the only bit of himself he had left. Emptiness cried from his insides, but he could only answer to the ache that encased it.

"God . . . Lord . . ." Words failed him—from without and within.

He stood there—unmoving and unfeeling—until the sun rode low in the sky and his stomach grumbled. "Best get back, boy. To-morrow we're leaving. Going with Col. Hayes and General Crook to join General Hunter. We're gonna take on the Shenandoah

Valley." What that meant, he wasn't sure. His brother-in-law had called it the "breadbasket of the Confederacy." Maybe they were going to burn the crops. But that hardly seemed humane. People gotta eat, don't they?

Kanawha Valley, West Virginia
July, 1864

Zander plodded along with the rest of the Fifth Regiment as it snaked its way down the Kanawha and James River Turnpike west toward Charleston. They escorted almost three hundred prisoners and some four hundred freed slaves. The Army called them contraband. Why, he couldn't figure. But Rampart was happy to be offering up rides to the freed children while his master walked. This was a long trek for short legs, after-all.

Word was, Blazer's Scouts were bringing in a goodly number of bushwhackers, but he had not seen hide nor hair of them. And if he didn't see Fin until after this whole mess was over, well . . . that was all right by him.

The little boy atop Rampart snagged his hat and giggled when Zander acted shocked. He tousled the boy's hair and perched the hat on his head proper.

Had he ever been so tired? They were going home—well, to where his family was anyway—and Zander should have been grateful, but fatigue had drained him of most every emotion. Not even a shred of pride in the U.S. Army remained—not after General Hunter's actions.

Zander dragged his boot heels, deep in thought, kicking up the dust. Disgrace rumbled inside him like an empty belly. How could someone like General Hunter be on the Union side and act like some power-possessing vigilante? The commander's mission into

Virginia had been only thievery and brutality—and destruction. In Lexington, he ordered troops to plunder the town and burn the Virginia Military Institute. The very school so many Union officers attended themselves. *Senseless!* Innocents burned out of their homes! *Senseless!*

Ol' Hunter's men even stooped to making off with George Washington's statue and burning Governor Letcher's house. What does burning a Governor's house have to do with warring?

Like the rest in Col. Hayes's command, Zander had stood there seething as black smoke rolled over the flames covering half the horizon. *Senseless!* He had pondered on the number of men under Hunter's command who resented their orders.

In Buchanan, after General McCausland burned the bridge, Union troops forded the river, only to have Hunter order them to burn the town. In every town they marched on in Virginia, innocents, homes, and businesses fell to General Hunter's wrath. But Lynchburg, the industrial heart of the Confederacy and only actual strategic target, was brushed aside. *Senseless!* The Federals could have taken it. They had the chance. But they set up camp outside of town allowing the Confederate Army time to amass a defense. *Senseless!*

After a brief artillery banter, Hunter's troops retreated like a bunch of jeering school boys—all bark and foolishness, but no action. Thanks to Hunter's inaction, the Confederate General Early had a clear passage all the way up through the Shenandoah Valley. *Senseless!*

Zander growled and shook his head. Pure folly and wickedness—at the expense of men who were just following orders. Replaying the whole Shenandoah Valley debacle in his head set his blood to boiling. How could he be proud when that's the kind of game the commanders were playing at?

Rampart seemed to enjoy this new duty, walking at the slow pace of the long train of wagons, ambulances, and humanity. Zander led him off to the side of the pike. "Time to give someone else a chance, I reckon," he said, lifting two children from Rampart's back, their curly black hair now dusted gray.

He left an elderly woman atop Rampart to continue riding. Her toothless grin and dark skin reminded him of Ol' Izzy somehow. At the memory of the dear family friend, a pang of bittersweet surprised him. The first real thing he had felt in weeks, unless you count disgust. He swallowed hard, then turned to the crowd.

"Who's next? The shorter your legs the better chance you get to ride."

"Me! Me!" Several children vied for the coveted spot on Rampart's back.

Did he miss his family? Yes. In some unexplained turn of events, Zander missed his family something fierce all the sudden. He plopped two more children onto Rampart and resumed walking. Those elated smiles were all the reason he needed to walk himself on his own two feet every inch of the way into Charleston.

The massive train stopped only at night and by the second day, the sheer number of horses, wagons, and bodies crowding the pike made travel in the opposite direction mostly impossible. Some folks trudged along in rhythm, keeping step to the jubilant songs of freedom that arose from the former slaves. Occasionally, from the other side of the Kanawha River, patriotic tunes of a drum and fife corps echoed across the roiling waters. Most everybody, except for the prisoners, seemed to be in good spirits.

He had been so proud to don this blue uniform just a few short months ago—to wear the pin of a U.S. Cavalryman. He fingered the buttons of his jacket. It had long since lost its appeal.

Zander spit, then sheepishly eyed Rampart's young passengers. He had been taught better than that. Too bad General Hunter hadn't been. This whole business stuck in his craw like a chicken bone.

Well, President Washington, sir. If discipline is the soul of an army, as you said, General Hunter is soulless.

Six

Fort Fuller, New Creek, WV

"Oh, no you don't." Lola snagged Felix's sleeve as he prepared to jump from the wagon. "You are *not* deserting me. I need your help."

"But I want to go watch the troops drill!" He pooched out his lower lip and crossed his arms. Eyes drooping longingly, he gazed past the mix of log and clapboard buildings comprising the fort. When shouts echoed from the hidden field in a staccato of noise, her brother pumped his arms and scowled. "I'm missing it."

"Felix Nathanial Wade, we have a family business and you, sir, are part of this family, are you not?" She shook her head, wondering if her expression duly conveyed the disappointment niggling at her. Whatever got into her brother at times like this, she hadn't a clue. But she would not have it.

Felix blew out a noisy sigh and his shoulders rose and fell dramatically. Shoving a hank of black hair from one eye, his expression and words dripped with defeat. "Yes, ma'am."

"That's better." She smiled and tapped his nose with one finger. "You help me get set up and *then* we'll see if you can go watch."

His eyes danced and just that quick his frown flipped. "You mean it?" Bounding to the ground, he rushed to the back of the wagon. "Let's hurry!" He heaved and grunted, struggling with the gate board.

"You're still a little short in the britches for lifting that board out, aren't you?" Lola grinned—her good nature renewed. She lifted the heavy board from its groove and set one end on the ground. "But you *are* strong for a man of your years, little brother. Would you help me with these barrels, please?"

Felix nodded. "Yep, I'm strong, all right."

He inched a barrel toward the edge of the wagon bed, and together they worked to set two barrels on the ground. After Lola laid the board over them to fashion a table of sorts, she sent Felix into the back of the wagon. He snorted and groaned, scooting the heavy crates to the rear until she could reach them.

"Hand me those clothing bundles now, and then you can go."

"Yes, ma'am!" He slapped at the hair on his forehead in a mock salute and tossed her the bundles before leaping to the ground. With a *WHOOP*, he sprinted toward the parade field, beyond the rows of log huts that dotted the hill.

Cupping her hands to her mouth, she shouted after him, "I want you to stay within hollering distance, you hear me?" She smiled when a reply drifted back to her. That boy did keep her on her toes.

Even before she could properly display the merchandise, Federals and civilians crowded around to see the wares of Wade Mercantile. Lola apologized as she squeezed in to arrange the rows of hand towels and wool socks beneath the customers' noses. Backing out of the chaos, she turned to set a tin of matches next to the lanterns and knives, bumping into a customer, apologizing again. A tall soldier doffed his hat, flashing a near-toothless smile, and she nodded politely. The business she pulled in from this sutler station brought in a large portion of the store's profits, so she would not complain one bit.

"May I have two yards of this, please, Lola?" Mrs. Magee waved a fold of brown fabric. Gray and yellow stains splotched her once-white apron, which covered much of her ample figure.

"Certainly. What are you making, Mrs. Magee?"

"A dress for my little granddaughter." She fingered a heavier blue fabric. "And two yards of this here for a new shirt for my Algern. It will be a surprise. Has the price changed since last month?"

Lola gathered up the scissors and fabric, pained to tell Mrs. Magee that yes, indeed, the price had gone up.

The woman pressed her lips together, then produced a disciplined smile. "Oh, let's just have the brown fabric for now, Lola. My Algern has enough shirts."

"Of course, Mrs. Magee." Lola cut the yard goods, regretting the circumstances that made her party to folks going without.

As soldiers jostled each other and crowded up to the wares, a fight erupted over the last can of peaches.

"'Taint yours, Heslep. I was just paying the lady for it."

"Well, now, it looks to be in *my* hand." Heslep brandished the can above the shorter man's head. "Whatcha gonna do 'bout it?"

"I'm agonna thrash yer sorry hide, that's what!"

Lola scurried to the side of the wagon and reached into another crate. "Gentlemen." She raised her voice over the ruckus, waving a can of peaches in the air. "Gentlemen!"

"Just you name the place, Turley. Anytime."

"I will. And you can bring yer own nurse to patch you up!"

"Gentlemen!" Lola pressed the can into Private Turley's hand. "I believe you each owe me for one can of peaches." She held out her palm, scolding them with a glare. Why couldn't army men behave with civility? It was moments like this that made her wish her papa was up to sutlering at the fort. She had practically whispered the price, embarrassed to be asking so much, although she was making but a pittance on each can.

Both soldiers stepped back, shaking their heads and leaving her with the peaches. Their voices trailed behind as they retreated amid grumblings about not buying a side of beef. Lola looked at the small crowd, embarrassed to realize those men were not the only ones unwilling to pay the asking price.

Just before noon, Felix showed up for lunch, and Lola set him to rest in the wagon's shade with some biscuits and hard-cooked eggs. He flipped through the pages of a book about the railroad, sharing his observations every few paragraphs. When his informative declarations halted, Lola stopped fussing with the displays and crouched down to check on her brother. She chuckled at the way he sprawled on the cool tarp, sound asleep with a crust of biscuit dangling from his lip.

The afternoon slipped by in a haze of customers and conversation, and eventually Felix arose and headed off to make his rounds with the other sutlers. The longer summer days yielded long workdays, too. Already, Lola's back ached from standing. If only she could sit for a spell. She squinted into the bright sun and pulled her damp dress away from her body. Her nose twitched, assaulted by the pungent odor of fresh manure—completely expected, what with the cavalry returning from drills, but most ripe on a hot day like this.

Fort Fuller was a little like a town all its own, with civilian folk bustling here and there. Handsome soldiers, too. She adjusted her spectacles, suddenly self-conscious. She patted her sweaty face with her sleeve and frantically tucked unruly hair into the knitted snood.

Why did she bother? It's not like anyone would take a second look in her direction—not the decent ones, anyway. They were only interested in the offerings spread on the makeshift table and stacked in the wagon bed.

Musket fire shattered her ruminations. Soon, the powerful stench of gunpowder wafted by. She fanned the air with one hand. She should be used to this by now.

Lola tapped a pencil to her list, trying to recall her earlier thoughts. She made a note to bring more tobacco next time. Seems she runs out sooner with every passing Saturday. And the men never even balk at the rising prices. She often set up her wares on other days of the week, but Saturday was by far the busiest. Maybe because the soldiers had more time on their hands—and money.

Was there even one thing unaffected by the Rebellion? Though not as bad as in the South, prices had done their share of creeping up. She hated posting the new flour and coffee prices today.

By the time Lola had loaded the wagon, a blessed breeze vanquished the day's warmth. Silvery clouds gathered against fading orange and ochre with the sinking sun as she guided the wagon through the tall fort gates. She smiled timidly at the guards as they returned Felix's lazy wave. In the mornings, he made a show of saluting as the wagon passed, but by evenings, he succumbed to the busy ruckus of the fort. He would likely be asleep before they even made the road.

Sweet thoughts of her own childish adventures brought a sigh as a symphony of tree frogs escorted them home. If only she could turn back the clock. Nay, the calendar! But she could not bear to lose Mama all over again . . . Horsefeathers! She did it again. Her thoughts were often as hard to tame as her unruly crown. Oh, to be a child again.

Her thoughts had yet to be taken captive, that was all. She would corral them by thinking on the chores waiting for her at home.

Her ruminating on supper, however, gave way to the concerns that had kept sleep at bay more than a few nights. Why were her figures and inventory amiss? How many times had this happened now? She needed to go over the numbers in the book again, uninterrupted. If she could find the energy, perhaps tonight was her chance. Just as soon as Felix was in bed, she would give it another look. There must be a logical explanation for coming up short. An explanation, she hoped, found in her bookkeeping, and not in somebody's pocket.

Seven

CHARLESTON, WEST VIRGINIA

"Just look at this!" Melinda Jane slammed the paper onto the table, seething with indignation. "God Almighty is gonna judge that man as surely as He judged King Saul."

Her sister-in-law shushed her with a frown. "You'll wake Addie. What are you going on about?" Gus clucked her irritation and snatched up the Charleston Daily Bulletin. "Humph. More General Hunter." Her eyes flashed and her hand flew to her coppery crown. "He burned the Military Institute?"

"And look right there—" Melinda Jane poked at the printed words. "All that palaver about how *Mr.* Hunter's gonna handle Southern sympathizers. Says if there is any property destroyed or jayhawked within five miles of their home, they'll be forced to pay five times the amount of the damage. And if a Union soldier is wounded within five miles of a sympathizer's home, their house will be burnt!"

"Does seem mighty harsh." Gus shook her head. "He's not from around here. He just doesn't understand how it is with folks this side of the mountains—mixed loyalties and all."

Door springs whined as Mrs. O'Donell pushed open the porch door with her backside. Turning, she dropped a basket of garden pickings on the floor with a groan. "Sure'n this decrepit back o'mine is giving up the ghost." She straightened with a grimace, her hand to the small of her back. Silvery curls clung to her moist brow. She brushed them away from her ruddi-er-than-usual face. "'Tis best I be leavin' more of the gardening to Bertie and Will, I'm thinkin'."

Gus scurried to help her to a chair, even as the woman swatted her away. "Oh, Mrs. O'Donell, I don't know why Will wasn't out there helping you with that."

"I'm not broken, las. Just old, 'tis all." She dropped into the chair with a *chuff*, accepting a glass of water from Melinda. "I told Will to never mind—I'd not planned to be so long at it."

Melinda Jane took a seat. "There's no reason for you to be working in the garden, Mrs. O'Donell."

Gus set the basket in front of the cupboard. "This is wonderful. Just look at these peas!" She split open a couple of pods and offered a handful to the women.

Melinda Jane rolled her eyes and moaned. "Not again—" She clutched her skirts and darted for the slop jar she had taken to keeping on the back porch. Surely this casting up her insides every day was bound to end soon. But with her stomach's every tumble or threat, she would smile to herself, imagining the look on Fin's face when she tells him he's going to be a pappy. How she longed for that moment. *Oh God, bring him home to me.*

She shuffled back to the table and dropped into a chair. A nap. She needed another nap. Her bones weighed like iron as she rested her head on folded arms.

Mrs. O'Donell patted her back. "There, there, las. 'Twill pass afore ye know it."

"You poor girl." Gus said, handing her a wet rag. "Am I making supper again tonight?"

"That depends. Do you want it cooked?" Melinda Jane mumbled, her cheek now resting on the table. She raised her head, dabbing her face and hairline with the cool cloth, remembering how the smell of bacon had sent her running for the outdoors this morning.

"I take that as a *yes*." Gus chuckled.

Melinda Jane offered a feeble nod and dropped her head again, thankful for the charitable care her dear friend lavished on her. If only she had been that considerate when Gus was carrying little Addie.

"Where is that girl?" With a hand on the doorjamb, Gus hollered upstairs. "Will? Willamina Dabney, you have work to do in here!" She turned with a sigh, eyes marred with concern. "I . . ." Her face puckered in thought. "I sure wish we'd hear something from Zander. I never figured him for falling slack in letter writing." She snatched a kettle from the shelf and started pumping water. "Now, Fin—that was a different matter. I did not much expect word from him when he first left."

"That brother of yours sure keeps the letters coming now, though—at least as often as he can get to a post." Melinda Jane knew Fin had been with General Hunter. And Hunter was in the Kanawha Valley again. She had been praying day and night that her husband would walk through that front door.

"It's been harder letting Zander go." Gus set the water kettle to boil.

"'Cause he's your younger brother. You feel responsible."

Shaking the coals in the bin, Gus reached over and opened the damper. "I do. But, he's different from Fin—more inside himself about things that matter."

"He is that."

Fifteen-year-old Will danced into the kitchen, one hand swishing her skirt with each step. "You wanted me?"

"Now I *know* you weren't out in the barn. What took you so long?" Gus dropped several potatoes into the sink before pinning Will with a raised brow. "Hmm?"

"I was rearranging my clothes."

Melinda Jane met her sister-in-law's shocked expression and grinned. Who was this child, anyway? "You . . . you were *rearranging* your clothes?"

"Yes. It says in Godey's Ladies Book"—Will closed her eyes and recited—"'a young woman's clothing should be neatly folded or hung, free from wrinkles and lint at all times.'" She nodded in satisfaction.

"*You* read Godey's Ladies Book?" Gus poised a knife in mid-air, ready to take on a potato.

"Is that so hard to believe?" Will huffed and donned an apron. "You makin' me wear dresses here in Charleston has greatly increased my wardrobe, it seems."

Melinda Jane shook her head, her amusement getting the best of her. "Honey, it's not just your wardrobe that has increased."

Gus chuckled and handed a potato to her sister. "You're . . . d*eveloping* into a lovely young woman, Will."

"Yes, *developing*," Melinda Jane repeated, glancing at Mrs. O'Donell and envying Gus's ability to come up with tactful words.

Mrs. O'Donell's stoic expression was much at odds with the twinkle in her eye.

"You just plain outgrew the clothes you wore in Gauley Bridge," Gus went on. "Your new wardrobe was a necessity. And you don't see any of your friends running around in britches, do you?"

Will eyed the women. "I didn't ask to become a woman, you know. I was happy as could be in my britches back at the farm." She picked up a knife and started peeling. "I feel like this war is never going to end. I'm spending my formative years in the city. Can't be good for a person. The air smells of coal smoke from the riverboats and the school is broken up by age. I would head home tomorrow if you'd let me." She puffed a strand of auburn hair from her eyelashes, looking forlorn.

Gus hugged her sister to her side. "I'd like to go home too, Will. But life doesn't always let us choose."

Melinda Jane stood, then sat again, not sure whether her stomach was trying to get her attention. "This war won't go on forever, you'll see. Then we can go home and rebuild."

"Oh yeah . . . rebuild. I almost forgot about the barn being burnt. Seems like such a long time ago now." Will bit her bottom lip and let the peelings fall into the sink. "I miss Zander."

"We all do." Gus sniffed, slipping several potato chunks into the steaming water on the stove.

"That boy is on me heart day and night." Mrs. O'Donell dabbed her eye with a hanky. "I miss him too, ya know."

"So do I." And Melinda Jane worried for him too—just as much as she did for her husband. *Walk through that door, Fin. For me. For our child.*

Eight

July 1864

Fire crackled under the mess skillet as beans and sowbelly sizzled. The tantalizing scent lured Zander's nose toward the vittles. He nodded with satisfaction. Not bad, for a simple fare. Must've been that onion he added in.

Morale was high in the ranks of the Fifth, for the first time since General Crook led them off into hell. From a few tents down, a raucous bout of laughter rang out, followed by a string of profanity. Life was returning to normal, all right. The hum of the base camp made for a striking contrast to the angst of a campaign—heading off to who knows where to do who knows what.

Zander stirred the beans one last time, then dipped out portions onto two plates. "Supper's on," he called, careful not to attract too much attention. Likely, others close by already suffered from the irresistible smell of his cooking, anyway. He shook his head, chuckling at his own thoughts.

Bass appeared from behind the tent, wiping his freshly shaven face with a towel. "*Mmm.* It smells like Mutter's cooking," he said with a grin.

"Then your Mama needs to learn to cook better."

Bass lifted his plate and breathed in the aroma. Eyes closed, he babbled something in German, nodding his approval. "Not bad, Dabney. But perhaps I am just too hungry."

"What we need is a pile of cornbread."

"Did I hear somebody say cornbread?" D.R. Leach seemed to magically appear with a wide smile across his ample cheeks. He reached into a poke and drew out a kerchief. Pushing a hank of yellow-white hair from his eyes, he made a show of uncovering two actual pieces of cornbread. His pale eyebrows lifted and his belly bounced with a silent laugh. "Wanna trade? Cornbread for those beans?"

Zander's mouth watered. Well, it wasn't his sister-in-law, Melinda Jane's cookin' or his sister Gus's, but it *was* honest-to-goodness cornbread.

"I do not know if we have enough here for you also." Bass wrinkled his forehead, eyeing the skillet.

Zander shot his tent mate a frown and an elbow jab. "There's enough. Have a seat, Leach. You got a plate?"

"Right here." Leach delved out cornbread for the three of them as Zander dished beans onto his mess plate. Leach paused for a minute, and Zander figured he was saying grace. When had *he* stopped saying grace before meals?

For a time, they ate in silence, but for the smacking of lips and incoherent mumbles of delight from Bass.

Leach poured himself a cup of boiling water. "Did I hear you're a baker, Bass? You might fix up a batch of biscuits to trade for some finer victuals while we're at camp." He produced a square of paper from his pocket and unfolded it, revealing two scant tablespoons of coffee.

"Coffee!" Bass's eyebrows shot up.

"*Shhh*! Keep your voice down." Leach glanced around and his words died to a whisper. "I'll share. This is all I got, though."

"If that's all you got, I don't need any." Zander drizzled hot water onto his plate, then wiped it with a kerchief. "You just keep my portion for yourself, for later."

"I will take his." Bass held out a steaming cup.

Leach sprinkled a bit into the two cups, then carefully folded the rest back into the paper. He grinned at Zander. "Well—if you're sure."

Zander nodded. "You been mighty generous already." *Coffee.* Maybe he would drink his fill tomorrow. His furlough started first thing in the morning, so he'd head into Charleston. The thought of home cooking made his mouth water. The high cost of sugar, coffee, and most of the vittles he loved gave him pause. He'd best rein in that imagination of his. But, if the women at home had managed a grand little garden like they did last year, he knew he was still in for a treat.

Odd to be thinking of food instead of his family—and he hadn't visited them since joining up in January. He missed everyone. Surely, he did. After where he'd been, what he'd done—maybe they would see right through him. He stared at his hands. Maybe they would know. Fin would know. All the more reason he did not want to see his brother just yet.

"Thanks for the cornbread, Leach." Zander slipped into the tent to put his mess kit away, grabbed his hat, and headed back outside. "I'm gonna take a walk," he announced, then strode off with the corral in mind.

"Do not forget you have a race in one hour!" Bass hollered.

He kept walking. One thing at a time.

Ignoring his friends' banter, Zander stared into the fire and stabbed a stick into the charred wood as the evening chill and quiet settled over camp. An odd sort of hesitancy had settled on him. Tomorrow he was going home—least ways to his Charleston home—to his family. He loved every one of them, but the truth alarmed him some. He didn't *want* to see them. Had he become so calloused? So uncaring?

"I wish I could see my family," Bass grumbled. "I do not know why you are not excited to see yours, Zander. I would fix machinery in the bake shop and chop fire wood. I would take my sister for a candy stick at the mercantile. Perhaps I would buy Mutter a new hat."

Leach and Bass jumped to their feet, gawking at something behind him. They mashed their hats into place and stood at attention, holding a salute, like two wooden soldiers.

"Attention, Private Dabney!"

Fin. Here?

Zander swallowed hard, drew himself up, and turned with a frozen salute as apprehension fashioned a knot in his throat.

"At ease, men. I need a word with Private Dabney here."

"Yes, sir, Lieutenant." Wide-eyed, Bass and Leach skittered into the tent.

Fin's jaw muscle twitched, and Zander marveled at the deep lines carved into the corners of his eyes. It was his father's face, with flecks of silver sprinkled in the neatly trimmed beard. And it was the sober face of a hardened officer, imposing, but for the trace of a smile—easily missed by anyone who didn't know Fin.

But did Zander *truly* know his brother?

This meeting was inevitable. As if the last few weeks had swept away all he held dear, he struggled to reclaim some trace of affection he'd once held for his brother. His mind craved that old familiarity, the sweetness of kinship, of acceptance. A shudder of something foreign crept its way up his middle, but he held his salute, directing his gaze straight ahead.

Fin stepped closer; his face now painted with a warm smile. He stretched out his arms in welcome, but Zander remained at attention, hand still frozen in a salute as his world faded out of focus like words on a page—words that wove a story so enthralling you wanted desperately to step into the pages and live it out, but you knew in your heart it was just a made-up story. It was not real.

Fin dropped his arms in a huff. "What *is* this?" His brow creased and his chin dipped, spiriting Zander back home for an instant—failing once again to meet Fin's expectations.

He didn't skin that deer the right way. He was riding when he was supposed to be cleaning stalls. He had set a bad example for his little brother. He brought in one turkey to Fin's four. A jumble of all the years he had failed to measure up. All Zander ever wanted was to ride, but his family did not see it that way. But Gus understood. His older sister knew him better than anyone.

Fin cleared his throat and shot an uneasy gaze across the encampment.

Zander's words fled like a spooked stallion. A flood of emotion he thought long gone blistered the back of his throat, pushing up to his eyes. He refused to blink, savoring the burn as Fin's single First Lieutenant bar distorted to a gold blur.

"Walk with me, Private." Fin ground out the words and struck off with long, deliberate strides toward a distant stand of trees.

Zander obeyed, sucking in an unsteady breath. He kept his sight fixed on Fin's back to avoid the meddling eyes sure to be taking in the whole affair. No doubt his brother had stirred up considerable attention seeking him out. They reached the musty coolness of the grove and walked several yards farther into the murky shadows.

Fin turned and wrapped his brother in a bear hug. "I thought I'd never see you again," he croaked. Zander stiffened as his brother's body pulsed with a sob.

His hero brother. *Crying?*

Zander clenched his teeth, but despite his efforts, the dam burst and he let go a flood akin to old Noah's. Long minutes passed before he eased from his brother's embrace and swiped a sleeve across his eyes and nose.

With a huff, Fin yanked a wadded kerchief from his pocket to wipe his own face. He spoke to the ground more than to Zander, appearing almost embarrassed. "I've been looking for you since we hit the Valley. Finally met up with your Colonel Hayes, then he directed me to Major Fleming, who sent me to Sergeant McNeer."

Fin shifted his attention to Zander. His stare probed too deep for comfort. But Zander would not look away—not anymore.

"Your sergeant had some mighty proud things to say about you, little brother. Mighty proud." Fin gripped Zander's shoulders and dipped his head in a solemn nod.

Even in the dusky light, Zander caught a spark in his brother's eyes. A spark of . . . pride? Had he ever seen it there before? He had yearned for it all his life.

But it had finally come at a high price. Too high.

Zander stared into the twilight as seconds ticked by. He ground his face into his palm and snuffed. The call of a hoot owl punched the forest's silence, jerking him back to reality and his own miserable self.

He drew in a shaky breath. "I was at Cloyd's Mountain."

"I know." Fin blinked, expressionless.

He needed answers. "Why didn't you tell me . . . wha . . . what it's like? How . . . how could you do this for three years?" His fists tensed as he fought the urge to pummel his brother's chest. He wanted to pound out the rage that had dogged him, taunted him, kept him up nights—even stolen his ability to treat others with decency.

Fin sniffed and frowned at his boots. He yanked off his hat and slapped it to his leg with a grunt. "Dag nab it, Zander! Just what was I supposed to tell you, anyways?" He paced to one side and back again. His pained expression, ripe with regret, begged for understanding and somehow Zander knew it sought forgiveness at the same time.

"No man knows what he's in for till he's in the thick of it. You put one foot in front of the other and you . . . you survive, man! You just pray you can keep it together. You . . .you commit yourself to God—then go in with all you got." He paused and his nostrils flared as he sucked in a loud breath. His expression pinched miserably as he clutched Zander's arm, and a tear squeezed from his eye. "God will never leave you, little brother. Word says He won't never forsake you."

Zander jerked away. "Musta been God's day off, cuz He was nowhere near that pasture!"

He whipped out his knife and strode over to an ancient fir tree, sensing Fin's scrutiny as he twisted the point into its bark. How quickly the dusk had yielded to a sort of eerie darkness here in the trees. The heavy gloom mimicked his mood perfectly.

Fin's hand clamped onto his shoulder. "God is always there with you. You just be durn sure you don't turn your back on *Him*."

Zander balled his fists. He wanted to lay into Fin in the worst way. Instead, he punched the tree. Pain sliced through his hand. He relished it, wondering if he'd been lucky enough to break a bone.

Whirling on his brother, he hissed out the venomous thoughts that had plagued him night and day. "God turned his back on my friend, Skanks. A whole lot of other men, too—cuz they didn't walk away from that field. And a thousand others—men just like you and me." He seized his brother's arm, desperate to make him understand. "I looked in their eyes, Fin!"

Zander slammed his back against the tree and slithered to the ground. Clamping his eyes shut, he shook away the images that had haunted his mind like banshees. Would he ever escape them?

"I'm sorry."

The words he had longed to hear suddenly meant nothing. He dug at the cool soil as the trembling subsided and silence thickened the air. "I lost the Colt you gave me." Bet his brother never lost *his* gun.

"Yeah?"

He heard the smile in Fin's voice.

"I've known men to lose everything they started with—even the shirt off their backs."

How could he be so cavalier?

"I see you still got your knife though."

Zander nodded, remembering how hard he had worked to clean off the blood. If his Pap had known what that knife was going to do to somebody else's son—

"Time is a great healer of the wounds we can't see, little brother. It's a long road a man has to travel. Just don't you try to go it alone, ya hear?"

Enough. Zander bolted to his feet and started walking. His body cried for sleep and his mind wanted to explode.

"I'm quartering here tonight." His brother's steps closed in from behind. "And I'll come by for you in the morning. We'll head home—to James's house." Fin caught up and grabbed his sleeve, jolting him to a stop.

Zander shook off his brother's grip, refusing to look at him.

"Do me a favor," Fin said. "Don't let the girls know you were at Cloyd's Mountain."

He nodded and took off walking again.

"See you in the morning." Fin's voice trailed behind him.

What did he care where Fin was sleeping? His sour attitude grew heavier with each step. Why was the walk back so much longer than the one to the grove? It crossed his mind to head over to the corral, but he figured Rampart might be tuckered out after beating that mare this evening. Even the extra six dollars in his pocket did not shake his sullen mood.

Time, Fin had said.

Zander smirked. Time or death—whichever came first.

Nine

If only the refreshing early morning would linger a while longer. The horizon had booted the sun off toward mid-morning, and already Fin detected a mugginess set to infringe on this most glorious day. But nothing was going to rattle his homecoming—not the weather and not his moody little brother. Giddiness stretched his smile and filled his insides just thinking about Melinda Jane and the surprised look on her face.

The woods skittered and chirped a familiar complement to the rhythmic steps of his bay gelding, Duke. Rampart held to an easy pace despite a healthy pent-up energy, tossing his head and snorting now and then, as if making up for Zander's silence.

Fin glanced sideways at his brother, noting the deep ridges on his brow. Chewing the inside of his cheek, he tried to figure a way to reach inside his brother's head. He'd had a hard time of it. That was true. But now he was heading home to his family. Wasn't that a balm of sorts, being with the ones who love you most?

"So, what did you miss about home?" Fin leaned forward, trying to make eye contact. Maybe he could get him talking.

Zander shrugged. "The farm, I guess. Earlier days."

Not home cooking or the family or even Bertie's and Will's antics? Truth be told, if it were not for Melinda Jane, Fin would pine for the earlier days too. But he was on the cusp of starting his own family now, and that was something mighty fine to look forward to.

"I missed Melinda Jane's cooking."

Zander cocked his head with a skeptical eye. "Her *cooking*?"

"Uh . . . well . . . among other things."

At last, one side of Zander's mouth twitched like it pondered a grin.

Fin swallowed, trying to formulate what he wanted to say. "I know it's been hard. Truth be known . . . like walkin' through hell. But you can't let on to the women. If they really knew what we go through, they'd puddle-up on the floor and tie us to our bed posts so we couldn't ever leave again. Some things are between man and God."

Fin breathed a prayer, because there was no missing the way Zander's cheek hardened as he stared ahead. Or the way his fingers tapped the hilt of his saber.

Charleston

Fin took in the old sites as they rode down Front Street past two colorful riverboats snuggled up to rickety docks on the Kanawha River. The boats hissed and clanked in preparation to leave their moorings, likely carrying supplies upriver to troops. Familiar odors of fish and coal smoke hung in the humid air, suspended there for lack of a breeze.

He could never live in the city. Who wouldn't prefer the farm scents of fresh hay and the smell of rich soil? He had seen enough of what life offered to know what he wanted now.

"I wonder if they've eaten yet." Zander said, angling north up Cox's Lane. "Breakfast sounds good."

Now that was progress. If Fin failed to put a smile on that boy's face in the next few blocks, it would be a mighty pathetic homecoming for the family. "I believe I can smell biscuits from here," he said, sniffing the air. Yep. Definitely biscuits. "Golden brown on the outside. White and soft on the inside. Mmmm."

"And maybe some flapjacks? I haven't had flapjacks since I left home."

"A whack-o-jacks tall as the milk pitcher." Fin grinned. "With raspberry or maple syrup?"

"Maple. But I don't expect any since we're in town and all. Eggs are kind of rationed here too—what with only a dozen layers at James's place." Zander sat a little straighter and Rampart stepped a little higher.

"I bet little Adelaide has grown a foot." Fin smiled. He had seen his little niece a couple months back, but it always fascinated him the way babies sprouted up so fast.

"Yeah. Might be she's walking now. That is—so long has she's grown *two* feet instead of just *one* foot." Zander's mouth kicked up at the edge.

"Wiseacre." It wasn't exactly a smile, but it would have to do.

James's house came into view, and Fin urged Duke into a trot. His chest swelled and his heart beat faster at the thought of his wife's beautiful face, and her lips and her . . . everything. God sure knew what he was doing—creating woman for man.

He had left Zander behind somehow, so he motioned for him to catch up. "Well, come on! We'll surprise 'em together." Fin tied Duke to the rail and waited on Zander, who moved along at a snail's pace. His brother squinted up at the house, not even trying to hide the grimace on his face as they walked together.

"Think of the family, little brother. It's what we men do, no matter how hard it might come. You're home."

Just up that sidewalk, beyond the faded shingle that read, DR. JAMES HILL, PHYSICIAN, was the house where those he loved waited—and that made it home, for now.

"Home is the peace you need right now, little brother. You'll see." He nodded to Zander, doffed his hat and combed his hair with his fingers. Swallowing down a holler of excitement with a smile plastered across his face, he reached for the doorknob.

Ten

Closing the door behind him, Zander breathed in yeast and orange oil, cinnamon and soap. It smelled of home and family and food. It warmed his chest and lodged an unexpected lump in his throat. The old hound Coot trotted in from the kitchen, whining an impatient greeting as his tail whipped the air.

Fin chuckled. "The first in the family to greet us." He scratched Coot's ears and crooned a hello.

Zander stooped to ruffle the liver-colored fur and give the dog a hug. "You're moving a mite slower old boy. You'll have to go out and get reacquainted with Rampart." He jerked his attention to a series of thuds as nine-year-old Bertie bounded down the last two stairs.

"Fin! Zander!" His little brother charged into him with a toppling force.

Gaining his footing, Zander snatched Bertie up in a bear hug, surprised at the laughter gurgling up from his insides. It felt good. Real good. "Whatcha been doing, brother—eatin' my share?"

"I been trying, but Gus just plain refuses me third helpings."

"I do not!" Gus pushed through the kitchen door, a wide grin on her face and tears already slipping down her freckled cheeks as crimson blotches mottled her brow.

Melinda Jane paused on the landing, eyes wide, hand to her mouth. "Fin!" She choked back a sob and tears sprouted as she flew down the stairs, still in her wrapper. "You're here! And Zander. Praise the Lord!" Fin met her at the bottom, swallowing her tiny frame in an embrace.

Zander no sooner released Bertie, and Gus grabbed him. His sister squeezed his middle like she was wrestling a steer as he hugged her right back.

He was home.

She let go and grasped his shoulders, scrutinizing him as if he were one of her patients. She blinked hard and turned pensive. "You're not hurt?" Her piercing gaze seemed to cut right through him—as if she could see beyond his fragile façade. For just an instant, a storm of knowing clouded those green eyes, splintering his resolve.

She hugged him again, tighter, and when the back door slammed, she stepped aside. "That would be Will."

"What's all the ruckus in here? I could hear you from—"

Will froze in the doorway, her expression an exquisite mix of surprise and relief. She bolted for Zander. "You're not dead! You're home! You're not dead!" She hugged his waist, chasing the air from of his lungs.

It had only been six months, not *years*. He pried her grip loose so he could catch a breath and look at her. "You thought I was dead?" Was there something he should know?

"No. I'm just glad you're not, 'cause I prayed every single day that you wouldn't be. You and Fin both." The summer sun winked through the lace curtains, setting her eyes to shimmer as they bounced between her two older brothers. She had sure done some growing the last few months. And he wouldn't be here to chase off the boys. Melancholy intruded on his homecoming, and he shook it off.

Will swished over to Fin, who stood with his arm around Melinda Jane, and his moony eyes glued to hers. As if it were a dance, Will and Melinda Jane traded places and Zander's sister-in-law snugged under his arm.

She gazed up at Zander, and a fresh round of tears dotted her lashes and leaked down her face. "You know, every time I did the cookin' and had to make half as much, it was a reminder to pray for you." She pulled him down to hug his neck. Her body trembled, and he wrapped his arms a bit tighter, wishing he could ease her concern. Pulling back, she wiped a tear from his face and set her palm to his cheek. "We missed you something fierce, Private Dabney."

"Well, I...I'll try to eat my share whilst I'm here," he scratched out, talking around a walnut-sized lump.

Fin had been right. He needed this place, this peace.

"There's someone else here who would like to say hello." His brother-in-law stood in the parlor doorway with little Addie squirming in his arms. No freckles, yet, but a head of coppery hair just like her mama and the same sweet smile. James set her down, and she toddled across the floor on tiptoes, each hand squeezing one of her pappy's fingers.

Zander squatted and held out his arms. "Come to Uncle Zander, Addie." James pried one chubby hand loose, and the little girl reached out to him. "I think she remembers me."

"She pretty much goes to anybody," Bertie said with a shrug.

"Bertie!" Gus scolded.

"Well, she does. But that don't mean she don't recognize Zander."

"It's all right." Zander gathered Addie into his arms. Such innocence. Seemed it wasn't so long-ago Bertie was about this age. Zander would set the little tyke in the straw to keep him happy while he tended to Rampart, just a colt at the time. Life had been so good, then. He had nary a care in the world. Another lifetime ago.

James gripped Zander's shoulder and pumped his available hand. A russet beard hid much of his scarred face, but not the warm smile. "It's good to have you back. How long is your furlough?"

"Five days."

Gus slipped her arm through her husband's. "We'll take good care of you whilst you're here."

Zander nodded and turned to Fin, but he must've slipped out of the room with Melinda Jane.

"WHOO-EEE!"

Zander jolted at the cry and clutched his knife. His heart hit the ceiling then plummeted to the floor. He shot a look around the room, trying to slow his breathing, hoping no one had noticed. But James met his gaze, his lips drawn tight and his eyes colored with concern. Or was it understanding?

Fin swaggered in, a ridiculous grin plastered across his face and Melinda Jane caught up in his arms, feet in the air. "I'm gonna be a pappy, everybody!" He kissed her smack on the lips. "We're gonna have a baby!"

"*We're* gonna have a baby?" Melinda Jane flashed a sassy look. "I don't know what part it is exactly that you plan on doing, Phineas Dabney, but I'll gladly give you this first watch with all the heaving I been a-doin'!"

"Is that why you been so qualmish? Cuz you're havin' a baby?" Bertie scratched his head. "I don't remember the cows ever losing their hay afore birthin'."

Everyone roared with laughter. Bertie frowned. Fin lowered Melinda Jane to the floor as if she were made of crystal.

Zander chewed the inside of his cheek, taking in his brother and his wife. How in blazes could Fin be so altogether full of joy—after everything he'd been through?

Time.

"Glory be! Me boys are home! I near dropped the eggs when I heard the ruckus." Mrs. O'Donell scurried into the room, flapping her arms like a mama bird, herding Fin and Zander to her. She stepped back and looked each of them up and down. "Praise the Almighty, yer both in one piece."

"I'm gonna be a pappy, Mrs. O'Donell!" Fin sounded and looked like a schoolboy. His enthusiasm brought a round of laughter.

"And so, ya are!" She winked at Melinda Jane. "This rebellion best be a-quittin' soon so the wee one will have his da home." She had not let go of Zander's arm and now she tugged his ear closer. "'Tis a glorious day indeed to see you've come to no harm. Gus has been beside herself with worry. Och, she doesn't let on much, ya know, but we could tell. We've all been miserable not knowing whether ye be alive or daid. So, why have ya not seen fit to write? Would it have hurt ya to set yer sister's mind at ease some?"

Her whispered words dripped with concern, but still scolded. He was eleven years old again, caught fiddling with Rampart instead of stacking the dry wood like he had been told. A week of rain taught him a hard lesson when the family had nothing to burn but wet wood.

He should have written those letters.

He forced a smile. "I'll write as soon as I'm settled at my next post. Didn't mean to cause worry." Why hadn't he been less selfish and thought about his family needing to hear from him? He would write real regular from now on.

"There, there." She patted his hand and her gray eyes gentled. She spoke up a bit as the room grew louder. "I dinna mean to make ya feel guilty. I'm guessing you were caught up in the newness of it all. 'Tis water under the bridge, as they say."

Gus batted the air with her hands, quieting the room. "I'll make us a big celebration breakfast. Will? Please come with me." She headed for the kitchen.

"But I wanna stay in here with the boys."

Gus passed her a look that sent her stomping into the kitchen.

Zander's heart swelled with belonging. Some things never change at home. It wasn't the farm, but it was home.

James held out his hands to Addie, and she sprang from Zander's grasp. She laughed and patted her pappy's chin whiskers. He barely remembered the somber Major James Hill who commandeered their barn for a Union hospital three years ago. Time marched on. It surely did, whether a body wanted it to or not.

Time. That's what Fin said he needed.

Zander called after James as he headed out of the room with Addie, "You're not using your cane?" The Dabney barn had burned the first year of the war and James nearly died in the blaze. He had used a cane ever since.

"I've been trying to get around without it here at home." James smiled adoringly at his daughter before locking eyes with Zander. "As I'm sure you know by now, just because it is not obvious to others, doesn't mean there's no pain."

Zander closed his eyes, letting the strong coffee-scented steam wet his face. No matter that the day was muggy and hot, the brew was a comfort he had not enjoyed since he left home. The swill his unit drinks around the fire tastes like you just showed the bean to the water. He would wait another minute, then chance a scorched tongue for a taste.

James gripped the carved arms of the parlor chair and gingerly lowered himself to the seat before picking up his own cup. "I brought the coffee back from Wheeling last time I was there. Prices aren't near what they are here."

"Ahhh . . . I'd forgotten what a good cup of coffee could do for your taster." Fin settled into the stuffed seat, still with the same smile he had worn since they arrived. "Thank you."

"Yeah, thanks." Zander blew across the rim, then cautiously slurped.

"The women and Bertie are off to town." James sobered. "I want to know where you two have been. What's happening out there?"

"You being a Major still, I thought you'd know everything already," Zander quipped, a bit more harshly than he intended.

James passed a look to Fin, then set his cup down before eyeing Zander directly. "I'm only privy to what the camp commanders happen to know when I visit the camps."

"Sorry, that came out wrong." He wasn't raised to be contrary. James only acted as an Army surgeon in a limited capacity because of his injuries, and Zander knew it.

"That's all right. I tried to keep track of you both, but it wasn't always possible." He smirked at Fin. "Especially with you."

"Even *I* can't keep track of me," Fin said with a chuckle. "Half the time I'm off on a minute's notice."

Zander eyed his brother. The question had been nagging at him. "What'd you do up in Lewisburg to keep those Rebs off of Crook's troops? We got a straight shot all the way to Cloyd's Mountain without a confrontation because of that."

Fin chuckled. "Not one of my prouder moments. We just lit a mess of fires and made a bunch of racket—us and the Fifth Infantry's band. Did a good job of fooling those Confederates into thinking Lewisburg was under attack again. When they pulled their forces in, we slipped out the back door."

"Wait." James leaned forward, arms on his knees, eyes drilling Zander. "*You* were at Cloyd's Mountain?"

Zander stared at his feet. Then he stared at his hands. He wiped them on his britches several times, unwilling to meet James's gaze.

His brother-in-law groaned, falling back against the tufted chair. "They figured the Union lost ten percent of its force to casualties there. The Rebs lost closer to twenty—including General Jenkins." He gripped Zander's knee. "Thank God," he rasped, directing his words heavenward.

Zander shot up, almost capsizing his cup. He set it on the tray. Unwilling to let his mind travel back to the battle, he walked over to the bookcase. He ran his fingers across the spines of Pap's books, brought from the farm when the family fled. The books were a piece of Pap—a piece of his family. "Can I take one of these back with me?" he asked, turning suddenly.

"I don't know why not," James answered, a skeptical tip to one eyebrow. "Best talk to Gus about that."

Zander took his seat again. He could talk about the campaign. But only that. "Fin, I looked for you on General Hunter's expedition. Were you in the advance or the rear?"

"Advance. Got a Birdseye view to General Hunter's *tactics*." He snorted as hard lines carved his jaw and fire blazed in his eyes. "Ten minutes. That's how long he gave the Governor's wife and daughter to vacate their home before burning it—supposedly in retaliation for some bushwhackers burning Governor Pierpont's place."

"Yeah, we watched it burn. Most of Crook's men were pretty disgusted with it, all right." Zander gulped the rest of his coffee. "'Tweren't right. Pert near every town we marched through caught Hunter's wrath. I can just imagine how terrified those families must've been." He shook his head. "My unit had nothing to do with all that. Only thing Hunter accomplished was to make the Union Army look bad."

Fin rolled up his sleeves and grumbled. When he scrubbed his beard, he exposed a jagged scar running from knuckle to elbow. Zander swallowed hard, figuring only a knife could've done that, the way that purple snake turkey-tailed all ropish-looking. Now that was a war-wound folks would notice. Another thing to add to his brother's reputation as the *Dragon Slayer*.

But what about his own scars? Seemed *his* wounds were out of sight, so no one would ever know. He'd have been better off with a scar like Fin's to show off. Then maybe folks would just leave him be. Why'd he get the sour end of the deal, anyway? He'd rather have a hundred stitches than—

His gaze shifted from the scar to Fin, who was frowning right at him. Zander glared back, daring him to look away. Resentment suddenly roiled inside him like a rapid as he fisted his hands.

Fin's jaw hardened and he squinted at Zander a minute before dropping his hand and slipping it under his leg. "Buchanan's only fit for owls and bats after what they done," Fin groused. "Poor folks."

"Zander? Are you all right?" James asked.

"Huh? Um...we bivouacked outside Lynchburg—not doing a durn thing." He shifted back in time, remembering. "Stayed so long, the Rebs had time to call in reinforcements—and we could hear them celebratin' from our camp." Zander wanted to spit out the rising bile. "What we should have attacked, we didn't. What we should've left alone, we molested."

James accepted a coffee refill from Fin and announced, "As of yesterday, Jeff Davis has publicly declared General Hunter a felon—to be executed upon capture for what he's done to the citizenry."

Fin shook his head. "At least ol' Bill Thurmond's been captured. Not quite sure how much that will quell the antics of Thurmond's Rangers, though." He yawned as he stood to stretch. "Thanks for the coffee, James. I'm goin' upstairs. And if I don't wake up for supper, that's fine by me."

Zander headed for the kitchen and the back door. "Yeah, thanks for the coffee. I'll be in the barn. Would ya mind telling Will I want to see her when she gets back?"

"Zander?"

He turned.

James stood awkwardly, brushing away Fin's help. His brow furrowed, and Zander recognized that look. *Pity*. "I wish I had noble words to assuage the ache I know is in your soul. Only God's grace and time can do that."

Time. Yeah. *Grace*? Where is that?

Zander nodded stiffly and strode through the kitchen. He paused with one hand on the back doorknob as James's voice scratched low, talking to Fin in the other room.

"He's not a boy anymore. Bloodiest, ninety minutes of the war, they're saying—Cloyd's Mountain."

"Yeah. His body may be home for now, but it'll be a long time before he's our Zander again. A long time."

There it was again. He gritted his teeth, mighty tired of hearing that word.

Zander wrapped his savings in last week's newspaper and tied the string in a knot that was never meant to be untied. He added another long piece of string and wrapped it around the rectangle.

"You wanted to see me?" Will stuck her head into the barn.

"Yeah. Come in and close the door will, you?"

"Ooo. What's so secretive?" She stepped closer, eyes twinkling with mischief.

"I want you to hang onto something for me. And I don't want anybody to know about it."

"I guess I can do that. What is it?"

He cocked his head to one side, shooting her with a look born of fifteen years dealing with his sister's antics. "If I don't tell you for your own good, are you gonna be disagreeable?"

She must've had to think about that, because for a rare moment she seemed speechless.

"Please?" It was the only plan he could come up with. He couldn't drag the money around with him anymore. It had been hard enough worrying about it stuffed in his saddlebags during those last two campaigns.

She propped her hands on her hips. "Alexander Dabney, you better not be getting me into any trouble here."

"You just have to promise not to open it." He grinned and held out the package. "'Sides, since when do you shy away from trouble?"

She chuffed and rolled her eyes. "All right. I'll take care of this here mystery package, but you have to promise to bring me something the next time you come home."

A bag of candy was a small price to pay for her silence. "You got it."

"I want earrings. Nothing ostentatious. Tiny pearl filigree maybe." Her eyebrows arched and a sly smile crept across her face. "Deal?"

Earrings? Ostentatious? When did his boy-whuppin', britches-wearin' sister start thinking about earrings? He looked her over. She'd grown up fast here in Charleston. *Too* fast.

"Deal. Thank you, Will. It means a lot to me."

Eleven

FORT FULLER, NEW CREEK, WV

Somebody in Zander's unit must've been spouting off, because here he was, challenged to a race after only three days at his new post. Surely, these Pennsylvania boys had not heard about his racing.

He eyed his opponent, sizing up the way he cranked on the reins and the telltale raw corners of his horse's mouth. Zander didn't have to swallow the bait, but something about this blackguard's attitude kicked up his dander.

"Come on, Dabney. I don't have all day." Ford's burly form dwarfed the black gelding as he reined it in a tight circle. He spewed a brown stream and shot a squinty-eyed dart in Zander's direction.

With the morning sun at his back, Bass waved them into position for the start of the race with a private wink for Zander. Ford tapped spurs to the horse, igniting a nervous shuffle in the mount.

The man's cruelty frayed a hole in Zander's usual calm. Men like Ford populated the cavalry at every post. Treat your mount with kindness and respect and the horse would show you the same, he always figured.

Bass stepped between them. "The odds are ten to one, Dabney's favor."

"No!" Ford roared. "My horse for yours."

Zander shrugged. "No race then." He turned Rampart about, raising a grumble from a growing crowd. Others had offered him this foolish proposition before.

"All right, then. Your fifty dollars against my horse." Ford's hard black eyes challenged him.

Scars striped the horse's sides. No government brand. Some men treated their mounts like throw-aways.

"Your sway-back, wet-footed nag can't take ol' Rubicon here. Or maybe you're just a coward, Dragon *Licker*." He fired the moniker like a cannon for all to hear.

Zander's ire flamed. Was there no escaping his brother's reputation? This big buffoon needed to be put in his place, and he was just the one to do it. He nodded his agreement to Bass, who looked none too pleased. Good thing Zander hadn't mentioned the little fact that his *savings* was now at the *Bank of Dabney* in Charleston.

"Dabney will take your bet, Ford. Still ten to one odds, Dabney's favor—for the crowd. If you win, you get your fifty dollars. If Dabney wins, he gets your mount."

A murmur trickled through the swarming onlookers as money changed hands. Bass collected bets while Zander repositioned Rampart next to Rubicon at the starting line. Ford threw a few shrewdly chosen insults into the air trying to gain support.

"You okay with this, boy?" Zander whispered, scratching Rampart's neck. The answer nickered back as tested muscle rippled beneath his hand.

The starting flag whipped the air, igniting man and beast to a fiery start as hooves sliced the sodden earth.

Zander held steady a length behind. "Easy boy," he crooned as Rampart responded to his will. Ford took advantage and leaned Rubicon directly into his path, and Rampart's ears signaled his annoyance at the tactic. Enough was enough. Zander shifted his weight and measured strides cut into the mushy ground, easily propelling him into the lead. When a boisterous string of curses colored the air, Zander looked back to see his opponent wiping mud from his eyes.

Part of him felt sorry for the braggart. A small part. But a race was just that, and this ol' boy needed to be knocked down a peg.

Zander slowed a mite as he rounded the last curve, allowing Rubicon to pull up even with Rampart.

Determination carved Ford's features as he squinted one eye. He transferred reins from two hands to one as his horse slowed, veered to the left, and then corrected while pulling ahead. He looked over, shocked as he realized Zander was dead even again.

The man spurred his mount forward with only twenty yards left, casting Zander a devilish grin.

Maybe Zander ought to let him have the race. But even as he considered it, Rampart practically leapt into the lead and finished a full two lengths ahead of Rubicon.

A cacophony of cheers erupted, peppered with Ford's expletives before he pulled a kerchief from his pocket and wiped his red eyes.

Zander dismounted and bowed to the crowd, as did his four-legged partner. He stepped to the right, then left, and turned a circle and Rampart mimicked his movements. The cheerful response brought another bow from each of them.

Somebody handed him a canteen, but before he took a swig, he poured water onto his kerchief, offering it to Ford. "This'll help."

Ford slapped his hand away. "I don't need anything from you, ya cheat!"

"How you figure I cheated?"

"You know exactly what you did." The words hissed through gritted teeth.

"I don't know what you think I did, Ford, but that was a clean race."

"What is this?" Bass stepped between them, a scowl rumpling his stoic appearance. He studied Ford's mud-covered face and cringed. "Um . . . you will want to take your saddle, Ford."

Zander shifted his attention to Rampart. If he wasn't careful, they could both wind up in lockup over the whole affair.

The whole kerfuffle drew bystanders, more than a little interested in their conversation by now.

"You're a cheat, Dabney." Ford swore and stalked over to Rubicon. "A cheat!"

Zander walked Rampart, cooling him down until the crowd dispersed, then approached Rubicon. "I won this horse fair and square, Ford."

"Shut up, Dabney." Ford slid the saddle from the horse. Sleek, black fur glistened in the sunlight. "Take him. Worthless piece of meat."

Zander lobbed a leather strap over Rubicon's head and handed Ford the bridle.

"This ain't over, Dabney!" His eyes flared as he ground out each syllable. "Not over by a long shot!"

The words held a telling edge, sharp as the knife on his thigh.

Lola blinked against the sting as sweat pooled in the corner of her eye. The sun showed no mercy today, honed as it was by a clear blue sky and the complete absence of a breeze. She dug a hanky from a pocket of her gingham apron and dabbed her cheeks and neck. New faces sprinkled the grounds of Fort Fuller today, likely a newly arrived unit since her last visit.

She stepped aside as Eleazar, her father's hired man, effortlessly moved barrels from the wagon bed. Her work was so much easier when Papa could part with him for a spell. It took her fifteen minutes to do what he could do in two. The last time the town changed hands, poor Eleazar had high-tailed it over the state line into Pennsylvania so Rebels wouldn't claim he was a runaway-slave. This awful war needed to be done with!

"*Now* can I go?" whined Felix. "I want to go see those yo-yos over there." He pointed to a merchant across the yard, busy with his own set-up.

"I don't believe I've seen that man before." She struggled to lift a heavy crate of canned goods, adjusting her grip a second time. "Do you know him, Eleazar?"

"Can't say I do." His dark arms glistened as he snatched up the crate with little effort. "I can finish setting-up if you want, Miss Wade."

"Thank you, Eleazar." She brushed the dust from her hands and skirt, more than willing to let him take over. "I won't be but a minute. I'll just introduce myself before the man gets too busy with customers."

She accompanied Felix to the yo-yo vender to make introductions. Assorted small items from chess pieces to pocket knives already cluttered the makeshift table while the squat, graying Mr. Nobly attempted to make room for more.

Felix beamed at the merchant. "Did you know the yo-yo is thought to have originated in Greece? Instead of wood, these parts here," he pointed to the round disks, "were made of terracotta. That's a type of clay."

"I didn't know that." Mr. Nobly's overly-long cheek whiskers trembled with a chuckle. "You are one very smart young man."

"I read a lot." Felix hovered over the neatly arranged dime novels. He gasped and reached for a book. "You have *Captives of the Wild Frontier*!"

Lola rolled her eyes, knowing what would come next.

"*Puh-leez* can I have it, Lola?"

She smoothed the mop of black hair from his forehead. "I don't think that's proper reading material for a boy your age."

Disappointment stole every bit of his excitement, drawing his sweet face into such a sad state that she nearly gave in. He was such a good boy, and she hated to see him disappointed. Better that he get used to it now, she supposed. Adult life held a host of disappointments.

"How about a book on birds?" Mr. Nobly slipped a pocket-sized book from the back of a crate. "Just two cents." He winked, seeming to understand her predicament.

Felix brandished a tilted smile and batted his eyes—a tactic he had perfected. And it worked its magic on her. Every time.

She smiled and dug into her skirt pocket. "Here you go, Mr. Nobly. And it was a pleasure to make your acquaintance. I hope to see you in Wade's Mercantile when you're in town."

"Likewise, miss." He tipped his hat and handed her brother the book.

Felix began thumbing through it. "Thank you, sir."

"We best get back. Can't let Eleazar do *all* the setting up."

"Can I look around after we're done?" Felix asked.

"*May* you look around."

"I might if you say I can." He pressed the book to his chest, looking every bit the part of a compliant child.

"You spend more time wandering than helping with customers. You'll be doing this on your own in another few years, you know."

"Me? I'm gonna be a professor, not a store clerk."

"Well, you'll not be going to college if you don't help with the family business to make the money to pay for your schooling, little brother."

"I'll write books for kids my age to read. Books with *appropriate* material. Then I'll sell them and make enough money to pay for college. Likely I'll be a famous author one day."

That was her brother—thinking like a grown-up and acting like a child. And she wouldn't trade him for anything. She lifted his cap and dropped a kiss onto his forehead with an eddy of pride and love swirling inside her. "You just keep thinking like that, my little entrepreneur."

Zander slid his hand down Rubicon's front leg. Sure enough, the warmth there told him what he suspected. He checked the other cannons. Swollen. And a jagged scar wrapped a rear fetlock—likely from a briar tangle.

He patted the horse's withers. "I'll take care of you, boy. No more harm will come to you." He would need some supplies.

"Come on, Rampart, let's go visit the sutlers and see if we can get this ol' boy fixed up." He left Rubicon tethered and led Rampart across the open yard. The livery and blacksmith sat on one side with the hospital and command buildings on the other, encompassing the entire wide area.

"That's a roan. And a gelding. Would you call him a chestnut roan?"

Zander looked behind him for the disembodied young voice.

"I've got a book on horses at home." A boy about Bertie's age with a mop of dark hair seemed to appear out of nowhere. "Am I right?"

"You are at that." He grinned and extended a hand. "I'm Zander, what's your name?"

"Felix." The boy pumped his hand.

"Good to make your acquaintance Felix. And this here's Rampart."

"Hey, boy. You're sure fine looking," Felix crooned, scratching the whiskery chin then beaming at Zander. "And you're a private. I can tell because of your sleeve."

"My sleeve?"

"Yeah. You don't have a rank insignia. If you had two *V*'s, you'd be a corporal, and three would make you a sergeant. But I can tell you're cavalry by that red regiment patch."

Was this kid for real? "You sure do know a lot for . . . what are you, nine or ten?"

"Ten last month." Felix nudged the hair from over his too-serious eyes. "Can Rampart do any tricks? Before the war, a traveling show came by and it had a horse that did tricks. I still remember it."

Zander chuckled. "I'll bet Rampart here makes that trickster show horse look like a dimwit." He lobbed the reins over Rampart's neck and stepped in front of him. He shook his head, and the horse did likewise. Then he nodded his head, rewarded with a deliberate nod.

"Can he dance?" Felix stroked the red mane.

"Well of course he can dance."

Zander bowed, and Rampart returned it. Next, he did a series of steps, and when he turned back to his *dance partner*, the horse repeated every step with trusting brown eyes fixed on his master. For the finale, Zander raised both hands in the air and Rampart reared on his back feet and pawed the air several times, whinnying in delight.

Felix's exuberance was the perfect reward. He clapped and clapped, collecting interest from passersby. "That really *was* better than that traveling show horse!"

Rampart nuzzled his master's ear, the soft tickle sending a shiver down Zander's spine.

"I do believe you like all this attention, don't you?" He reached up to scratch between the twitching ears. "We're on a mission to get some supplies, for doctoring a horse," he told Felix.

"Follow me. I know right where you can get them."

"All right. You wanna ride?"

"I never rode bareback before."

Zander hoisted him onto Rampart and handed him the reins. "I'm right beside you."

Half a dozen sutler stands drew a smattering of customers and it was not hard to spot the most likely merchant to have what he needed.

"What do you think you're doing with him?" A bespectacled woman about Zander's age stood on tiptoe and slid Felix off Rampart's back.

"He's just giving me a ride on his trickster horse. Don't be mad." Felix shook off her grasp.

"We are here to do business, sir, nothing more." She scolded both of them with her eyes.

Zander doffed his hat. "I'm not a sir, ma'am. Just a private. We didn't mean any harm. My apologies." He had stumbled across a mama bear, for sure.

"We?" She glanced around and pulled Felix close, protectively.

"This is Rampart. We were just giving your son a ride."

"My *son*? Are you saying I look old enough to be his mother?" She jammed fists onto her hips and glared. He stepped back a few inches. That feminine form and pert nose were deceiving.

"Oh, no, miss." Zander eyed the apothecary supplies on the far end of a table. "I think I'd better just get me some of that liniment right there and be on my way." Growing up with three females in the house had taught him a thing or two about women. He knew when to retreat.

A black man rounded the wagon and acknowledged the woman with a nod. "Is there a problem, Miss Wade?"

The woman hesitated, looking like she was trying to decide whether to send Zander off or put him in his place. The fire in her blue eyes settled a bit, and she stepped behind the table.

"Everything is fine, Eleazar. Thank you." Her look still held a skeptical squint.

The man stood every bit of his own six feet plus, and had a kind look about him. Zander thrust out his hand. "I'm Zander."

"Eleazar Franklin." He looked at Zander's hand for a second, then grasped it, exposing a toothy smile. Eleazar regarded Miss Wade, whose stern expression had twisted into a confused pout. He shook his head, amusement passing over his features. "I'll be back come time to pack up."

"Thank you, Eleazar." Miss Wade pulled her shoulders back and picked up the liniment, thrusting it toward Zander. "That'll be twenty cents."

"Might you have some bandages and mustard, Miss?" He dipped his chin and flashed a hopeful grin. He was pressing his luck. She huffed under her breath, and Zander turned to check on Rampart, who seemed pleased as everything to have Felix rubbing his neck. "He likes to be scratched between the ears."

"But I can't reach."

"Just ask him real nice-like to lower his head so you can reach."

Miss Wade held out a roll of bandages. "Really, Private . . . I don't think—"

"Rampart, would you please lower your head so I can scratch between your ears?" Felix asked as polite and sincere as if he was requesting seconds at the supper table.

Unbeknownst to Felix, Zander bowed his head. Rampart did likewise, holding it low and still as the boy scratched between his ears.

Zander turned to Miss Wade, purely pleased to see her sour expression replaced by a broad smile. A very *fetching* smile. He grinned and caught her eye. She quickly frowned, nudging her spectacles higher.

"You . . . you have a talented horse there." She jutted out her palm, all business again. "That'll be twenty-five cents."

He dug the coins from his pocket. "You come here every week, Miss Wade?"

She nodded, one hand fussing with the angelic spray of yellow curls framing her face. "On . . . on Saturdays."

He would make sure he needed something next Saturday, too.

Twelve

Drill—a colossal waste of time. Zander smoothed the impatient ripple that skittered across Rampart's loins. Neither of them was happy to have to wait for the rest of the troops. *Good thing there wasn't a war going on or anything.*

The sarcasm tasted more bitter than sweet. Being with family had shown him just how far down river that attitude had dragged him. He was not altogether sure how to climb out of the water, though. Likely, he'd just let the current carry him along—alone.

The rest of his unit jockeyed into position amid curses and good-natured jabs. Other horses snorted and stomped to Rampart's composure. The parade ground fell silent as the artillery arrived, filing into their familiar positions, rehearsed a dozen times.

Following inspection, the order rang out for a volley. Twelve-pound howitzers and ten-pound Parrot rifles exploded their charges. Zander tensed as blasts fogged the air with clusters that seemed to wag black fingers of disapproval as he drew his saber and the unit simulated a charge.

Only after the charge did they retire from the field—at a pace to try the stoutest of patience. Had they ever actually used these precise maneuvers in battle? No. Not once this entire year. Was there really any way to prepare for the chaos of battle, though? He shook his head. So, they continued to drill like they were fighting the War for Independence. Well, he would not be moving at a snail's pace while men were being cut down. No sir.

And when had he even squandered a thought on fighting another battle, anyway? Not so long ago, hadn't he considered deserting—before he would allow some medal-wearing, paper-pushing officer to force him into battle again? From the way James and Fin let on, no two battles were alike. But what if he *was* up against another like Cloyd's Mountain? Darkness shuddered through his body and the lonesome space inside him expanded a bit more.

Leach trotted up to him as the unit split apart. "Hey, Dabney, you wanna head into town with us?"

"Sure. I could use a couple of things."

Kyle Stille, more disagreeable than not, rolled his pock-marked neck and stretched his back. "Wish I didn't have gate duty. Only time it's at all interesting, is when we got visitors."

"Be happy it is not latrine duty." Bass added. "I put in my time last week. Your turn will come soon enough."

Captain Giles trotted closer, cutting across the grounds to meet up with Zander. "Private Dabney."

"Yes, sir?" Hopefully he wasn't in trouble.

The captain slowed to a walk. "Sounds like Blazer's Scouts are holding up their reputations over in the Shenandoah."

Zander sighed inside. Did he honestly want to know? Of course he did. Fin was his brother, after all. If he continued to carry this chip around and something happened to Fin . . . "How's that, sir?"

"Seems General Sheridan has been none too happy about Mosby's guerillas harassing his supply lines so he sent Blazer's men after them. Set them up as sharpshooters at Snicker's Gap. Put Mosby back in his place real fast."

"That's good news, sir."

"Just thought you'd like to know." He circled back to the rear again, out of sight.

Stille leaned forward in his saddle, yellow teeth shaping a crooked grin. "When you gonna live up to your brother's reputation, Dabney? When you gonna slay your own dragons, huh?"

"When he is good and ready." Bass's eyes flared a warning.

"I guess it ain't your fault you weren't born with no kind of grit." Stille jabbed.

"Maybe he just didn't inherit the Dragon Slayer's skills, being the little brother and all." A voice snarled from behind.

"Naw. He don't have the guts. I seen the way he is. Why, I bet he apologizes to the chicken afore he rings its neck." Spittle squirted from Stille's mouth as he howled, miming the action.

Zander trained his eyes ahead, fighting the urge to pull out ahead of them. He'd had plenty of practice. The more they thought it bothered him, the worse it would get.

Leach turned in his saddle, shooting daggers at the man. "Stille, you don't know what you're talking about."

"You did not see Dabney here, at Cloyd's Mountain—did you?" Bass led his horse in closer, cutting in next to Stille. "And do you know why you did not see this man?"

"Cuz he was dug into a hidey-hole, wetting himself and crying for his mama?"

Boisterous laughter erupted. And multiplied. The whopper-jawed fool had collected a bigger audience than Zander realized. If Bass would just shut his pie hole . . .

"*Quatsch*! You did not see him because *you* did not even make it as far as the breastworks before you turned yeller." He muttered something in German and continued. "This man fought through every inch of the Rebel line. He has killed better men than you, Stille." Bass picked up his pace, hurling the last words behind him. "Think on that."

"Hey." Leach bumped Zander's knee. "Don't give that fool another thought. Let it slide right off your back."

"Yeah. Sure."

Killed better men than you?

And he was supposed to let that slide off his back too?

Zander perused New Creek's main street. A quaint little town with only a handful of businesses. Even so, it dwarfed Gauley Bridge. Clapboard and log houses sprinkled the sloping landscape on either side of the street, some with property stretching behind the stores. A lush field of knee-hi corn encroached on a white-washed barn at the near end of town, its gaping haymow door reminding him of happier times. He craned his head, trying to make out just what kind of buildings lay at the far end of this main road.

To his right, the post office shared a porch with a barber shop. Across from that and down aways, just past a narrow alley, looked to be a little cafe-type establishment. Likely more a saloon than anything—no doubt the most prosperous establishment this near the fort. Next door to that, a faded, but colorful sign announced in bold gray letters, WADE'S MERCANTILE AND DRUGS.

"I'm going in there," Zander told Bass and Leach.

Bass eyed the saloon. "And *I* am going in there." His eyebrows switched like two fat black caterpillars.

Leach pulled off his hat, running stubby fingers through shaggy, straw-colored hair. "I'm getting me a real haircut—and a close shave. Always a possibility of making the acquaintance of a God-fearing woman." He grinned and aimed his mount toward the broken hitching post in front of the barber's.

Zander hopped down and led Rampart to the town drinking trough before lobbing the reins over the rail in front of the Mercantile. He froze for an instant, hairs bristling across the back of his neck. It sure felt like someone was watching him.

He settled his hand on his new Colt and scanned his surroundings. Probably just his mind playing tricks on him. It would not be the first time.

A lone figure leaned against the saloon building with his face obscured in the shadows. The stranger seemed to stare directly at him. Something familiar about the way the man held his head niggled at Zander—cocky, daring. The stranger pushed himself away from the wall and turned, limping toward the alley.

It couldn't be!

"Hey!" Zander yelled, stepping out, hoping his eyes were playing tricks on him. The figure disappeared around the corner and Zander took off in a jog. "Wait a minute!"

He rounded the building, but the man was nowhere in sight. He sprinted to the back of the saloon and glimpsed the stranger, moving at a good clip for somebody who was obviously lame.

"Wait!" Whoever it was, didn't intend to get caught.

Zander ran past four houses, turned north, and circled back. There, behind the old barn, the man crouched, still as anything as if he had successfully evaded capture.

He surprised the man from behind. "Carter?"

Carter Dabney stood and swore before turning. A disgusted look gouged his face before splaying into a flashy, insincere smile. "Well, what do you know? If it isn't Zander Dabney. How ya been, *Cousin*?" He extended a hand in greeting.

Zander chewed the inside of his cheek, eyeing him with suspicion and ignoring the proffered hand. "Why aren't you in prison?" The last he had seen him, Carter Dabney was a little singed, shackled, and headed for a Union prison.

"Nice to see you, too." He dipped his head befitting a Southern gentleman. Having been raised on the Dabney plantation in Virginia, he and his family proved quite the contrast to Zander's family—especially where ethics were concerned.

"Why aren't you in prison?" Zander stared, injustice rankling his manners. What was he supposed to make of this?

"I was there all right. Over a year at Camp Chase, then almost another at Johnson's Island before they paroled me." A storm clouded his features. "No thanks to my kin in this counterfeit state—this bastard offspring of political rape." His jab wielded the saber of a challenge.

"Now just a minute. My family had nothing to do with you getting wounded or ending up a prisoner in our barn."

He sneered. "And here I thought blood was supposed to be thicker than water."

"There's nothing we could've done for you, Carter, and you know it." The memory rode a spiteful wave, the image of his smoke-blinded, heartbroken sister so clear. "We'd be all too happy to never see you again after what you did to Gus—"

"I was only thinking of her, Zander. There was no future for her with a man like James Hill. It was for her own good." Sincerity, real or false, colored his words. "Surely you understand that."

"You don't lie to family just because it suits you. You put her through hell, thinking James was dead for all that time. And what about burning down our barn?"

Carter shrugged and pulled a mangled, mud-colored cigarette from his pocket. He rolled and straightened it with his fingers. "The barn was unintentional. You can thank your dear Dr. Hill for that."

"He didn't start the fight, Carter, you did." Zander drew his Colt. "I'm taking you in as an escaped prisoner."

Carter chortled with an excess of amusement. "Not *escaped*. Paroled. And this leg gives me such fits as to prevent me from serving the Confederacy—*my* country." He struck a match on the barn's foundation and lit the cigarette.

Something did not ring true to his story. Hadn't he done a fair job of evading Zander just a few minutes before? "You shouldn't be here. If you're really paroled, why aren't you back in King William County?"

"I'm free to travel wherever I desire."

"But you're a Confederate and this is Union territory."

"I happen to know that there are plenty of Southern sympathizers residing in this state. And I am *very* sympathetic to the South." He flashed a victorious smirk and turned to leave. "Check out my story if you like." He tossed the words over his shoulder in a dare.

Zander would do just that. He did not believe his cousin for a minute, and he knew how to find out the truth.

PART TWO

For he commandeth,
and raiseth the stormy wind,
which lifteth up the waves thereof.

Psalm 107:25

Thirteen

Resentment dogged Zander as he headed back to Wade's Mercantile. Coming face to face with his cousin had raised more than just bad memories. Carter was kin, sure, but that didn't give him the liberty to wreak havoc in the family like he did. And that old vendetta of his had taken its toll on a whole lot more than James, Gus, and the barn. Carter's way of looking at life was twisted. Zander pressed his fingers to the dull ache in his head. Carter never did say what he was doing in New Creek, and he'd bet his last dollar it was nothing good.

He spied Felix Wade sitting on a bench outside his family store, untangling a yo-yo. The boy looked up with a big grin and saluted. "Hi!"

"Well hello to you, too, Felix. Looks like you got yourself a rat's nest there." Zander plopped down on the seat next to him.

"Yeah. It's a whopper all right."

"Want me to see if I can do anything for it?"

The boy dropped it into Zander's outstretched hand. "I thought about cutting the string and putting on a new one."

"Well let's not get ahead of ourselves." He worked the main knot loose, then threaded another one through the tangle. "Looks to me like this will work for you a mite longer." He let the yo-yo drop from his hand, dangling it until the spinning slowed. "Just like new," he said, handing it to Felix.

"Thanks, Private! I guess I need to be more careful with it. I was trying to do *around the world,* but it kept getting tangled."

"It's Zander. And you just keep practicing. You'll get it soon enough. I hear you can do other tricks with that thing too." Zander ruffled the boy's hair just like he had done to Bertie's so many times. He already missed the little troublemaker. "I got me a brother about your age."

"What's his name?"

"Bertie. Well, Bertram, but he doesn't like to be called that. It's reserved for when he's in trouble with my older sister."

"I know what you mean." Felix looked up, shoving a hank of hair out of one eye. "When I hear, 'Felix Robert Wade'—I know I better put on my best politeness or make myself scarce."

Zander chuckled. Isn't that the way of a boy? A diminutive woman approached, lifting her skirt hem as she stepped up to the porch. Zander jumped up to open the door. "Let me get that for you, ma'am." She toddled into the store, a silent scowl connecting her sagging cheeks. No doubt one of those Southern sympathizers Carter alluded to.

He shrugged, determined to see to his business. "Got some shopping to do. I'll be seeing you, Felix."

The boy was already engrossed in his yo-yo.

Zander closed the door behind him and took in the fair-sized store. Well-stocked shelves lined the walls and, as if someone had drawn an invisible line right down the middle of the room—food stuffs and kitchen supplies were on the left and all manner of other items on the right.

A cold stove stood in the center of the store, like a guard separating the two sides. An eye-catching display of cookware, crockery, and utensils lent a colorful hominess to its blackened pot-bellied face. To the right, a shelf of colorful fabric bolts hung above a sewing machine and darker bolts stood upright to the side. A sideboard with wide shelves held ready-made clothes, hats, and galluses. Endless wall shelves touted knickknacks, clocks, picture frames, games, ammunition, and guns. A counter ran the length of the food side with barrels tucked beneath decanters and dispensers above.

Coffee beans, spices, and tobacco mingled in the air. Two baskets—one of apples, pears, and plums—the other of tomatoes, sat above barrels marked oatmeal, flour, and cornmeal. A larger barrel of vinegar set at the end.

He doused a low whistle. So much merchandise for a town this size!

Whale oil lanterns in tin, pewter, and even brass lined up on a shelf like artillery. A style he had never seen before had a sign taped to its base: WE HAVE KEROSENE LANTERNS AND FUEL. *Kerosene*, huh?

He kneaded his chin. He had not shaved since Charleston, as that required borrowing somebody else's strap every time. He'd be sure to get a new razor while he was here. Why hadn't he written down what he needed?

"May I be of assistance, Private?"

He turned to face a woman in her forties. Her face smiled, but her eyes didn't appear to agree. "This Kerosene fuel. I'm not familiar with that." Zander pointed to the sign.

"Oh, yes. That is quite new. It will catch on quickly, I'm told. Brighter than the whale oil lamps." She folded her hands at her waist. "I am Mrs. Tesley. If there is anything else I can get for you, Private, please just let me know." She dipped and floated over to a woman who was fingering the yard goods.

Zander scouted the room, making a mental note of what he needed. He strolled over to the catalogues on the counter and leafed through them. A body could order just about anything from the busy pages—furniture, farm machinery, even steam engines and lumber.

Miss Wade emerged from the back of the store through check-ered curtains. An *all-business* smile sprouted on her face. "Can I order something for you, Private?" She donned an apron and approached the counter. "Perhaps a deluxe butter churn or a plow for your field." She tipped her head in thought, tapping her chin with one finger. "I know. How about window panes for that house of yours?" She appeared so pleased with the suggestion.

"Uh . . . I'm living in a hut, Miss Wade. Not a house. I don't have a farm or . . ."

She laughed, shaking her head. "I'm sorry. It has been such a drab, busy day. I just had to create my own entertainment for a minute, and if you'd seen the look on your face, you'd have enjoyed it too."

"You making fun of me?"

"Oh, no. Not at all, Private. I am merely entertaining myself at your expense." She sighed. "If you came to see my brother, he's out front."

Two could play at this game. "Out front? Are you sure about that, Miss Wade?"

She puffed a coil of blond hair away from her face and pushed her spectacles up her nose. "Oh, that boy! He had better be out there." She spun, marched around the edge of the counter and toward the door. "Felix Robert Wade!"

Now they were even. Unless the boy wasn't still sitting on that bench—then there'd be a whole different matter to not get in-volved in. Zander stepped over to the jars of sugary treats. Rampart would sure like something like that. He turned when the door slapped shut behind him.

Miss Wade strode through the gap in the counter and turned her attention back to Zander. Her face was a bit red as she brushed invisible dirt from her yellow apron. "I did not need that rush of concern today. Thankfully, my brother was still right where I sat him earlier." She switched her lips to one side. "I suppose if I had given him a book, then I wouldn't have been so worried about him wandering off again."

"Sounds to me like he's bored. Maybe the boy's in need of some adventure. When is the last time he went out hunting or swimming in a creek?"

She gasped. "Felix finds his adventures in books. He is too young to hunt, and I don't have time to take him swimming in a creek. And he is *not* bored." Her brow wrinkled, and a hand flew to her hip. "Now, is there something I can get for you?" Her eyes darted around the store, as she just seemed to realize her voice had risen and drawn attention.

"I got a brother about his age, and since he's been forced to live in town the last couple of years, he has to work hard to stay out of trouble for want of adventure."

She leaned closer. "Felix is *not* your brother. He is mine," she practically hissed.

He hadn't meant to get her dander up. "My apologies."

Her shoulders slumped, and she suddenly looked exhausted. "No apology necessary, Private . . ." Half of her mouth lifted in a smile. "Now, about your order."

He figured there was a soft side there. It just got tangled up in that brood mare kind of instinct. That was something he understood.

A man stepped from behind the curtain, the spitting image of a grown-up Felix with an added thick mustache. He pulled an apron from a nail, limped over, and stood beside Lola as he tied it in place. "I'll take over here, honey."

"Oh! I didn't realize the time." Lola caught Zander's eye for an instant, then scurried off through the curtain.

"What can I get for you, Private?" The man's stern face wore a shadow of pain, much like the one his brother-in-law carried with him.

"You must be Mr. Wade." Zander extended his hand. "I'm Zander Dabney."

Mr. Wade stared at the hand, then drilled Zander with a hard look. "Listen, son, I appreciate the Union Army's business. And I've tried to be tolerant of the way this town of ours keeps changing hands like a ball in a school yard—and I've managed this long to avoid making friends with any of you soldiers, whether Rebels or Yankees. I don't intend to start now. So, if you'll just give me your order."

Mr. Wade's attitude was not surprising. Hadn't Zander's own best friend joined up with the Confederacy and taken a Yankee bullet? People were people no matter where you went. It was just this confound war that made them enemies.

"Yes, sir. I'll take two pounds each of flour, cornmeal, and beans, please. A razor and a strap, too, if you don't mind."

Zander pulled several coins and a couple of bills from his pocket as he waited for Mr. Wade to collect his order.

"Will that be all?" Mr. Wade poured the beans from the scale into a bag.

"I'll have a pound of cracked corn and a little molasses, too."

The man's brows tilted. "You mean ground corn. I took care of that already."

"No, sir. Cracked corn, for my horse."

"I can appreciate a man taking care of his horse, but isn't that a waste. Those Federals will just issue you a new one if that one breaks down."

"Rampart isn't a Federal pony. No, sir. I raised him from a colt." The neighbor's mare had died giving birth, and Pap had offered up five dollars he couldn't spare, knowing that little spindly legged foal would be a salve to a ten-year-old little boy who had just lost his mama, too.

Zander swallowed away the emotion. "Got him the year my mama passed and I nursed him from a newborn. Why, I guess he's been my best friend, you might say."

Mr. Wade's features softened. "Then you best take real good care of him. I'll get your corn and molasses."

Lola sat with her dear friend, Ann Benoit, still puzzling over the handsome private in the store. He had noticed her. *Truly* noticed her. Most of the soldiers at the fort and the ones who came in the store treated her like she was either invisible or just a clerk to take their money.

"Lola, dear, you look deep in thought. And you're smiling." Ann looked down at the cheese sandwich on the plate. "And you've hardly touched your lunch."

Taking a sip of tea, Lola stared at her plate. "It is a divine lunch, Ann. I'm sorry," she said taking a bite and smiling as she chewed. "Delightful."

Ann chuckled. "You cannot fool me. I think you have much too much on your mind, and I think there is a man in the mix here."

"Oh, I may have been thinking about a certain soldier I met at the fort. I see a lot of soldiers there, I know, but this one I actually *met*. I mean, he truly talked to me. And Felix. And Eleazor." She felt absolutely silly now that she heard herself.

"And what is this young soldier's name, may I ask?"

"Private Dabney. He's so polite and amicable, Ann. And he's witty, and charming. He's different from the rest."

"Well, perhaps God has a plan for you to do more than bury yourself in that store day and night. A young woman should be thinking of her future, Lola."

"My *future*?" Lola wagged her head. "My future is burying myself in the store day and night because Papa can't do it all by himself, and I worry about him. He needs me, too." Her heart pinched as she recalled his painful movements and awful coughing attack that brought him to his knees this morning. "And my future includes caring for Felix for several more years."

She sighed. "I'm not complaining, mind you. It's where God wants me and I want to be with Papa and Felix right here in New Creek. I am perfectly content with the way everything is. By myself—I mean, with my family." She set the cup rattling and put it down, suddenly uncomfortable with the conversation topic.

"But Sarge, I'm telling you, something smells fishy. He's a Rebel, and he was in a Federal prison." It was no use. Zander had spent several minutes explaining to Sergeant McNeer about seeing Carter, and all he got was a questioning stare.

"I've heard enough, Dabney." The sergeant let out an exasperated breath. "Even if it was your cousin you saw in New Creek, the government has traded thousands of Rebel prisoners for our own so far. Prisons are over crowded on both sides. No one expected the war to last this long. But here we are."

"If you knew how low-down and conniving Carter is . . . If I could talk to the captain about—"

"Enough! You're dismissed, Private. And I'd better not hear about this from the captain, either."

Zander stalked away, optimistic that he had one more dollar in his poke. He would write to James.

Fourteen

August 1864

Zander leaned into the warm rain as it slapped against his cheeks. Squinting to make out the silhouette, he sent up a *whoop* when Fort Fuller finally came into view after three long days. He'd be the first to alert the garrison.

Word was Confederate General McCausland had demanded the Chambersburg citizens pay a ransom. When they couldn't pay, his men looted and burned the town—all in retaliation for General Hunter's atrocities in the Shenandoah Valley. The Rebels fled after doing the dirty deed. Zander's detail had been scouting them ever since—until those Johnnies turned their sites on Fort Fuller and the railroad.

Something in his gut told Zander that he was somehow responsible for General Hunter's actions. Even if he had not personally burned folks out of their homes or robbed them willfully, he was there. Oh, he knew deep down that he could not have stopped it—or even made a bit of difference. But guilt still dogged him.

He rode through the gates at a hot gallop and slid to a halt at the command office. Major Fleming stepped onto the porch.

"They're coming." Zander said, flinging his leg over the saddle and landing on both feet. "General McCausland is about ten miles out."

"Good work, Private." Major Fleming wrinkled his brow and looked across the yard. "Where are the rest of the scouts Captain Giles sent?"

"Oh, they're coming. I just figured you'd want the news as soon as possible."

Several riders galloped into the Fort, striking a beeline to command.

"I believe Private Dabney has beat you to it, men." The Major turned to Captain Giles, just stepping onto the porch. "I wonder if a bit more cooperation in the ranks might be in order, Captain?"

"Private Dabney here has a penchant for outrunning the others, sir. I'll see it doesn't happen again." The captain saluted, then hurried down the stairs. "To your stations, men!" His voice carried across the growing flurry of activity. He turned to Zander. "I will speak to you about this later, Dabney. Right now, we have more important things to tend to."

Zander saluted. "Yes, sir." Why did he have the feeling that latrine duty was in his near future?

The fort burst to life as men rushed about. Artillery had taken its place on the high ground two days ago in the event that General McCausland headed this way. Units made haste to man the cannons scattered throughout the town and surrounding the New Creek Valley. The bugle sounded and sergeants barked orders as Zander cooled down Rampart.

Bass pulled up next to him. "You in trouble?"

Zander shrugged. "Probably. I just figured we were in a hurry is all."

"We're both in need of a rest, huh boy?" Rampart nickered in delight as Zander ran the currycomb across his rump. Turning a weary head, Rampart gently butted his master's side.

By midday, after a proper show of force, McCausland's fatigued troops seemed to change their mind about taking the garrison. Zander and a few scouts from Company D shadowed the Rebels until McCausland's troops hunkered down just north of Moorefield.

As Zander and the others pushed through on the twenty-mile return trip to report, Rampart picked up the scent of a crab-apple tree a few yards off the road, which he made sure his master knew about. Even though Zander caught quite a ribbing from everyone, he took the time to stop. He loaded up his saddlebags and made a good-sized pouch with his bedroll, filling it up too. And he still caught up to them within fifteen minutes.

Upon their return, he offered some juicy treats to Rubicon and Rampart before turning them out. He was sure looking forward to that bed tonight. Let General Averell worry about McCausland.

He walked through the darkness with a smile, realizing there was something to look forward to—Saturday. Yes, indeed. And a particularly pretty little sutler gal.

By the time Zander finished with his regular garrison duty followed by latrine duty, Saturday was wearing thin. A panic set in when he spotted Mr. Nobly's wagon heading out the gates. It would've been preferable to clean up first, but not at the expense of missing Miss Wade altogether.

He jogged around the corner of the livery and breathed a sigh of relief. From the looks of things, she had just started putting away her wares. And it didn't look like Eleazar was there to help.

He slowed to a steady stride. No reason to seem anxious. Felix appeared to have mastered that yo-yo of his because he stood there throwing one *round the world* after the other.

"Now, put that thing in your pocket and help me." Lola started lifting a crate, then put it back on the ground. "Felix!" She stood and shoved her glasses up her nose. "Now!"

"Yes, ma'am." He stuck the toy in his pocket and took hold of one side of the crate.

Zander reached for the crate, lifting it to his chest. "Please, let me. Where do you want it?"

She stepped forward, attempting to take the crate from him, but tripped on his foot, colliding with the crate and tipping Zander off balance.

"Whoa!" He righted himself and caught the crate from slamming onto the ground just as she toppled over, landing smack on her backside.

"Of all the . . ." Fire sparked in those violet-blue eyes.

Zander plunked the crate into the wagon bed and rushed to offer his hand. "Real sorry about that, Miss Wade."

Her glasses sat all crooked and halfway down her nose, and her crimson face looked about to explode.

He had never seen anything so fetching in all his days. He fisted his hand to keep from nudging those spectacles back into place. Entirely out of his control, a whopper of a smile commandeered his face, but that was his downfall—his Napoleon's Waterloo.

Her mouth hung speechless. And if Zander had learned anything from living with women, he knew that look—plus silence—was never a good thing.

She sat there with her face blooming more plum-colored. It was all he could do not to shout, *"Breathe!"* But he was not that stupid.

No sir. Zander withdrew his hand and stepped back, realizing Felix was doing the same.

Miss Wade fiddled with the lay of her skirt, brushing dust from its folds. The muscle in her jaw bulged, relaxed, then bulged again.

He grabbed off his hat and crouched down so he could look her in the eye. "You sure are pretty when you're mad." And he meant it with all his thumping heart. Maybe he should sit on the ground and just wait for her. What would Fin do? He had to laugh. Fin was ten times more awkward around women when he was Zander's age.

"You think this is funny?" She gaped at him, her face changing to a more strawberry sort of red now.

"Oh, no, ma'am. I wasn't laughing *at* you. I was thinking about my brother Fin and how—" This was not helping. He jumped to his feet, stepped right up to her, bent down, and scooped her up in his arms.

She slapped his shoulder. "What do you think you're doing? Put me down!" Felix peeked around the edge of the wagon from where he now hid.

He set her gingerly on the wagon bed. "I am truly sorry for my part in any of this . . . mishap, Miss Wade. You just sit tight while I load your wagon, and if you'd like, I will be happy to take you to see the post doctor." Swallowing back the odd feeling rising in his chest, he watched the frown lines melt away and the red turn a petunia pink.

An uncomfortable silence nuzzled between them as he loaded up the wagon. He started to lift her again, but she stopped him with the first smile she'd ever treated him to.

"I believe I'm fine now, Private," she said, and accepted his help down.

He smiled to himself when she squeezed his forearms an extra time before letting go. With nary a word, he hoisted the two larger barrels into place and assisted her up onto the wagon seat.

"Thank you," she said, all serious, as Felix scrabbled onto the seat.

"Least I could do, Miss Wade." He wanted to ask her, but after all of this . . .

She unwrapped the reins from the brake and looked straight ahead, but there was still that one side of her mouth that wanted to smile.

Courage triumphed over lack of confidence, and he pulled back his shoulders, standing tall, cap in hand. "Miss Wade?"

"Yes, Private?"

"Would you consider going on a picnic with me on Tuesday?"

Her eyes widened, unblinking as silence hung between them. Didn't he read somewhere in the Bible about a long pause in heaven or something? This kind of seemed like that.

At last, she cleared her throat. "I believe I can make arrangements to do that. We'll have to take Felix as a chaperone, of course." She glanced his way for an instant.

"That's just fine with me." He winked at Felix, who winked right back.

Miss Wade adjusted the reins in her hands. "But I can't keep calling you 'Private' now, can I?"

And God said, let there be light. "Private Zander Dabney at your service, Miss Wade."

"One o'clock?"

"Yes, ma'am."

"And, Private Dabney?"

"Yes, ma'am?"

"I hope you'll consider bathing before our picnic." She shook the reins, and the wagon rolled off.

He watched the wagon all the way out the gates and turned at last—to an audience of four merciless, hooting soldiers who had clearly been treated to a grand bit of entertainment at his expense.

Lola warmed, thinking of the scene she had just left. My, how she wanted to turn around and watch how the private handled all that ribbing from his comrades. But she had her pride, and she did not want to add to his embarrassment. But he was a bold one, she would give him that.

She slowed the wagon, realizing Felix labored to keep his eyes open. "Set that carpet bag up here on the seat and rest your head. You look plum worn out."

Without a word, Felix took her suggestion and made himself as comfortable as one can on a wagon seat. He was asleep within seconds, appearing almost angelic. How thankful she was for sweet moments like this in her hectic life.

The train whistle startled the horses, but not her brother. She gazed at the iron snake as it neared, rumbling and belching black smoke. Her mind went to the polite private who had so brazenly asked her on a picnic. *Zander.* She tried the name in her mind, wondering if his given name was Alexander.

She could still feel his powerful arms around her as he scooped her up as if he was picking up a kitten. Heat flooded her at the way his eyes had so honestly met her own. A strange mix of courage and sweetness and shyness in that one. *Zander.*

Tuesday! She was going on a picnic with a U.S. Cavalryman in three days! Her stomach flipped like a fish as reality reared its head. She gulped, feeling her heart kick up. What had come over her? He was nearly a stranger to her. What would Papa say?

Feeling equal parts qualmish and excited, she hupped the team, surprised she had enough focus to consider what she would wear. "Zander." She didn't mean to say it aloud. Thankfully, Felix did not stir. From deep inside her, a smile sprouted and climbed to her face. *Zander*.

Fifteen

Soldiers crowded around the news board outside the command office and Zander meant to investigate the hubbub. He stepped up to the small crowd and a dozen soldiers parted like the Red Sea. A poster read BLAZER'S SCOUTS RECRUITING.

Was there no place to hide? What was so wrong with being a lowly private in the U.S. Cavalry, minding one's own business? He knew what kind of hero Fin was, all right, and it galled him to no end.

Kyle Stille slapped an iron grip on his shoulder. "Seems your moment has arrived, Private Dabney. Blazer is looking to make up for losses from their spring campaign. Here is your chance to join up with that brother of yours and make a name for yourself."

"Leave him alone, Stille. If he wants to join he will. Not everyone aspires to be a Blazer Scout," Leach said, coming to Zander's rescue.

He could hold his own with Stille, but it just seemed like a waste even talking to the man. Truth be told, Rampart had a better shot with the Scouts than Zander did. Naw. He was not giving this bag of hot air any satisfaction.

"I'd do it just to get me one of them Spencer Repeaters," Stille said, taking his hand off Zander, closing one eye and feigning a grip on a rifle.

"You can buy one for yourself if you got thirty-five dollars," somebody added.

Stille aimed his imaginary firearm and pulled the trigger. "I hear you can load it on Sunday and fight all week."

"And if you're lucky, you live to tell about it," Leach said. "Come on, Dabney. We've got guard duty." He motioned with his head and stepped off the porch.

"I'll walk with you," Bass said, joining them. He turned to Zander. "Why did you not put Stille in his place? You could take him in a minute."

"And what would that accomplish?" Zander huffed.

"It would get him off your back. Everybody else, too, probably."

Leach picked up the pace, and they followed. "Dabney's right, Bass. It wouldn't accomplish anything worthwhile. Might even make matters worse."

"You are talking about turning the other cheek and all, Leach, but I am talking about stopping some loud mouth from tearing a man down in front of all those other men." He turned to Zander. "Do you not have any pride?"

"Now, my pap would remind me that pride goes before a fall. Not so sure about that exactly, but all the same, I'd just as soon not add fuel to that fire." And what a fire it could be if he was not careful. He was already in trouble for running on ahead of his unit.

Before they split up, he had to get this over with. "I need a little help with something."

Leach glanced at Bass. "We'll help if we can."

"I've invited Miss Wade on a picnic—"

Bass yanked him to a stop. "Is that what you were trying to do earlier? We thought you were just trying to see how mad you could make her!" He laughed long and hard, aided by Leach.

Truth was, Zander could see the amusement in it too as the entire scene played in his head again. "All right. All right. As I was sayin', I invited her, but I've got no picnic fixin's. I suppose we can lay out my bedroll blanket, but what kind of food should we take? And I'll have to use my saddle bags instead of a basket." Zander slumped, overwhelmed with the implications of providing a woman like Miss Wade with the type of picnic that would make her say yes again.

"Is that all?" Leach said, thumping Zander on the back. "You just let ol' D.R. take care of that, sonny. I'll have you wooing that girl from the minute you go to callin'."

Leach's enthusiasm set a bundle of nerves to buzzing inside Zander. Whatever that boy was thinking, at least it was better than whatever he could come up with on his own.

"Eleazar, are you sure you unloaded every barrel off that supply wagon?" Lola tapped her pencil.

"Yes, ma'am, Miss Wade. I stacked them five across and two high in the stock room." He pulled the bandana up from around his neck and wiped at the sweat trickling into his ears. "I counted everything again and compared it with the bill of lading before I gave it to you."

She had no second thoughts about Eleazar's count. She'd known him for half her life, and would trust him with it, too. Mama had hired him when he was just a teenager and discovered right off that the man had a head for business and did not shy away from hard work.

There just had to be some explanation for the missing barrel of salt. And it represented no little investment. "Have you seen anyone in here besides us?"

"Nope. Just Mr. Wade, you, and me since the order came in."

"And Mrs. Tesley," Felix added. He slipped a yellow candy stick in and out of his mouth with one hand and held a book in the other.

"When was that?" Why would she have been in here? Either Lola or Eleazar did most of the stocking.

"This afternoon, just before you and Eleazar came back here."

"I wonder what she was doing?"

"Don't know. I don't think she saw me, though, cuz I was sitting in the corner. Did you know if you drop a trail of cornmeal and sit real still, you can coax a mouse out of its hiding?"

Lola plucked the candy from his hand. "Think now, Felix. Did she carry anything out of here with her when she left?"

"I don't know. She never came out this way. I just figured she went out the alley door because after the mouse saw me and ran back into its hidey-hole, I went back out front." He nodded at the candy, suspended in air just inches from his face. "Can I have that back, now?"

Lola adjusted her glasses and began to pace. What to do with this information? She did not want to out and out accuse someone of stealing. She'd need proof. But Elmira Tesley was such a fine employee. The customers adored her.

"Lola?"

Maybe she could set a trap for her? What could she use in place of cornmeal for this thieving little mouse?

"Lo-oh-la."

Maybe she should talk to Papa about it first. He would know how to handle this. But lest she get ahead of herself, prayer must be her first course of action. God would show her what to do.

"Lola!"

"Oh!" She stopped short of putting the candy stick behind her ear as if it were a pencil before handing it back to Felix.

"Thank you." Her brother stomped away, shaking his head. "Sisters!"

Sixteen

"There ya go, boy." Zander winked at Rampart as he straightened the brass buckle on the sleek black sidecheck. "You're lookin' pretty spiffy—like a regular city carriage horse with this fancy harness."

He jumped up into the conveyance, compliments of D.R. Leach's acquaintance at New Creek Livery. Leach didn't tell him how he had struck the deal, and Zander wasn't asking. That boy was all heart, and a romantic to boot. And probably never took a gal of his own on a picnic, but Zander promised to give him all the details about today's excursion. Bass had a hand in procuring some cheese from the mercantile and the picnic "basket".

He pulled to a stop in front of Wade Mercantile. He was early. Now what? A delivery wagon halted just ahead of him and Eleazar trotted out to meet the driver from behind the store. After a brief exchange, he started unloading sacks from the wagon.

Zander jumped to the ground and hailed Eleazar. "Let me help with that." He trotted over and threw one sack over his shoulder.

"Why, thank you, Zander. Much appreciated. But if you're here for Miss Wade"—he grinned and tossed a look at the carriage—"and by the looks of that fancy buggy you got there, you are, I doubt she'd take kindly to you helping me and working up a sweat and all."

"I'd rather be totin' flour sacks than sitting in the sun biding my time."

Eleazar shook his head. "Follow me then."

"You live here in town, Eleazar?"

He nodded. "I got me a little cabin on the south end." He laid his sack down, adjusting it so Zander's sack fit squarely on top of it. "It's not much, but my Juliette makes it homey for us. Got us a little one, too. A boy, Matthew."

They trekked back to the wagon for another load, and Zander looked to make sure he wasn't keeping Miss Wade waiting.

"Where you hail from, Zander?"

"Fayette County. Not so far by horse, but seems a thousand miles away." Had any place felt like home since this whole rebellion started?

"You missing it, aintcha?" Eleazar hoisted a sack.

"I am at that." He slung another over his shoulder. "I'll sure be glad when all this is over."

"Me too. Seems every time those Confederates take this town—and there's been a lot of times, I tell you—I gotta skedaddle north and stay put until you Federals chase them off again."

"Must be hard on you and your family."

"It sure is. I got me a home here, but nobody and no place to live up north. Only thing I can do up there is find odd jobs and pray a farmer lets me throw up a tent on his land while I'm there."

"One thing I miss about being home is fishing. You think you and your boy might want to come along with me and Felix fishing sometime?"

Eleazar laughed. "That'd be a mite hard, since my Matthew's only six months old, but I'd be happy to join you."

And hopefully, Eleazar would know where there was a good fishing hole. "Well, I guess the little guy can sit this one out, then. At least for a couple of years."

Zander glanced at his watch. "Well, 'carpe diem' as my pap would say. I best let Miss Wade know I'm here."

⌘

Lola looked up from the ledger at the sound of the bell. Private Dabney stepped in and removed his hat, kneading it in his hands. His blond hair was slicked back and his face without the beard. My, he was handsome.

She glanced at the store clock. "You're ten minutes early, Private Dabney. I'll be with you in just a few minutes. I have a couple of things to finish up here, I'm afraid."

"I don't mind waiting, Miss Wade. I'll just be out front." He stood awkwardly for a couple of seconds, then bolted out the door.

After closing the book and removing her apron, she pushed the curtain aside to check her hair in the round mirror. The face that gazed back at her was too round, the neck too long, the hair too wispy, and the awful spectacles simply an eyesore. But she had worn them since she was young and there was no getting by without them. She adjusted the gold frames, then squeezed the nose piece together between her fingers. They were always slipping down her nose, and she had tried everything to stop it short of wiring the earpieces around her ears.

Slipping through the door into the family's kitchen in search of her father, she smiled at Papa's snoozing figure resting peacefully in a chair with his legs propped up on the table. She'd just as soon have Eleazar tend the store, but some of the customers wouldn't have it.

"Papa." She gently squeezed his shoulder. "Papa, I am going out now."

He opened his eyes and smiled. "I guess I dozed off. What time is it?"

"It is 1:00 and I am taking my lunch. Remember? I said I had plans today for a long lunch. I'm taking Felix with me."

He dropped his feet to the floor and stood. "Just the two of you?" One eyebrow lifted, and she knew when she answered his question, both would smash together in a scowl.

"No. We are picnicking with Private Dabney. I believe you met him in the store a couple of weeks back."

"The Federals come in and out of here all the time. How would I remember one of them?" He grumbled, stood, then traipsed through the store and out the front door.

Poor Private Dabney.

She followed her father out and found the roan horse hitched to a quaint little buggy. Felix sat on one side of the single seat.

Private Dabney stood at attention, waiting to assist her like the hotel doorman she had seen in Baltimore. He nodded to her father. "Good afternoon, Mr. Wade."

Her father seemed to relax his shoulders. "You'll have her back by three o'clock, then?"

"Yes, sir. Not a minute later."

Private Dabney offered his hand to help her up, and they headed down the street. She could still feel her father's eyes on her when they rounded the next corner.

If Lola sat any closer, she would be in his lap! She squeezed next to Felix, but he wiggled and pushed back.

"Where are we going?" Why hadn't she asked before leaving? Suddenly it didn't seem so wise to be riding to who knows where with this stranger.

"Can Rampart dance when he's pulling a carriage?" Felix asked, leaning forward so he could look at the private.

"Felix, that's preposterous," she said.

"Well, now, I don't mean to be contrary, but your brother has every reason to ask such a question. Let me see if Rampart is up to it."

Private Dabney pulled to a stop and jumped down. He whispered in the horse's ear and the horse nodded emphatically. He looked up with a broad smile. "Rampart says he'll give it a go."

He danced a finger back and forth in front of the horse's face and said a few words she couldn't understand before jumping back into the seat. He lifted the reins high and clicked his tongue, and Rampart moved nimbly from side to side.

"He's doing it!" Felix cried, jumping up from his seat. "See, Lola. I told you he could dance!"

Lola pulled him back down. "Amazing. Truly amazing." The beautiful gelding was prancing a little to each side with every step, lifting hooves and head high.

"Well, look at that." Private Dabney's face beamed. "Wasn't sure he would do it wearing a harness. He does love an audience." He chuckled, then lifted the reins again and tugged lightly. Rampart shifted into a trot and tossed his head with a snort.

"What's that mean when he snorts like that?" Felix asked.

"Well, it depends. In this case, I think it means he was having fun and didn't want to stop."

"I do believe you think that horse is near human, Private." Lola watched the light dance in his eyes. He was awfully handsome. Much too handsome for her.

"I confess, I do think of him that way. He's been my best friend most of my life."

Felix pointed off to one side. "We're here. The creek's just over there."

"I figured Felix would know a nice picnic spot for us so I let him pick the place. Not too far away though, so you can run home if I scare you off." He grinned, then guided Rampart off the road into the shadow of a spreading maple.

"If you think for one minute that I will allow you to act untoward, Private, perhaps you should turn this carriage around this instant." Oh! She had been foolish. Papa was right to tell her to ignore these Yankee boys.

Zander held up both hands in surrender. "I didn't mean anything by it, Miss Wade. Just a bad joke is all. I'm a mite nervous, I guess."

His honesty was her undoing. "Nervous?" She had every reason to be nervous, but him? Why ever would he say such a thing?

"Yes." He clamped his mouth shut, looking sheepish. He jumped down, and rounded the back of the buggy.

She twisted in her seat as Felix bounded out of the buggy. Where was the picnic basket, anyway? A touch of alarm squeezed her chest. There was nothing in the buggy but a wool blanket atop a box.

"If you're looking for the picnic basket, I don't have one." Zander said. He uncovered the rectangular box setting on the floorboard. "I kind of had to make do."

Zander's hands circled her waist as he helped her down. Large hands. She pulled at her skirt and adjusted her spectacles, feeling out of sorts. Understandably so, since her last jaunt out with a young man had been two years ago—and ended in disaster when she refused to wear her eyeglasses and tripped over his feet, falling face-first into a mud puddle—thankfully, injuring only her pride.

After leading Rampart to a grassy area to graze, he spread the army-issued blanket on the ground. "I brought a little something extra for Felix." He dug into his pocket and produced a tight bundle of string.

"For me?" The boy leaned his face over the private's hand. "What is it, Zander?"

"A fishing line. Go find a pole. A switch about as long as you are tall would be best."

"Fishing! Oh boy! I'll find me some worms, too."

"I must admit, Private, you do know how to win over little brothers." Lola started to sit.

"Let me help you." He held her hand while she lowered herself as gracefully as she could onto the rough blanket.

"Thank you."

He wiggled a fishhook free from the cluster of string and untangled the length.

Felix waved a thin branch through the air. "Will this work?"

Her poor brother. How many times had he asked Papa to take him fishing, and he had declined each time due to busyness.

"That'll do fine." Private Dabney tied the length of string to the end of the branch. "If you don't get this on here good enough, your supper might just get away." He bit his bottom lip in concentration as he pulled the string through again and again.

"I still need to find the worms." Felix dipped the stick through the air, immersing invisible bait into an invisible creek.

"That's it. You know what to do from here?"

"Just get me some fat, juicy worms and stick 'em on the hook. Did you know worms are neither girl or boy, but both—in one?"

"I *did* know that. Now, you be careful with that hook. It's sharp." Private Dabney chuckled as Felix trotted off and over the creek bank just a few yards away.

"I hope it's all right." He tossed his head toward the creek. "I have a ten-year-old brother and he'd be bored to tears if he had to sit here on a blanket and listen to grown-ups talking about nothing important."

Nothing important? If the conversation was unimportant, what did he have planned exactly? She folded her hands in her lap, considering her next move.

"Oh. I didn't mean that talking to you wasn't important, Miss Wade. I meant it wasn't important to a young boy. The topic of discussion, that is." He wrinkled his brow, then tossed his hat on the ground and sat cross-legged on the edge of the blanket. His chest rose and fell as he looked up and the lines of his face relaxed. "This is a mighty pretty tree, wouldn't you say?"

He was just an over-grown boy himself, it seemed. She gazed into the lacy leaves above, squinting against blades of bright light. She was tempted to lie on her back and watch the breeze move the green canopy in a dance—something she had done on occasion when she was younger. The tension slipped from her shoulders.

She smiled at the thought. "Yes. It is a mighty pretty tree."

"I'm planning on going fishing with Eleazar sometime soon. You think Felix would wanna come with?"

"I have no doubt he would be thrilled."

"Good."

"Good." She smiled politely and indicated the odd box. "Are we going to eat, then? Or do we just wait for Felix to catch us our lunch?"

His eyes widened. "Oh. No, ma'am." He sprang to his knees and opened the box lid. "I have a feast of sorts in here for us." He lowered his eyes, and she was sure a soft pink crept up his neck.

He suddenly looked right into her eyes, and a lump on the front of his neck bobbed. "Now, when I say feast, I mean that metaphorically."

"Metaphorically?"

"Yes. As in *like* a feast." He pulled out a canteen and two tin cups. "This is fresh, cold water, and I washed the cups real well. I figure we'd pretend this canteen's filled with apple cider." He filled each cup, then unwrapped a generous wedge of cheese.

"Is that from our store?" How had he managed that without her knowledge?

He avoided her gaze and rubbed his chin. "My friend, Bass, went in and bought it for me." He swept his hand over the food. "This whole endeavor took a bit of combined effort. Bass procured the cheese and loaned me his cup. Leach borrowed our picnic hamper here and that fine buggy."

He pulled two neatly folded calico kerchiefs from the box and spread them. He set an apple and an egg on each, then produced another cloth-wrapped bundle. "I picked the apples myself—with permission from the farmer. Boiled the eggs. Sure hope they're done in the middle. And I made these biscuits myself." His shoulders shrugged. His countenance fell. "Burned 'em. Don't tell my sisters, I'll never hear the end of it."

"You have sisters?"

"Boy do I! Willamina, but we call her Will, is fifteen, but likes to pretend she's fully grown. Kind of big for her britches now and then, if you know what I mean. And Augusta, we call her Gus, she's my older sister, about four years older than me, sort of the mother hen to all of us'ns. And then there's Melinda Jane, who is really a family friend, no relation. But she fully counts as a sister seein' how she's lived with us most of my life."

She smiled, covering a chuckle with her fingers. It was obvious he cared for them. "You definitely have sisters, and I have only Felix—and Papa, of course." Suddenly, a big family sounded so divine. Sisters! She could only imagine what it must be like to have sisters.

Next, he unwrapped a purple cloth. "Tsk. Tsk." He shook his head and sighed. "Picked the blackberries myself, too." He squinted up at her. "Squished."

"I'm sorry. I'm sure they were wonderful. You have quite outdone yourself, Private." She realized why her brother was so taken with this soldier. Resourceful. Polite. And handsome.

He grinned and a divot appeared in his cheek. "I hope you don't think it's too simple. You deserve a real picnic, but I just wasn't sure how to get everything without going right into that store of yours and buying it all. I didn't figure that would be as special either."

Springing to his feet, he announced, "I'm gonna run the rest of this down to Felix. I'm sure he's working up an appetite. Be right back."

She watched him leave, overcome by the the urge to giggle. She was not a school girl! What was wrong with her? Would she even be able to eat with her stomach fluttering so?

He returned in a short time and took his knife from a sheath on his thigh and sat across from her. Dribbling a bit of water over the blade, he wiped it clean with the edge of his napkin. "I washed the knife earlier, when I washed the cup, but—" He stilled, fixing his eyes on the blade. Those blue depths darkened and his smile vanished. With slow, deliberate movements, Zander picked up the cheese and cut thin slices.

He squeezed his eyes closed, and when he opened them, he had apparently returned from wherever his thoughts had journeyed. "Sorry I don't have any butter. If you want, we can slice the apples and make us some cheese, apple, and biscuit sandwiches?" His smile reappeared and hope seemed to glisten in his eyes.

It moved her he had taken such care to please her. How he had planned out everything. "I think that sounds wonderful."

"It does at that."

She watched in silence as he deftly cut the apples and created a sandwich from each biscuit.

"Thank you, Private."

"Miss Wade, I do have a first name, you know. I don't hear it much these days, but I think it's still mine." His eyebrows raised and his gaze seemed to pin her to the blanket.

"Yes, I know. Zander." If only he knew how she had rehearsed that name. Not that it would mean anything. It was just a name, after all. Not like they were courting or anything.

He leaned forward, amusement obvious in the creases of his eyes. "If you don't like it, you can't blame me. My mama and pap named me Alexander, after Alexander the Great. I like plain old Zander better. Fewer expectations that way."

"It's not that, Pri—Zander." She sipped her water. "I'm not in the habit of calling the soldiers by name, that's all." She fought the urge to slide her glasses up the bridge of her nose.

"I'll bet you meet a lot of military men, owning the only mercantile in town and all. And selling at the garrison, too." He fiddled with his sandwich. "So, Miss Wade—"

"Please, call me Lola."

He relaxed his posture. "All right. I will. I mean, thank you. I have to admit, I've been having a hard time not doing it in my head."

"Oh?"

"I . . .I didn't mean anything rude or improper by that. What I meant was, I've been rehearsing talking to you, and I just kept forgetting to say *Miss Wade* in my head."

Different. He was just plain different from most of those army types. They would generally come into the store all self-important. As if the uniform alone should make a girl fall at their feet. Either that or they'd just plain ignore her.

"Are you always this honest, Zander?"

"Yes, ma'am. Hard not to be."

"I got one! I got one!" Jubilation rang in her brother's voice from the creek bank.

"I best make sure it doesn't get away. Excuse me." Zander stood.

"Wait, I'm coming too!"

Her heart flipped like that fish as she grasped his strong hand and let him lead her off to the creek.

Seventeen

Zander struck out for his quarters with a spring in his step. First, the picnic with Lola boosted his confidence, and now he had won another race. He fingered the bills in his pocket. He needed to find a safer place to stash his savings up here at New Creek. The closest bank was twenty miles east and real inconvenient.

As soon as this rebellion ended, he was not wasting any time collecting his funds and heading west. All the planning and dreaming soothed his mind more and more. He could lose himself in thought for hours, picturing the ranch he would build. Without warning, a perky little blond gal squeezed into the picture. Zander smiled, shaking his head. A little too soon for those kinds of dreams.

"Dabney!"

A yank on his arm spun him around. Ford stood there in all his brawny-ugly. "What do you want?"

"A rematch. A fair one this time." Ford hissed the words and furrows creased his brow.

Zander jerked away. "I'm not racing you again. And it *was* fair." He glanced around, hoping for more foot traffic before he kept walking. The last thing he needed was a dustup with this yokel.

"You'll race me again, Dabney. And I'm getting my horse back!"

The voice trailed behind Zander as he quickened his steps, forcing his mind on more important matters. He owed his family a letter and figured he'd work on that before turning in. Just four more days and the sutlers would be at the garrison. Four days to figure out some sort of something he needed to buy from a certain pretty little angel-haired gal.

Slipping through the curtain, Lola stood behind the counter, hoping to go unnoticed. Mrs. Tesley closed the cash drawer and plunged one hand into her apron pocket. She spun around and her hand flew to her neck.

"Miss Wade! You startled me!" She visibly slowed her breathing. "I didn't hear you come in. Is there something I can get you?"

Lola had caught the woman red-handed. She pulled back her shoulders suddenly feeling vidicated. "I'd like to see what is in your pocket, Mrs. Tesley."

"My pocket? Why whatever for?"

"Is there a problem with that? Is there some reason I shouldn't know what is in your pocket?" Lola propped her hands on her hips.

A customer pushed through the front door, setting the bell to ringing and pulling Mrs. Tesley's attention from the subject at hand. "I must see to this customer. I'll only be a moment."

Lola touched the woman's arm. "First—" she nodded toward the pocket.

The clerk huffed, "Oh, all right." She slipped a crumpled envelope from her pocket and knitted her eyebrows together. "It's really none of your business, Miss Wade."

"A letter?"

"Yes, a letter. That is all." The woman showed Lola the empty pocket. "See? I suppose now you want to read it."

How could she have been mistaken? Heat climbed her neck. The woman had acted so guilty. "I apologize, Mrs. Tesley. Truly. And I do not wish to read your letter."

The woman lifted her chin high. "*Now*, may I see to the customer?"

"Of course." What a miserable, embarrassing turn *that* had taken.

Maybe her numbers were just off. But how could they be off in both cash *and* merchandise? Something was not right, and she was determined to find out what it was.

Eighteen

September, 1864

A complete waste of a decent Saturday! Sorely exaggerated reports of an enemy detachment had sent Zander and his patrol on a wild goose chase. The *Rebels* turned out to be farmhands and their *rifles*, pitchforks. He galloped back toward the fort with the unit, hoping to salvage at least some of the day. If only he could make it back to the garrison before Lola and Eleazar packed up their wagon.

A shot rang out somewhere in a nearby stand of trees and Sergeant McNeer pulled up, frowning. "And I thought we were done with this nonsense. Dabney and Bass, go check that out. We'll wait under those trees," he said, heading off with the half-dozen men in the detachment.

Zander and Rampart struck out at a fast clip with Bass on his heels. Another shot rang out as he slowed, entering the cover of trees. Swallowing back a keen reservation, he motioned for Bass to keep quiet and picked through the undergrowth until movement caught his eye. His mouth went dry. He felt for his knife.

Both of them dismounted, ground-tied their horses, then set out on foot. Zander's chest tightened, reminding him to concentrate on the *now* and not the *then* as they jogged between trees barely big enough to afford any kind of coverage.

"Gotcha!" A scrub of a boy, no more than twelve, set his musket on the ground and raced across a patch of clearing to collect his trophy. He held the limp carcass of a fox squirrel high with one hand and let out a *WHOOP.*

"There is your Rebel shooter," Bass said, a disgusted look on his face.

"Better the squirrel than us, all the same."

Zander tamped his breathing as he headed back to the horses. He had dodged the bullet again. Garrison duty was boring all right, but he had grown to like it that way—while the other men chomped at the bit for battle and glory. *Glory!* His stomach roiled, and he yanked his thoughts from the horror of Cloyd's Mountain.

Dusk crowded the sky as the unit returned to the garrison and the first sutler lumbered through the gates. Bass and Zander dismounted and made a beeline to the Wades' mostly loaded wagon. Felix waved and trotted over to meet them.

Zander handed his reins over to Felix. "You wanna ride him?"

"Yeah. Can I?" The boy rubbed at the white star on the horse's forehead.

Zander caught Lola's eye and, at her smile and nod, he lifted the boy onto Rampart. "Just stay close-by where I can see you." Felix beamed, and it warmed Zander's heart. He sure missed Bertie. It was good to have a free-spirited boy around. It helped keep life in perspective. When he turned, Lola was still smiling at him, and it kicked up his heartbeat—and his nerve—about ten notches. He had better go claim his territory before somebody else did. With one eye on Felix, he crossed the ground between them in an instant.

"Dabney!" Leach strode up, a newspaper in one hand. "I heard about your successful foray. Rebels with pitchforks, huh? What will Granny Lee's boys think of next, huh?" He laughed and handed Zander the paper. "Thought you might wanna take a look. I gotta git. Guard duty." He was off before Zander could even open it.

"I already saw that one," Bass said. "More about the Blazer Scouts. I am going to try to catch the post with a letter home. I have not had a letter from my *volks* for over a month now." He frowned, staring at the ground.

Lola finished with the last small crate, and Zander eased it from her hands, loading it into the wagon bed. "Where are your parents, Private Bassoom?" she asked.

"Winchester, ma'am. And my younger sister, Hannah." He doffed his hat and headed off. "Good afternoon."

Lola's eyes grew round. "Here he is fighting for the Union and his home is in the Old Dominion? Must be weighty for him."

"Unfortunately, there are plenty of fellas in his shoes. I feel bad for the ol' boy. He tries hard to follow the action, always worried about his family. But he's a good sort. And I trust him with my life." He opened the paper, caught by the headline right off.

"What does it say? Is your brother in trouble?"

Zander snorted. "Hardly."

"What's that supposed to mean?"

"'Mosby's Rebel Guerillas have met their match in the Blazer Scouts, a foe more familiar with the mountain passes and river fords than his own men. Captain Blazer's Federal Scouts have met Mosby's forces head-on with success at every turn. At Myer's Ford, the celebrated Scouts got the bulge on the First Squadron of Mosby's command and drove them from the field in typical Blazer Scout fashion. First Lieutenant *Phineas Dabney* of Fayette County and Sergeant Noah Hicks of Greenbrier County received commendations for extraordinary valor.'" His brother's name rang irksome, so he handed her the paper. "More of the same."

"That long face does not become you, Zander Dabney." She leaned across the table and placed a hand over his own. "Aren't you proud of your brother? Or are you moping because you wish you were him?"

Wish he was Fin? If Lola could see inside him, she would never ask such a question. "I'm glad I'm not him. I couldn't do what Fin does. And I wouldn't want to. I . . . I couldn't." Zander hefted the make-shift table into the wagon. "I'm not him, all right?" He whistled for Rampart, fighting the odd panic thumping in his chest.

Lola stepped closer. "I'm sorry. I didn't mean to upset you."

"I'm not upset." He pulled Felix down from the saddle, shrugging off Rampart's affectionate nuzzle.

"I'm sure he wishes you were proud of him."

"Proud?" It came out louder than he'd meant.

"Yes, proud." Her eyes flashed before searching his, and he turned away to mount up, afraid of what she might see with that probing way she had.

"I guess I am proud of my brother. But I wouldn't trade places with him for all the land out west." And he meant it. He fiddled with a buckle on the halter. What good was a ranch and a thousand horses out west if you couldn't enjoy it? How could a man find happiness if he had to face his own ghosts every time he closed his eyes?

"Are you coming with us to church tomorrow?" she asked, her voice hopeful as she touched his arm.

Zander turned to face her. At least that was one place no one would expect anything of him. He squeezed her fingers and smiled. "I'd like that. I'd like that a good deal. I'll see you there."

Lola watched Zander ride through the gate. She ached, wishing she understood him better. His presence would make her feel light as a feather, as if she hadn't a care in the world. But so suddenly he could look as if a storm was brewing inside, all lost in thought, like she was not even there. She had never known anyone like him, truth be told. And certainly, no other boy had ever made her feel this way.

"Let's get going, Felix." She climbed onto the seat and unwrapped the lines.

"I wish Rampart was my horse," Felix said, scrabbling up to the seat. "Do you think if I asked for a horse, I could have one?"

"I don't think now is a good time to ask for a horse. Why don't you just wait another month or two and see how you feel about it then?" Another horse they did not need. Things were hard enough without the added expense. They could barely afford their two employees as it was.

She gave the lines a shake, and they aimed for the tall gates. By the time they rolled into town, it would be near dark. Why hadn't she asked if Zander could accompany them? But he seemed to have other things on his mind.

Since when did she need an escort? And since when had she wanted *him* to be that escort? The thought warmed her middle. She smiled to herself, remembering the way Zander lit up when he talked about his sisters and his little brother, which endeared him to her all the more. But there was some small, niggling thing she could not put her finger on. Maybe it had to do with his relationship with his older brother. Or maybe it was something else entirely.

Felix snoozed on the seat with his head bobbing lazily. She sighed with the realization: her dear little brother was already attached to Zander—and so was she.

Nineteen

The piano music halted as the preacher shuffled his way to the podium. Zander figured the man to be all of eighty years old, but his voice rang true and clear without a waver or crack. His spectacles balanced precariously on the tip of his bent nose, and how they could remain in place during an entire sermon was truly a thing of mystery.

"I read from Saint Matthew, chapter fourteen verse twenty-nine, continuing where we left off last week." After a few wisps of page turning, the preacher seemed satisfied. "'And he said, Come. And when Peter was come down out of the ship, he walked on the water, to go to Jesus. But when he saw the wind boisterous, he was afraid; and beginning to sink, he cried, saying, Lord, save me.'"

The sermon waxed verbose as minutes passed like hours, and Felix fidgeted on Zander's left. Leach sat on his other side, focused on the sermon. Zander watched a fly light on the shoulder of the woman in front of him. Hadn't he heard this story a thousand times?

"'And he arose, and rebuked the wind, and said unto the sea, Peace, be still. And the wind ceased, and there was a great calm.'"

Lola sat beside Felix with hands folded in her lap. Her head turned in response to his gaze, and the corner of her mouth turned up. His chest warmed to that smile. They were so seldom alone, but when they were, all he could think of was lifting those spectacles from her face and capturing those lips with his own.

"'And he said unto them, why are ye so fearful? How is it that ye have no faith?'"

He would trade places with those disciples any day of the week, yes he would. Fearful. Hah! Those boys didn't know fear.

"'What manner of man is this, that even the wind and the sea obey him?'" The preacher stepped away from the podium and wet his lips.

Here it comes. Just like every other sermon he had heard a thousand times, and what difference did it make? He wasn't here for the preacher. He was here for Lola, because she wanted him here.

Leach nudged his arm and caught his eye, nodding his approval at whatever the preacher had just said. Zander watched another fly and counted how many congregants the little buzzer landed on before flying so far afield that he lost sight of it. A flurry of fabric and seats creaking brought his mind back as everyone stood.

The pianist banged out the recessional and the congregation filed from the pews. Zander stepped aside, allowing Mr. Wade to go in front of him. The earlier sunny promise of morning had given way to pewter clouds. Already they spit raindrops at the departing church goers.

"You seemed rather serious during the sermon." Lola bumped her shoulder against his as they stood on the covered porch.

"Some things to give thought to, I guess."

She broke into a wide smile. "Well, maybe you can tell me all about those thoughts sometime. Are you sure you and Private Leach can't stay for Sunday dinner?"

"I wish we could, but we both have duty at the garrison."

Her bottom lip pooched out only for an instant, then she pushed her glasses up that little nose. "I understand. And so does Papa." She stretched her neck and grinned in her father's direction.

"He likes you, you know. I never thought I'd see him take a liking to a Yankee soldier, but he does. He told me so."

That was a good first step. A real good first step. Zander adjusted his belt buckle just to give his hand something to do. It was just itching to grab hold of Lola's hand and squeeze it tight, but this was not the time or place.

"Did you hear what I said?" She plunked her arms over her chest and a hurt look crossed her blue eyes.

"I heard you all right. I was just busy trying not to reach over and hold your hand."

"Private Dabney! You are bold, aren't you?"

They shared a laugh and Felix pushed between them. "What's so funny?" he asked, his eyebrows raised in anticipation.

Lola covered her mouth and turned away, her shoulders vibrating with amusement.

Zander pulled Felix closer and yanked off his hat, holding it high as the boy jumped for it. "You missed it, little man. You just missed it is all."

After polite goodbyes, Leach and Zander set off for the fort. In minutes, they had covered a good distance at a steady lope in silence.

"So, what'd ya think of the preacher's message?" Leach's voice oozed enthusiasm.

"It was all right, I guess," Zander said, hoping this wasn't going to feed into one of Leach's sermons.

"You didn't even give it much thought, did you?"

"Sure, I did. I thought about how I'd trade an hour on the battlefield for a stint in a boat on a stormy lake."

Leach twisted his lips to one side and seemed to grow a couple of inches in his saddle. "Well, I figure them boys in that boat were fighting their own kind of battle."

Zander huffed. "How ya figure?"

"Every one of them was fighting against their own fears. Fighting against their faith, even. Do you doubt for a minute they weren't terrified?" He drilled Zander with his pale blue eyes.

"Sounds like they were, sure enough."

"The way I see it, it doesn't matter what you are afraid of. If the fear is real, it's real." He held up one arm. "Pretend there's a skeeter here on my arm. Now, you and I know this hand of mine is really nothing much to fear, but to that skeeter, this hand means death. Is that little critter right to be afeared of my hand? You bet he is. Yes sir. Because this hand can end his life just as sure as anything."

"Stop waxing all philosophical, Leach. You're hurtin' my brain." That boy surely did like to carry on. Zander galloped on ahead and into the garrison, leaving Leach in his dust. He had more important things to think on just now—like the race coming up after his shift. And counting his money.

Lola shifted uneasily in her chair and passed on the platter of venison. Sunday dinner was not the place to discuss what had her stomach in knots. And it wasn't worth causing her papa grief if her suspicions were incorrect. The last time goods went missing, she told herself, the *next* time, she'd talk to him about it. Well, *next time* had come and gone—twice. Was it more disconcerting that the till did not balance with the receipts or the fact that odd amounts of sugar and gunpowder and flour seemed to go missing?

She only had one suspect, and she had yet to catch Mrs. Tesley red-handed. And worse, the woman was onto her. Lola was certain of it.

"Did you know the fancy name for a bean is leeg-youm?" Felix waved a speared string bean in the air. "And not all leeg-youms are eatable. Some are just for looks. Did you know a peanut is a leeg-youm?"

"Is that so?" Papa patted Felix on the head and winked at Lola. "And to think, I used to worry about this boy's schooling."

Lola stood and began gathering the dishes. "And I figured he would end up sitting in the streets begging because Miss Clovis nearly banned him from attending school."

"She was boring. The most boringest teacher a boy could have." Felix shoveled his last bite of potatoes into his mouth as his sister slid the plate right out from under his fork.

"You seem to be in an awful hurry, daughter."

"I have some things to tend to in the store." She headed through the doorway, her arms laden with dishes. "It won't take long, I promise."

"You work hard enough during the week," Papa called after her. "I don't like you working on Sundays."

She reappeared and scooped up the glasses. "It's not really work. Just a quick double check, then I'll join you in the parlor."

Stacking the dishes in the sink, she doused them with hot water to soak, then slipped into the storeroom and opened the safe. Money spilled from the cloth bag onto the table and she recounted for the third time, this time noting on a paper scrap the denominations of coin and currency.

Lola hissed a breath through clenched teeth. A whole five dollars short! She replaced the money and closed the safe a little harder than was necessary. After hefting a bag of coffee onto the scale and noting its weight, she counted the cans of tobacco on the shelf and wrote that down too.

Just let Mrs. Tesley try something tomorrow. Lola had set a trap and had every confidence the mouse would take the bait. If even one pound of coffee was missing or one can of tobacco unaccounted for, she would know it. Not until then would she approach the woman.

Twenty

October, 1864

Zander spread his jacket aloft over Lola's head, pulling her close to shelter her from the sudden deluge. He laughed, blinking the rain out of his eyes. "Don't believe I've ever seen this much rain come on this fast before!"

"Neither have I!" She lifted her skirt and raced up the two steps to the safety of the Mercantile porch. She turned and her hand flew to her mouth. "Oh, Zander. Just look at you! You're drenched!"

"Anything to spare the lady." He bowed gallantly then shook his head like a wet dog, sending water flying.

She turned her back and covered her face. "*This* is what you spared me for?" When she faced him again, giant drops of water dotted her spectacles. And she was laughing!

And she was lovely. His heart kicked to a trot and his gaze fixed on her lips. If she only knew how he'd dreamed of kissing those lips. He glanced across and down the street, just in case anyone else was foolish enough to be out in this torrent. If he was going to embarrass himself, he'd prefer no witnesses.

"Allow me, ma'am." Feeling equal parts giddy and daring, he carefully removed her eyeglasses. It was now or never. He stepped closer, and tipping her chin, met her lips with his own for just an instant. "As sweet as I imagined."

Her mouth formed a little *O*. Silence hung heavy between them. Painfully heavy. He withdrew and concentrated on cleaning her glasses with his drenched shirt, afraid to look up. *If only she would say something!* He'd been a fool. Maybe even scared her off. She was the best thing about this whole blasted rebellion, and he messed that up too.

"Um," she mumbled, and he looked up at last.

He couldn't even see her face for she was concentrating on his soggy jacket in her hands. Feeling defeated, he reached for it. "Reckon I oughta take this and be going."

Suddenly, as if just realizing where she was, she gasped and searched the street for any witnesses. "I . . . I think I should be going. But I need my spectacles." She squinted, reminding him of a mole.

"I . . . I don't know that I did these justice, but . . . here." He started to put the spectacles back on her face, but she took them from him and did it herself. "Don't worry, I wasn't going to try to steal another kiss. I apologize if it was unwelcomed."

She handed back his jacket. "You needn't steal kisses, Mr. Dabney. I am quite in favor of giving them for free at the proper time and place." Picking up her skirt, she opened the door, and then turned to him. "It was a very nice kiss." Her coy smile unraveled him right up until the door gradually creaked to a close.

Yes, sir! One down and a whole lot more to go. He turned with a heavy sigh. That girl was worth having, and anything worth having was worth waiting for. Wasn't that what his sister, Gus, would say? He donned his heavy wet jacket and jumped over the steps, splashing in the mud like a boy. His heart hadn't felt this light since . . . before. He remembered Fin telling him once that a man had cause real often to take his thoughts captive. Until now, he figured his brother was talking about women, but what if he meant to take them captive about other things? Like unpleasant sort of things.

Lola leaned her back against the door, her heart thumping and head spinning. What was she thinking? If Zander had known how much she wanted those stolen kisses—that she wanted more—what would he think of her? Putting a finger to her lips, she smiled, remembering. She could still see his drenched uniform and soggy cap, hair in his eyes. She chuckled. Even soaked and a little silly, there was something about him that filled her right up to overflowing.

These last few months had been the happiest she ever remembered. Perfect, had it not been for the problems at the store—and the war, of course—both of which were out of her control.

Charleston

"Well! It is about time we got some word from that brother of mine!" Gus carefully pried open the envelope.

"What's it say?" Melinda Jane asked, balancing little Addie on her hip. "Go ahead. It won't hurt to read it twice since I know everyone will want to hear it at supper."

She unfolded the missive and scanned the page. "It says here that he's found a way to make some extra money to save for after the war."

"Now, how would he do something like that?" Melinda Jane lowered the squirming toddler to the floor.

"He doesn't say." She read some more. "And he's got himself a girl, sounds like. Her name is Lola, the mercantile owner's daughter in New Creek."

Melinda Jane broke a cookie in pieces and handed one to little Adelaide. "That's what you want, isn't it, sugar?"

"And he says he saw Carter Dabney a while back. Right there in New Creek. He wants James to look into it."

"His vision must be blurred on account of that girl. Carter is in a Federal prison." Melinda Jane's eyebrows knit with concern. "Isn't he?"

"Well, we all thought so. I know he was, but maybe he escaped. James is going to be none too happy about this."

"I'll pass that on to Fin and see what he says about it. Maybe he knows something. I'm sending him a letter tomorrow."

"The only other news is that garrison duty is dull as ever." Gus shook her head and slid the letter back into the envelope. "I worry about Zander. He's got such a tender heart, always has. What does this ugly rebellion do to a boy such as him?"

"He'll be all right, Gus. Fin says it's just forcing him into manhood in the worst way possible, but he's a Dabney, so he'll get on."

Gus snagged the table cloth just as her daughter pulled it over her head. "I hope you're right. There's nothing I can do but pray. I'm so weary of praying."

"I think we've come to figure out what the Apostle Paul meant when he said to pray without ceasing." She squeezed Gus's hand. "I'm praying right along beside you, sister."

Gus sighed and pulled out a chair. "And I'm grateful for that."

Will jogged into the kitchen doorway. "Sorry I'm late. Do you need me for supper?"

The two women shared an amused look. Will *asking* if she was needed? That girl was full of surprises.

"Since you are asking, I'd appreciate you collecting some potatoes from the cellar," Gus said.

Will disappeared as James entered the room with his nose buried in a newspaper. "Apparently Colonel Oley will be taking the command post here in Charleston." He glanced up, then limped over to the chair Melinda Jane scooted out for him. "And Captain Reynold's command was attacked in Winfield by 400 of Thurmond's men. Seems Captain Thurmond died in the altercation before they were run off by our Seventh Cavalry.

"After that Rebel, Witcher, captured Bulltown and Weston . . . and after making off with all those prisoners and supplies—well, I just hoped things were settling down this side of the mountains." He shook his head, wearing a forlorn mask.

Several seconds of silence passed before he lifted his face from the paper. "Is something wrong?" His gaze darted between the women. He let the paper fall to the table. "Is it Fin? Zander?"

Gus covered his hand. "No, dear. They are fine so far as we know."

"Then what?"

"It's Carter . . . Dabney." Gus watched the volley of emotions play across his face, settling at last on hardened inquiry.

"What about him?"

"Zander says he saw him and talked to him in New Creek."

"New Creek?" His voice punched the air as he stood abruptly. "Don't hold supper for me." In a whirlwind, he strode out the door and disappeared.

Will stood with her mouth agape. "What was that all about?"

Indeed. What *was* that all about? No doubt James would sort this out. And when he did, Gus hoped it would be before Carter wreaked more havoc on her family.

Twenty-One

Zander stood at attention as Captain Giles paced back and forth, waiting for the rest of the company to report. A familiar queasiness settled in his stomach and his feet faunched to do anything but stand still. What was taking everybody so long? The sooner he knew what this was all about, the sooner he could get back to the stables. He opened his fists and scrubbed sweaty hands against his pant legs, trying to ease his aching fingers.

"Men, it has come to our attention that General Jackson has once again attacked Colonel Youart's men at Beverly. That is the only information we got before the wire was cut. Three companies will ride, but it's ninety miles and we'll likely be too late for reinforcements, as will the other commands directed there. Dabney!"

Zander swallowed the sudden rush of bile into his throat. "Yes, sir."

"You will ride on ahead to let them know we are coming. Since I know no one can keep up with you, you'll be on your own. Let them know we are right behind you. Encourage them to hold out if they can."

"Yes, sir."

"You're dismissed. The rest of you fall in. We leave in fifteen minutes. Dismissed!"

Zander whistled for Rampart as he jogged to the paddock, his pulse racing. He would saddle up first, then swing by the hut for his saddlebags and canteen.

The first day of riding, Zander saw but one wagon. He had ridden well into the night before he rested for an hour, knowing his unit likely was doing the same, albeit twenty miles behind. By mid-morning, he began seeing signs of Jackson's men, their great numbers leaving an unmistakable swath across the land.

Beverly had been a Confederate supply depot early in the war, but remained in Union hands after the Battle of Rich Mountain. The town straddled both the Parkersburg-Staunton Turnpike and the Beverly-Fairmont Turnpike. Whoever controlled the town had a base of operations for striking the B&O Railroad and an inroad to the Kanawha Valley. A perfect position to hold.

The thought of running headlong into retreating Rebels left Zander's mouth dry. He gambled they'd return to Virginia through the gap and planned his route accordingly.

He had given up on prayer of late, but fear drove him to the Almighty. He uttered a cowardly prayer that he would arrive too late to help—that he would miss the Rebels entirely. Some soldier he was!

Beverly, West Virginia

Zander galloped through the gates, spent and thirsty. The wounded sprawled across the open ground inside the garrison, several bodies covered with blankets and others writhing in pain. Bandaged men offered words of comfort and shared their canteens.

Seeing the carnage riddled him with shame for his earlier pathetic prayer.

A dozen Federals stood guard over a cluster of bound Rebels leaning against the fort's wall. And after someone directed him to Colonel Youart, Zander delivered his message. Reinforcements were no longer needed. According to the report he was to take back to Captain Giles, the garrison had lost eight men, twenty-three wounded and thirteen captured. The Confederates had fared about the same but lost eight times as many in prisoners.

Zander watered Rampart, talking to him in a low voice mindful of sounds of suffering around them. Two men busied themselves arranging the dead in a row like blanket-covered logs. A long, wide crimson stain marked one blanket. Zander looked away, reigning in his mind as it sorted through the weapon that would bleed a man that way. A saber? A bayonet? A hunting knife like the one he wore strapped to his leg would do the job. Just like gutting a deer.

His hands shook as he gathered the reins and mounted. He would take his rest outside these walls, then head back to meet up with his company. There was nothing he could do here that was not already being done.

New Creek

Lola watched as Mrs. Tesley swiped the feather duster across the wall shelves. She lifted each item, dusted it, then returned it to its place. The bell sounded, and she quickly tucked the duster into her apron pocket.

"Why Mr. Anderson, what brings you in today? I received that new fabric Mrs. Anderson was wanting." She fairly skimmed across the floor to the bolts of yard goods. "Or might I interest you in a fresh shipment of chewing tobacco?"

The woman knew just how to work a customer, that much was certain. But Lola was putting her foot down. She would take no more excuses.

Several minutes later, Mrs. Tesley closed the door behind Mr. Anderson and turned the OPEN sign to CLOSED. "Well, now. Another day, another dollar." She smiled at Lola, her clear complexion and firm skin crying foul, for the woman was forty-five and not a day younger.

"Mrs. Tesley, might I have a word with you?" Lola stepped in front of the counter.

"Why of course, Miss Wade." She approached with eyes the mirror of innocence.

"It has come to my attention lately that we seem to be . . . losing merchandise. And the till has come up short on numerous occasions."

"Surely you have mistaken your figures, dear Miss Wade. I am absolutely certain of my transactions and record keeping."

This was not going to be easy. "Mrs. Tesley, I am wondering if you have been . . . borrowing from the till." There. She said it.

The woman plucked a hanky from her bosom and blotted her eyes. A most forlorn expression shadowed her face as tears appeared on command. "Surely you aren't accusing me of stealing, Miss Wade." She grasped Lola's hand. "I could never, ever, do such a thing to you or your father. You have been so kind and generous to me all this time that my dear Samuel has been fighting and sacrificing for the Old Dominion and her cause. Whatever would I do without you and your father's kindness? Why, you are like family to me." She gulped back a sob and dabbed at her eyes with a quivering hand.

"But Mrs. Tesley—"

"I am so sorry there seems to be some sort of error. Perhaps I've been a bit distracted of late, not hearing from my Samuel for so long." She hung her head and massaged her temples. "Perhaps I am not well."

"Mrs. Tesley—"

"Oh, please allow me another chance, Miss Wade. I'm sure any miscalculations will right themselves in time." She clasped her hands together, begging. "Please, Miss Wade. I'm so certain there's been but a small unintentional error."

Lola couldn't just throw the woman out on the street without even a husband for support. Maybe there *had* been an error in calculation. The trap she had meticulously set was a complete failure. And she so did not want to bother Papa with this.

"Please consider yourself on probation, Mrs. Tesley. I will be double and triple checking the inventory and numbers from the till. If it comes up short again, or I find more goods missing, I'm afraid you must leave our employ." There, she'd said it. And she had insisted. Hadn't she?

"Thank you, Miss Wade." The woman's eyes were suddenly dry, and she replaced the hanky. "I will see you tomorrow at noon. And I will be punctual as always." She spun and quit the room before Lola could formulate an appropriate final warning.

A male voice boomed, "Miss Wade?"

"In here, Eleazar." Lola pulled the shade down on the front door and turned the key in the lock.

"I didn't mean to eavesdrop. I was just bringing in these supplies."

"No matter. Just tending to an uncomfortable task."

"I think there's something wrong with your brother, Miss Wade."

"Felix?" Lola rushed toward the back of the store and zipped around the counter, colliding with an apparition with stark white eyes.

"It's just war paint." The boy smiled, his red lips and white teeth stark against the black stripes of his face. "I read that Indians mix charcoal and water to paint their face before going to war. They make other colors too out of crushed berries and even their own blood."

"Well, your face looks more like a zebra to me."

Eleazar chuckled. "I just wanted you to see him so you could stop him from going to war."

"Has Papa seen you?" She planted her hands on her waist. "And who all has seen you like this?"

"Not yet, and nobody."

"Well, you show him real fast, then get yourself washed up. Supper will be on soon enough." She smiled at Eleazar. "Thank you for bringing him in."

His face lit with a smile. "I always try to keep an eye on that one."

"How is little Matthew? And Juliette?"

"They're doing real fine. Seems the little one is cutting a tooth, I think. Gnaws on your fingers somethin' fierce if he gets the chance."

"You're a wonderful papa, Eleazar. And Juliette is a lucky woman."

He kneaded his hat in his hands. "That's real nice of you to say, Miss Wade. I'm beholden to you and your papa for this job all these years. Makes a man feel proud to support his family—put food on the table and a roof over their heads."

She patted his arm. "We're blessed by you, too. Give Juliette my best."

"See you tomorrow morning, Miss Wade." He donned his hat and headed out the back door.

Lola blew out the lantern and set off to the kitchen, her mind more on a certain private than on the evening meal. Her fondness for him and thinking about him multiplied every day. She even fancied herself married to him someday when she allowed herself to daydream. But he seemed distant at times, and she couldn't figure out why. It was as if he was right there with her, sharing in a laugh or talking about important matters. Then he was somewhere else. And on the Sundays when he sat with her in church, he didn't seem to listen—like his body was there, but not the rest of him.

But Papa liked him—the way Zander was all cordial and respectful around him. Which was the real Zander Dabney? Was it the polite, fun, honest one? Or was it the silent, pensive one—whose eyes darkened for no apparent reason and whose jaw tightened and flexed in the middle of a prayer at church?

As much as that man was a mystery, he was growing on her. And when he wasn't around, she wished he was. Lola sighed, resigned to wait out their relationship until things seemed just a little more *right*.

Twenty-Two

November 1864

Zander set the crumpled letter aside. He had read it at least a half dozen times. He never should've left the comfort of James's house in Charleston. Why hadn't he just waited to be conscripted?

Bass lay on his cot with one arm shielding his eyes from the lantern light. Nothing seemed to excite his friend anymore. Even the prospect of a race turned him surly, and he claimed he didn't need any more money.

"You heard from your folks lately?" Zander made a feeble attempt at conversation, trying to get the boy talking.

Bass slammed his feet to the floor and sat up. He glared at Zander, as owly as anything. "No."

"Well." *That's why he was in such a surly mood?* "I'm sure you'll hear something soon."

"You think the mail just slides through easy as you please between the Old Dominion and here?" Bass stood and grabbed his hat. "I need some fresh air."

Zander passed a questioning look to Leach. "What'd I say?"

Leach shrugged. "Beats me. He's been contrary for days now."

"I'll be back later." Zander stuck his letter under the thin mattress.

"You know, Dabney," Leach ventured, "you might try talking to your friends sometimes instead of that horse of yours."

"Yeah, well, Rampart doesn't talk back." He strode out into the night, pulling a folded paper from his pocket and pinching a bit of tobacco between his fingers. He didn't even like the stuff. Couldn't figure how some did. He sighed and returned it back to the paper.

The next morning, Zander rode with a half-dozen men in escort of two supply wagons en route to Fort Piano. Perched just east of town on top of a steep mountain, the trip there and back would prove time consuming with a wagon.

As the convoy turned off the main road, Zander glimpsed a horse heading into a dense stand of trees. Bass's horse.

"I'm going to check something out. I'll catch up in just a minute."

"It's your hide," quipped the private, bringing up the rear with Zander.

"Back before you know it." Zander galloped away, entering the woods where he had seen Bass disappear.

Rampart picked his way over fallent branches, following the fresh trail. Zander heard voices and stopped. He couldn't make out the words, but he recognized Bass's voice. In a flurry of cracking branches, a horse broke through the undergrowth not fifteen feet from his position. The rider turned and met Zander with a look of surprise, followed swiftly by a devilish sneer.

Carter!

"Hiyah!" Carter Dabney turned and bolted off into the trees.

"Bass?" Zander moved forward, listening for a reply.

Silence.

What if Carter hurt him? A keen mix of anger and panic swelled in his middle. "I know you're in here Bass. It's me, Dabney. Come out, will ya?"

Nothing. He needed to return to his detail, but he wasn't leaving his friend to die. Zander prodded Rampart farther into a crowded over growth. He breathed a sigh of relief when he saw Bass sitting on his horse, seeming not to notice he had company. He sure didn't look hurt.

The concern vanished, replaced by full-fledged anger. "What were you doing with that man?" He didn't try to hide the contempt in his voice.

"I don't know what you are talking about." Bass stared straight ahead.

"You know what I'm talking about. You were talking to that Rebel!"

Bass blinked, and his face hardened to stone. "I said, I do not know what you are talking about." The words pounded like a hammer to an anvil.

"Tell me. Now!"

Bass whipped around his mount and kicked it into a furious escape through the trees and out of sight. Zander seethed, but he dare not follow, or he would face a court martial for deserting his post. He would have to deal with this later.

Zander paced in front of the hut, his mind roaming places that made his blood boil. Bass had managed to avoid him for the last twenty-four hours, but no more. He had to come back and sleep at some point.

Leach opened the door wide, calling him in. "You're wearing a path like a hound with a treed coon, Dabney. Have a seat, why don't you? Bass will be here when he gets here."

"And when he gets here, he's gonna wish he'd stayed away."

"Wish you'd tell me what's got you so riled up. Whatever it is—"

"Maybe I will come in. Catch him by surprise." Zander stomped inside and dropped onto the cot. He grabbed a book and pretended to read to thwart any more questions from D.R. A half hour, then an hour, ticked by before the door creaked open.

Bass stuck his head inside, his face registering disappointment when his eyes met Zander's.

"You can't avoid me forever, Bass. We're gonna talk about this whether you like it or not." Zander stood, tossing the book onto the cot.

Bass pushed past him. "We don't have anything to talk about."

"Oh yes, we do! Like why you're talking to that no good Rebel cousin of mine."

"Cousin?" Bass's face fell slack.

Zander stepped closer. "Yeah. And he oughta be in a Federal prison. You got no business even talking to the likes of him. It's treason!"

"Lower your voice," Bass growled. "Like I said. There is nothing to talk about." He slumped onto the bed. "Now, leave me alone."

Zander jerked him up. "How can I trust you if you won't tell me the truth?"

Leach sprang up between them, trying to pull them apart. "Maybe ya oughta leave him be, Zander," he said, eyes pleading.

Heat burned in Zander's chest. He clenched his jaw. "I'll let him be just as soon as he tells me why he was meeting with a Rebel in secret."

Bass jerked away, but he tightened his grip. A fist slammed into Zander's jaw and he staggered backwards.

When Bass turned his back, Zander lunged at him like an angry bear, wrapping his arms around his middle. He yanked him sideways and Bass crashed to the the floor.

"Tell me!" Zander roared.

"You fools! The whole camp will hear you!" D.R.'s panicked gaze darted to the door. "There's better ways to settle this."

Bass charged at Zander and they both flew through the door, slamming the ground with a thud. He drove his fist into that smug face, and Bass threw a handful of dirt into the air, just missing Zander's eyes.

"Break it up!"

The voice barely registered as he pummeled away on Bass, one blow after the other until two sets of hands dragged him off.

"Looks like both of you boys will need a couple of days to simmer." Sergeant McNeer motioned for another private to haul Bass to his feet. "You want to tell me what this was about?"

Bass stiffened. "No, Sergeant." He pinned Zander with a desperate look and a silent plea.

"Dabney?" Sergeant McNeer growled.

He didn't have a shred of evidence, no way to prove anything. And he had to know what Bass was doing talking to Carter. "No, Sergeant."

"Take them both to the stockade!"

"I will never understand a man's need to settle an argument with his fists." Lola sighed and brushed a lock of Zander's hair from his swollen cheek. "Does Bass look this bad?"

Zander tipped his head away. "He looks worse."

"Oh." Maybe if she didn't push him, he would tell her what all this was about.

"It was nice to spend Thanksgiving with a proper family. Makes me miss my own." He winked. "And the food was just as pleasing as the company."

"Why, thank you, Private Dabney." She handed him her wrap, and he eased it over her shoulders. "You want to take a walk?"

He shrugged, and she took that for a yes.

"Last year, with President Lincoln declaring the day of Thanksgiving and all, I was settled with my family. And sadly, itching to join the cause." He took her hand, guiding her down the porch steps. "This year, I'm thankful as can be not spending it with the rest of my unit at the fort. I don't know what they're eating, but in no way can it compare to that fare you served up. No sir."

They rounded the corner of the saloon and followed a well-worn path toward the creek, walking in silence for several minutes.

"It wasn't an argument." Zander reached for her other hand to face her. "I caught Bass in a meeting in the woods with my cousin."

"Your . . . cousin? I didn't know you had kin up her."

"He's not supposed to be here. Carter is a Rebel—least ways he used to be—and he should be in a Union prison. I know he is up to no good, and Bass is up to no good meeting with him like that." His eyes settled on their joined hands.

It was a comfort, the way he was willing to share more of himself, when at times he was so closed-off. But to fight with a close friend over bad blood with his cousin?

His eyes lifted, peeking at her through straw-colored lashes. "You won't say anything, will you?"

She squeezed his hands. "No. I won't. Besides, who would I tell? Why do you hate this cousin of yours so much, Zander? I can't imagine–"

"Remember how I told you that our barn was a Union hospital during the first few months of the war?"

"Yes."

"It's a long story, but Carter was responsible for the death of my brother-in-law's friend. He got himself wounded near our place, and ended up in our barn. Even after my sister nursed him back to health and we all took care of him, he lied to us about James being dead." He started walking again. "He claims he just happens to be here in New Creek, but I know he's up to no good."

"And you think Bass is in some kind of trouble?"

"I don't know what to think." He stooped, picked up a twig, and broke it into pieces. "He won't talk to me about it, so I can only assume the worst. I've got no proof."

She ached for him. It was obvious he wasn't just mad, but mighty worried, too. His heart is tender, for sure. A tree branch fell into the creek with a splash, interrupting the comfortable silence that had settled between them.

He stood, tossing the last piece of twig aside and meeting her gaze. "I can't trust him anymore." The stormy blue of his eyes matched the dark clouds that had drifted over them. "I have some . . . some savings that he's been holding onto for me. Savings to build that ranch out west I was telling you about."

"Do you want me to ask Papa if we can keep it in the store safe for you?"

"Would you? If New Creek had a bank, I would deposit it there."

She hugged his arm and turned back toward town. "I don't think he'll mind."

He smiled and stood taller. "That's one problem out of the way."

"We'll ask Papa just as soon as we get back to the store."

"Thank you." He took both of her hands and tipped his forehead to hers.

Flames kindled insider her as an invisible cord drew her to him.

"And thank you for being my shelter in this storm." He pulled her close. "No matter what foul matters I have to deal with out there"—he jerked his head—"you are my home, my shelter. You are everything in my life that is safe and beautiful."

He captured her in an embrace and a kiss she did not want to end. She savored the sweetness of him, somehow sharing both pain and joy. Every piece of her wanted to be what he needed. But deep down, she knew Zander needed more than any human could give him.

Twenty-Three

November 28, 1864

Pewter clouds sprinkled the road, leaving tiny divots in the dust as Zander dismounted at Wade Mercantile. He looped the reins over the hitching post and unbuckled the saddle bag, slipping a paper-wrapped bundle into his jacket. Two hundred dollars. Except for the money he had left in Charleston with his sister, it was the entirety of his savings.

Thankfully, few townsfolk were out and about on this sleepy Monday morning. Two soldiers stood talking at the corner of the post office and a dog chased a cat at the end of the block. Zander bounded up the steps. Grabbing the door handle, he glanced at those soldiers again, and when one of them turned, he stiffened. That Federal bore an uncanny resemblance to his cousin. The man looked right at him and all doubt vanished.

The fury ignited by that smug face burned clean through his common sense as Zander bolted into the store. Mrs. Tesley was the only one in sight, so he pushed the package across the counter to her. "Would you be sure to give this to Lola or Mr. Wade, please, Mrs. Tesley? It's real important they get it." He charged out the door with his Colt drawn before she could answer.

Zander raced across the street and rounded the post office, taking precious seconds to figure out which footprints were freshest. He jogged around the back and past the livery. Could be Carter was close by, or maybe he had made a run for it.

Pain exploded in the back of his head. His knees gave way to blackness.

Shouts sounded in the distance. Familiar manure and hay odors lured Zander back to consciousness. Rain pounded against the building, a hammer pounded the back of his head, and a gag crushed painful lips against his teeth. He writhed in an attempt to free his hands, bound behind him and tethered to his hobbled feet. *He had been hog-tied!*

The coarse rope tore at his skin, unyielding in his attempts at escape. Chest and legs screamed as muscles cramped. He scanned the tack and hand tools hanging on the wall. If he could just reach them. He was in the livery. But where were the horses?

Shots rang out, and a woman's scream sent him into a frenzied, thrashing, revived attempt at freedom. More shouts. Feet buffeted the streets. Horses whinnied. He rolled onto his side, thinking to crawl toward the door. Whatever was happening, the livery is *not* where he should be. He kicked and bucked, inching across the filthy floor, since his ankles were bound as tightly as his wrists.

Shouting through the gag was useless against the noise outside. *Pray.*

He had not prayed seriously since Cloyd's Mountain. Why would God help him now? Hadn't the Almighty led him to this point? Helpless, while others needed him.

An insidious voice hissed through his mind, telling him he was safe right where he was.

Another scream rent the chaos over the thrum of horses—lots of horses—galloping through the town as shots rang out.

If he could just get the gag off, he could yell for help.

Smoke filtered under the door, and a haze settled inside the livery. His throat erupted with spasms, so he concentrated on breathing through his nose to keep from choking. The door blossomed black as flames licked the edge of the charred wood. Zander rolled over, his back to the wall. He bucked and kicked, hammering lumber with his boots. One board rattled loose, then another, so he kept at it. Just as the door crumbled from its hinges, he rolled into the open, gasping past the gag to fill his lungs as rain washed his face.

The ruckus in the streets had settled into an eerie silence. Great smokey plumes rose above the town.

He log-rolled, muscles shuddering and knotting with every movement until he rounded the corner of the now-engulfed livery. Mud clung to all but his eyeballs as he rolled into the street, cringing at the results of what must have been an attack. A handful of people drifted into the street. He spotted Lola with Felix held fast in her arms. They leaned over a body . The boy flailed, and she struggled to keep him with her.

Look at me, Lola. Please, look at me. He stared at her, willing her eyes to fall in his direction until she suddenly raised her tear-streaked face and saw him.

"Zander?" She stood. "Oh, Zander!" She hitched up her skirt and dragged Felix with her, making her way to him.

Feeling equal parts relief, anger, and embarrassment, Zander could only watch as she stumbled toward him, sobbing.

"You're here. I can't believe you're here." She fumbled with the rope, then tried to untie the gag. "It's no use. I'll be right back." She pushed Felix to the ground. "You stay right here. Do. Not. Move!"

She ran back to the figure in the street and returned with a knife. Only then did he realize the Mercantile was ablaze. Black smoke funneled from the upper windows of the family's bedrooms. How long had he been unconscious, anyway?

She cut the mud-soaked gag first. He worked his mouth, testing his voice. "Are you all right?" he asked, trying to read through the fear in her drenched face.

Tears flowed and she gulped back a sob, sawing at the ropes on his wrist. "They took Papa. And . . . and they killed Eleazar." She motioned toward the body in the street.

At once, his hands were free. He engulfed Lola and Felix with mud-coated arms, holding them close as the boy shivered against him. "I'm so, so sorry I wasn't there for you. For them."

How could this have happened? And what of the fort? And what of Rampart? Confusion erupted into desperation. Not a horse was in sight. He'd have to head back to Fort Fuller on foot.

After long seconds, he loosened his hold on Felix and lifted Lola's chin. "Tell me what happened."

She clung to him. Fresh tears sprouted. "It all happened so fast. They rode in shooting and rounding people up like cattle, marching them out of town so fast. Papa will never be able to make it very far."

Zander grabbed the knife from her and cut the ropes around his ankles. "How long ago did they leave?" He stood on feeble legs, helping them both up.

"I don't know. Maybe 30 minutes."

"Does Eleazar have a horse at his place?" Zander needed a horse, and likely the Rebels made off with any they could get their hands on.

Felix slipped his hand into Zander's. "He has a mare in a little shed out behind his cabin."

"Then that's where we're headed." He felt Lola tense. "Lola, you need to tell Juliette."

"Oh, Zander . . ."

"She mustn't find out some other way."

Fear still colored her blue eyes, but she squeezed his hand and stood a little taller. "Let's go."

Zander galloped the chestnut mare through rain and mud all the way into Fort Fuller. Thick smoke columns rose from the warehouses of quartermaster and commissary stores.

Chaos reigned as soldiers fought fires and tended to the wounded. Shouted orders sent men running, others streamed in from outside the garrison, drenched and confused.

Sergeant McNeer and Captain Giles were not at the garrison. The only man from his unit he saw was Bass, who rode one of the few horses in the entire place. Zander approached him, wondering for an instant how he had kept his horse when the paddock was obviously empty.

"Bass! I can't find the sergeant or the captain. I'm going after Rampart and Mr. Wade."

Grim-faced, Bass handed him one of his pistols. "Lead the way."

Gray storm clouds and drifting smoke gave the appearance of dusk as the sun continued to climb. Zander and Bass followed the unmistakable trail west toward Piedmont. Hundreds of humans, horses, and cattle from Fort Fuller and New Creek had churned up an enormous swath of mud. Shivers plagued him from the icy rain, sucking at his uniform and sluicing into his eyes.

Bass rode by his side, crouched down into his gum blanket. At least someone was dry. And he'd said nary a word.

"If I can get close enough for Rampart to hear me, I know I can get him to cut loose. Probably bring a bunch more horses with him," Zander shouted over the fury of rain and galloping hooves. He pulled up, signaling for Bass to listen. The sound was unmistakable. *Cattle. And horses.*

Steering clear of the road, they paralleled the pike, meeting first a handful, then a dozen escaped prisoners making their way back toward Fort Fuller. Only one townsfolk appeared to be among them, and after some questioning, Zander was more certain than ever he would find Rampart and Mr. Wade.

Darkness shrouded the herd of horses, loosely guarded by Confederates. And off to the south, the prisoners huddled under a cluster of trees which afforded little shelter from the rain that continued to fall.

Zander dismounted and handed the mare's reins to Bass. "Stay here."

He circled around as best he could, counting the guards. Two of them were swilling whisky—no doubt taken from Federal stores. If he could just take out even two of the guards, he figured the prisoners could slip away one by one in the darkness. But without mounts, they would stand little chance when the Rebels discovered them missing.

He soon returned to share his plan with Bass, who followed his instructions without so much as a comment. After picking off the two nearly drunk guards, they led the prisoners two at a time to a grove of trees across an open field.

"Just two more or we risk being discovered," Zander whispered, keeping an eye out. A hand clamped Zander's shoulder. He grabbed for the knife that was no longer in its sheath.

"Zander." Mr. Wade had aged years, it seemed. "Do you know if Lola and Felix are all right?"

Relief swept through him. "Am I glad to see you. They are both safe. She's the reason I'm even here." He pointed to the woods. "Follow Bass to those trees. In just a few minutes, I'm going to be leading a bunch of horses by there and you need to make sure everyone is ready to ride. It's our only chance and it's going to happen fast."

"We'll be ready," Mr. Wade said, limping off.

Zander watched as Bass led the last of the group of prisoners into the trees.

"Hey. What do you think—"

He whirled on a Rebel, surprised to see his rifle slung over his arm instead of aimed at him. Zander threw a punch to his midsection, then cracked his skull with the handle of his borrowed revolver, catching him as he collapsed to the ground, unconscious.

Slipping through the darkness past a guard, Zander walked several more yards. He whistled low and soft, rewarded with a familiar whicker. He repeated the process twice more, aware of the subtle movement among the herd as Rampart made his way to him.

He rubbed the familiar muscled neck and marveled at the way Rampart's coat appeared ghostly in the dark. The saddle and tack was still in place, but he doubted that was the case with many others. Hopefully, the prisoners could mount and stay mounted in the escape.

He crept into the press of horseflesh and leaped onto Rampart, chucking his way in a tight circle to arouse the other horses. With a flail of reins, he bolted off with the horses close behind.

Shouts punched the air as he galloped for the trees, slowing just long enough for the prisoners to each snag a horse.

"Hurry!" He reached down and pulled up an older man who seemed confused. "Bass, you lead them back. I'll bring up the rear." He would leave no one in the group behind, either.

Rebels followed them only for a short time, then he figured they had thought twice about heading back toward the Federal garrison. What sweet relief washed over him when Fort Fuller's silhouette came into view.

Circling around the perimeter inside the fort, Zander made his way back to the gate while horses continued to pour into the confines of the garrison. Men scurried to close the heavy gates as the last of the rescued horses made their way in.

"Dabney!" Sergeant McNeer jogged toward him, slapping horses out of the way. "Is this your doing?"

"I . . . uh . . ." Zander dismounted, not sure whether he was in trouble for going off without orders or about to be congratulated.

"Where are the rest of the men?"

"What men, Sergeant?"

"The ones we sent after the prisoners."

"It was just Bass and me, and we didn't see anyone else. Just prisoners, Sarge."

Wearing an odd scowl, he scratched up under his hat. "And you freed these prisoners and horses on your own? Just the two of you?"

"That's right." Zander caught sight of Eleazar's mare, wishing he could snag her before she ended up in the paddock. "I couldn't find you or the captain neither one when I got back to the garrison, and I knew I had to move fast, before the Confederates got too far down the road."

Sarge ran a hand along Rampart's rump and chuckled. "Captain Giles is gonna want to hear this. Heck, Colonel Latham is gonna want to talk to you—after he explains to General Kelly how the entire advance guard of General Rosser's Confederates acquired Federal uniforms and walked right into the garrison."

Carter was wearing a Union uniform earlier. He knew his cousin was up to no good! If only he had proof. And what about Bass? Was he involved in this, too?

"We need to get these civilians back to town." Sergeant McNeer waved over a few men.

"I'm happy to escort them back, Sarge." Zander scanned the horses being herded out to the paddock.

"All right. Take several men with you, then get right back. We can pick through the horses tomorrow in the daylight."

"Yes, Sergeant."

Zander made his way through the press of horses and grabbed Eleazar's mare, leading her off to one side. Now, to find Mr. Wade.

Twenty-Four

Fire crackled and sputtered as Zander shoved more pitchy sticks into the belly of the stove. He had never been so glad to be out of wet clothes. The icy rain had soaked every fiber and chilled his skin to the bone.

He thought of the Wades and their loss. Not just their home, but their livelihood. Tonight, they found shelter with another family from church, but what about tomorrow? Would they even stay in New Creek?

"You and Bass are sure the talk of the Fort," Leach said, stretching out on his cot. "Still kind of a hard story to swallow—how you two freed the prisoners and then managed to get back all them horses too. God sure has a fine sense of humor, I tell you what."

"God probably had more important things to tend to. He doesn't pay much never mind to me these days, D.R.," Zander said, snugging the blanket to his chin as shivers rolled through his body.

Leach leaned on one arm. "Are you serious? There's nothing more important to God than taking care of His children."

He would not argue with his friend. But he knew the truth. Sometimes God just looks the other way, leaving his children to flip and gasp for air like a fish on dry land.

"Go to sleep, Leach. It's been a long day," Bass growled, turning his back.

"Where were you two when those Rebels came through the gate anyway? It was sure a sight, the way everybody scattered. I mean, what were we supposed to do when a hundred Union soldiers let loose with that Rebel war cry and then hundreds more come barreling inside the walls? I hear Colonel Latham and Captain Holmes hid in the bushes during the attack. Some of our guys even jumped into the creek."

"Goodnight, Leach!"

"Well, I just thought since the two of you weren't there—"

"Leach!"

"Oh, all right."

Tomorrow would bring its own set of extra work, cleaning up after the fires, taking inventory, and sorting through the horses. If only he could get into town to see how Lola was doing. He could almost feel her in his arm, all helpless and sorrowing.

The thing he wanted most in this whole wide world was to take care of that girl. To protect her and provide for her. She would make a fine pioneer woman. She was strong and hardworking. Smart, too. Real smart. And good with money.

And the possessor of his heart.

"What can I do to help?" Zander asked, stepping over charred crates lined up on the boardwalk.

"Oh! You startled me." Lola stilled the broom, and gray dust sifted to the ground.

"Sorry." He stepped closer, wanting to be near her. Wanting to comfort her. She allowed him to hold her for but a moment.

"I assumed you had your hands full at the fort. Papa said there were buildings burned there too."

"Yeah. They put everybody to work. This is the first chance I had to get away."

"I understand." Her lips curved in a fragile smile. "We buried Eleazar in the cemetery."

"I'm sorry I wasn't here."

"It was a simple service. Not very many folks there. Guess they had other things to do." She pulled the broom across the floor, her eyes fixed on the task yet so, so sad.

"What's Juliette gonna do—being it's just her and little Matthew now?"

"She says she's got kin up north. Probably gonna leave next week." She finally met his eyes. "Thanks to you, she at least has a horse to pull their wagon."

A rough cough broke through the quiet and Zander turned to see Mr. Wade pulling boards off the back stairwell. He covered his mouth with a kerchief, hacking in a way that brought back hard memories of Pap, gone three years ago now.

Zander shuffled through debris and scooted in front of Mr. Wade. "Let me do this. You need to rest."

"I'm fine. It's just all this smoke," he said, dropping his hands to his side. "There's just so much to do."

"I've got a couple of hours," Zander said. "Let me see what I can do to help."

Mr. Wade nodded in concession and backed away.

"There's a jar of water over on that barrel, Papa." Lola pointed with the broom. "Why don't you take a break?"

Mr. Wade ambled over to the barrel. "Just for a short spell, though." He put his hand to his chest, racked with violent coughs.

"I see the safe held up just fine in the fire," Zander said, thinking about his savings. "I surely do appreciate you letting me keep that money in there, Mr. Wade."

"Money? What money?"

"I gave it to Mrs. Tesley to give to you or Lola."

Lola dropped the broom. "Mrs. Tesley? Oh, Zander, you didn't!" She traded disgusted looks with her father.

Mr. Wade shook his head, looking like his dog had died.

"What?" Zander looked at each of them in turn. "What?"

"Nobody has seen Mrs. Tesley since the attack, son. And she sure never gave us anything to put in the safe for y—" A rack of coughing stole his words.

An invisible cannon ball struck Zander in the gut. His savings. Gone. His dream of settling out west. Gone.

Lola squeezed his arm. "I'm so sorry."

If this was God's way of shutting down his dreams, it worked real well.

"Look at this!" Felix dangled a charred mouse by the tail. "Roasted rodent, anyone? A mouse is a rodent, you know." He lifted it to his sister's face.

"Put that down. Are you finished with the job I gave you?" Lola's face signaled trouble like an approaching squall.

Felix hung his head. "No. I'm going. I'm going," he mumbled, shuffling off.

Lola shifted her attention to Mr. Wade. "He looks so tired," she whispered to Zander.

"That cough doesn't sound too good either." He had been around a lot of sick people in his life, and Mr. Wade sounded more than a little tired. A night of being soaked and near frozen could not have helped—and breathing in all that smoke.

They worked until dusk and Zander walked the Wades over to the Benoit home, where they were staying.

"I'll just be a few minutes, Papa," Lola said, standing aside as her family entered the house.

Zander offered his arm. "Walk with me?"

Her face lit up for the first time since all this trouble. She took his arm and fiddled with her spectacles. "I'd be delighted, Private Dabney."

"It pains me to see your family without a home. What will you do now?"

She sighed, plucking a few scarlet leaves from a bush as they walked. "I haven't asked. I'm afraid to ask, actually. Papa wrote a letter to his sister, but I didn't even ask what it said."

He fought the notions swirling in his mind. Any way he figured, he couldn't see the Wades staying in New Creek. A man has to put food on the table.

"You . . . you're not thinking of leaving, are you?" He focused on the worn path ahead, afraid to meet her eyes.

"Zander, it's not what I think that matters."

He stopped, pulling her to him. "I can't lie to you, Lola. You plum set my heart a'quiverin' every time I see you or even think of you." He drew a deep breath, taking in every wispy golden curl. "You have an effect on me like I never imagined possible."

She pressed into his chest, her eyes searching his. "And you on me."

He encircled her in his arms, relishing the feel of her body against his—her smallness and the way she fit to him, breaking him. He captured her lips, suddenly hungry for more of her as desire erupted, welcomed and wonderful. And so right.

Her body responded to his yearnings and the moan that escaped her lips only fanned the fire that roared in his belly. His lips roamed her cheek, her neck, her ear.

"Zander . . ."

She had whispered against his hair and he dampened the heat that bid him take what wasn't his. But how could he be without her for another minute? His heart ached at the thought of leaving her here in New Creek while he returned to Fort Fuller.

"Lola, I can't lose you." He tipped her chin and sought comfort in the depths of her startling blue eyes. "I love you."

Her eyes glistened and her smile was a salve to the growing pain in his chest. "I want what God wants, Zander. And I pray he wants us to be together."

He stiffened and stepped back, his fingers still caressing hers. "I . . . I'm not so sure God wants much of anything for the likes of me."

"But how can you say such a thing? He loves you, Zander. He wants only the best for you."

"Well, He's got a strange way of showing it." He turned back toward town, engulfing her hand in his. "If I don't get you back, your pap is going to come looking for you."

The disappointed look on her face made him feel like the worst kind of varmint. Why'd he have to go and say anything? Everything was going so well. The last thing he wanted was to cause her pain. They walked back in silence as Zander thought of ways to ease their parting words.

"I'll be back to help any way I can day after tomorrow."

She batted away a tear and forced a tremulous smile.

He cupped her cheek with his hand. "I made you cry." He was lower than a snake's belly. "I never want to make you cry, Lola. Never." He kissed the wetness on her cheek. "Forgive me."

Her shoulders rose and fell before a reluctant smile graced her lips. "Of course I forgive you. It's been a hard day. A hard time for all of us."

"I'll see you Sunday afternoon, then."

Her sweet smile slipped. "You can't come to church?"

It was the last thing he had planned for Sunday, but how could he let her down? "I'll try." He squeezed her hand and let it slip from his fingers as she closed the door.

Confounded war. He'd finally found a woman he would die for, and all he could think of now was staying alive for the rest of the war—and not dying.

Lola closed the door. A battle raged between her head and her heart, and she wanted to do the right thing. Oh, how she wanted what seemed out of her reach.

"Lola, dear, are you all right?"

She startled and turned. Ann Benoit's gaze held nothing less than kindness and concern. Lola glanced behind her, making sure no one was listening. She swiped a tear away and nodded.

"If you need an ear, you know I am always willing to listen."

Lola forced a tremulous smile, so very thankful for this woman, old enough to be her mother, yet more of an older sister. "I'll be all right. I'm just confused about some things right now. And I don't know what tomorrow holds."

"Do any of us?" She led Lola to the bench beside the hall tree and bid her sit. "Do those tears have anything to do with your young man?"

Lola fiddled with the hanky she'd found in her pocket. "How did you know Charles was the man you should marry, Ann? How did you know he was the right one?"

"Oh, well, I suppose because I didn't want to live without him. I remember the deep ache when we were apart. That is a rare and beautiful thing to have in a marriage."

Lola thought hard. She had that with Zander, didn't she? He occupied her every thought. Her heart flipped just seeing his handsome face. He was so considerate and tender with her. She warmed inside remembering the way he had kissed her. Zander saw *her*. Not some peculiar, short girl with spectacles and fly-away hair.

"But we humans are all flawed and those wonderful feelings come and go in a marriage. If there isn't something deeper holding two people together, neither will be happy for long," Ann said with a spark of wisdom shining in her eyes.

"What do you mean? What is deeper than love?" Lola squirmed as something niggled at her uncomfortably.

"Love is powerful. There is no force greater. It sent our Savior to the cross, Lola." Ann patted her hand. "Marital love is wonderful, but marriage needs a foundation of faith, mutual trust in the Almighty, dependence on Him and His Word. That is the only foundation that makes a marriage strong when the nice feelings come and go and life gets hard."

Deep inside, Ann's words resonated painfully. *Oh God, please heal whatever is making Zander hold You at arm's length.*

Twenty-Five

CHARLESTON

December, 1864

Augusta dropped onto the settee beside James, placing a fresh cup of tea on the low table. "Finally got the little one down. I didn't think she'd ever give up."

"See what you have to look forward to, Melinda Jane? Sleepless nights and sleepy days." James grinned and patted his wife's hand. "But motherhood does render a woman her most alluring beauty."

She smiled and snuggled closer to her husband. "And motherhood is most successful in provoking words of flattery from the husband who is washed fully in shame because he is not so tired and over worked as the mother of his child."

Melinda Jane set her tea down, shaking with laughter. "Is that how that works?"

"Now don't you two gang up on me. Can't a man offer a compliment to the love of his life without getting heckled for it?" He feigned a pout, then stood. "Bertie, what say you and I disassociate ourselves from these vexing women and seek out some comfort victuals?"

"Huh?" Bertie looked up with a wrinkled nose. His hand stilled above the cabin he was building from whittled sticks.

Gus swatted at her husband's backside. "Oh, he just wants some cookies."

"Well, why didn't he say that then?" Bertie jumped up and followed after James through the kitchen door.

Augusta chuckled. "I wonder which boy is more trouble sometimes—the one too big for his britches or the one too short for his." She sipped the tea, relishing the peace and quiet of the evening with family. But two holes remained in her heart, waiting earnestly for this horrid war to end so she could get her brothers back. Only then would she truly rest.

"I might just bypass motherhood altogether." Will lowered the book she had buried her nose in for the better part of an hour. "Maybe I'll be a writer. Like Charlotte Bronte. I'd get more sleep."

Melinda Jane *tsked*. "And you would have fewer people to love and love you back."

"But I'd have folks that loved me for my books."

"I think you'd find that love short-lived compared to marrying for love and raising up a family."

Will sighed. "Well, I have some time to consider my options."

Augusta winked at Melinda Jane and then patted her sister's knee. "You certainly do, Will. And I hope you'll consult the Good Lord when you are making your decisions."

James limped into the room with crumbs on his beard and Bertie in his shadow. He had a paper folded under one arm and a stack of cookies in his hand. "We haven't heard from either of the boys lately, have we?"

"I did hear from Fin two weeks ago, so I expect something soon." Melinda Jane rubbed her growing belly. "That boy is regular as a layin' hen with his letters."

James settled next to his wife. "I don't mean to alarm you, but it appears there's been an attack on Fort Fuller." He opened the paper and scowled. "I have the Wheeling Daily Intelligencer here, but it's a week old."

A sudden trembling in Augusta's middle snaked its way to her fingers, so she set the cup and saucer down abruptly, looking to her husband for more information.

"'The history of the late disaster to our arms at New Creek station, as far as we have been able to learn, is about as follows: On Saturday last, a small force under Major Fleming' . . . um, let me skip some of this." He scanned the paper as his brows pinched in concern.

"Well?" Augusta scooted to the edge of her seat. Her little brother could already be with the Almighty. Oh! She could not think like that!

James continued, "'On Monday morning the *A* Confederate force under General Rosser, about 1,000 in number, came slowly down upon New Creek, the advance being attired in our uniform. Supposing the approaching force to be the returning command of Major Potts, our men allowed the Rebels to come within thirty yards of the fortifications when the Rebels set up a horrible yell and charged down with great fury upon the fort. Our men were completely panic stricken and abandoned the fort without firing a gun. In fact, the whole command was completely demoralized, and it was in vain that some of the officers attempted to rally the confused squads.'

"Says here they burned the stores after helping themselves to several wagons of supplies, captured 250 citizens and soldiers, 250 cattle, and 800 horses."

Augusta stood, wringing her hands. "What if Zander was taken prisoner?"

"It says here that two privates were credited with the rescue of forty prisoners and two hundred horses."

"And it didn't give their names?" Melinda Jane shook her head. "I bet if they were officers, it would've said their names."

"Unfortunately, I agree." James turned the paper over, still reading.

Melinda Jane reached for the paper. "Can I see if there's any news about Blazer's Scouts?"

His scarred face brightened. "It does mention that 65 Scouts bested Mosby's force of 300 at the Vineyard last month. But we already knew that."

Melinda Jane slapped her knee. "That makes twice the Scouts have rattled ol' Mosby. They surely have been a thorn in his flesh, I'd say."

Augusta paced the floor, her mind visiting all number of dark places, speculating on Zander taken prisoner.

James rose, handed his last two cookies to Bertie, and wrapped his wife in his arms. "Now, Gus, you know we can't think the worst. Our trust in God's faithfulness to hear prayer is all we really have in this life."

She snugged her cheek against his chest. "I'm so weary. Weary of praying, weary of not knowing. Surely this ugly conflict has played itself out." His muscular arms cradled her. She felt safe, which was not fair because her brothers were in harm's way. Since Fin and Melinda Jane wed, she had felt more connected to her older brother through his more frequent letters home. But Zander was another matter. She could count on one hand the number of times he had written. And only one letter since that awful Cloyd's Mountain battle.

She could not explain it, even to James, but something was going on with her brother. And all she could think of was that he needed her. A silly thought. He was a grown man now. But his sweet nature was not the stuff of soldiers. She had heard enough from James and Fin to know that much. *Soldiers do what needs doing and don't think on it too much*, they said. But how does someone like Zander—so sensitive and compassionate—face such hellish goings-on?

"If I could, I'd scoop you into my arms, carry you upstairs, and tuck you into bed," James whispered in her ear.

This man always seemed to know just what she needed. "And then you'd take care of Addie when she wakes at 4:00 in the morning?"

He smiled, lifting her chin, leaving a suggestive kiss on her lips. "Gladly." He tugged on her hand, heading for the stairs.

"Now?"

"Yes, now."

"But, James, the dishes . . ."

"Don't you worry," Melinda Jane said, gathering cups and saucers. "I'll take care of these and see that the children say their prayers." She winked, none too discreetly at James. "You just go get a good night's rest now."

"There. You see? Problem solved." He grinned.

"And I expect a turnabout the next time that man of mine is home." Melinda Jane chuckled as she glided through the kitchen door.

Augusta mounted the steps, with James right behind her. Maybe she'd dream of happier times tonight. It had been so long, so many years. But God had truly blessed her family with safety . . . and love. She smiled. The man behind her was not the man she had met three years ago. That man was bitter and cynical. *Thank you, Father.* She had trusted God with so much already. And she'd have to keep on trusting. For her family's sake and her own.

Twenty-Six

Z ander jogged to catch up with Bass. "Hey. What'd you take off like that for?" he asked, cuffing his shoulder.

Bass shrugged him off. "I find the whole idea ridiculous. You practically forced me to come with you. All I did was what you told me to."

"You deserve that commendation just as much as me, Bass. I couldn't have set those townsfolk and the rest free without you. We did that together."

Bass trudged forward in silence.

Zander shook his head. Well, there's just another thing that made no sense. Bass's attitude was growing old. He was cantankerous in the morning, tetchy at night—and no fun in between. Maybe it was just the war, going on and on as it was. Or the fact that his family lived in occupied enemy territory. Except for Lola, there had not been one thing about this God-forsaken war worth holding onto.

But things could always be worse. What if he was seeing the kind of action his brother saw? He shuddered inside, knowing he was not the soldier Fin was. But at least he did something right, getting Mr. Wade and the others back. And Rampart. But what about those other prisoners? They for sure weren't feeling obliged to Zander and Bass, now, were they? He should've figured a way to get more out.

Bass whirled on him. "You know, Dabney? You can just keep my medal. I do not want it." He plucked the medal from his chest.

"But—"

And I do not want to talk about it anymore." He stormed off toward the new Quarter Master's building.

D.R. Leach waved Zander down and strode toward him. "I just overheard Captain Giles talking to Sergeant McNeer. Seems the Fifth Cavalry will be no more. We are consolidating with the Sixth Regiment here at New Creek." He stood tall, mimicking the sergeant. "'And will hereafter be known as the Sixth West Virginia Veteran Volunteer Cavalry.'"

"That so?" Zander grunted. "Under Colonel Latham?"

"Yessir."

"Seems kind of odd to be part of a Veteran unit since I've only been in the army since January."

"Sometimes I wonder who decides all this stuff. There's so many brass buttons up the line, I don't think the one knows what the other's doing half the time." A wide grin split D.R.'s full red cheeks. "I hear congratulations are in order, Private Dabney." He snapped a salute.

"Yeah, thanks. But don't go offering compliments to Bass. He's liable to bite your head off."

"Hmm. Judging from the way he's been acting, I think I'll take your advice."

Zander reached into his pocket to check the time, then snugged his overcoat up around his chin. If he hurried, he would have a good two hours to spend with Lola.

"Good afternoon, Mrs. Benoit, is Lola here?"

"Certainly, Private Dabney. Won't you step on in where it's warm?"

Mr. Wade's coughing sounded from an unseen room, unsettling Zander with memories of his own pap's illness. One that eventually took him from them all. Hopefully Mr. Wade would get better.

"Hello." Lola entered the tiny parlor with her usual grace, but dark circles under her eyes stole the sparkle he had come to adore.

He rushed forward to grab her hand, and she relinquished it only for a second, then claimed it again. "Lola?" Her eyes shimmered with unspent tears.

She closed the door to the rest of the house and motioned for him to sit.

But he didn't want to sit. "I've got good news." Maybe his news would take her mind off of her father for now. "They gave me a commendation, see?" He puffed up his chest to make sure she saw the ribbon and gold medal there.

"For saving those prisoners?"

"Yep. And I didn't even have to get all shot-up to earn it." He smiled, hoping to coax one of her own.

She nodded politely. "I'm happy for you."

He made another effort to take her hand, and this time she allowed him to pull her closer. "You've been crying. Is it your pap?"

She sighed and passed a look behind her. "He's not been quick to recover from his ordeal, that much is for certain. I'm afraid he might be getting worse."

He pulled her close, setting his chin atop her head. "I'm sorry. I truly am. I remember how much it hurt when my pap was ailing."

She melted into his arms for only a moment before she stiffened and pulled back. "We need to talk. Please sit down."

His stomach twisted as she took the chair across the room. He sat, his mind foraging for something he had said, something he had done to bring this on. "Am . . . am I in trouble?" He flashed a lopsided grin. If she would just smile.

The misery on her perfect face was intolerable as she fiddled with her spectacles and twisted a hanky into knots. "There's no easy way to say this, Zander. I'm just going to say it."

The child in him wanted to bolt for the door. He swallowed, unable to breathe. A hammer seemed perched to beat his life to dust. "I'm listening."

"We are leaving in the morning to stay with Papa's sister in Wheeling. There is nothing left for us here." Her attention shifted to the floor as she took a deep breath before continuing. "And, I think . . . I think this will be a good time for us to reconsider our f-feelings for one another."

Zander sprang to his feet. "Our feelings? I don't understand. What are you saying?"

"Oh Zander. Please don't make this harder than it already is."

He covered the gap between them in two long strides. "I love you, Lola. I've never said that to another woman. You're all I can think about. All that really matters to me anymore." He grasped her hands. "And I've never kissed another woman before you." There. He laid himself bare. What was there to reconsider?

She looked down at their hands. "I think . . ." She lifted that perfect, now tear-streaked face. "I . . . I do love you, Zander. But I'm not sure if we're meant to be together, because for some reason that you won't tell me, you are mad at God. Until you figure out why that is and decide to make up with Him . . ."

Not sure if we're meant to be together? How could she not be certain of it? Wasn't her mind filled with images of him every waking hour like his was of her? Didn't she dream of spending the rest of their lives together as he did?

"Until you work out whatever this is that's caused you to keep God at arm's length, there can be no *us*." A flood of fresh tears washed her cheeks. "I don't want to hurt you. Maybe . . . maybe when this horrid war is over. Maybe then . . . we . . . can . . ."

She pulled her hands away and stepped back. "I will never forget you and I will always be forever thankful to you for saving my papa." Her hand flew to her mouth to stifle a sob as she rushed out the door.

The empty room mocked his broken heart, calling out names like *idiot* and *coward*. Crumbling dreams crashed and splintered into a thousand pieces as he charged from the house.

Frigid wind sliced his ears and tore at his clothes through his unbuttoned coat, but he welcomed the icy chill. He ducked into the new livery where Rampart waited out the wintery weather.

"Seems it was a short visit after all, old friend." He pressed his face against the soft, warm neck as tears stung the back of his eyes. So Lola thought he held God at arm's length, huh? Well, she got that all wrong. It was God who just kept pushing him away. And God's arms were a heck of a lot longer than his own.

He shoved the pain deep into his boots, out of reach—just as he'd learned to do since Cloyd's Mountain.

Twenty-Seven

Christmas, 1864

Never had there been a more deplorable Christmas. Ice pelted the Fort with a keen vengeance, strewing a frozen coating across everything it touched. Troops had gathered together in shifts for food and song, a sorry substitute for the merriment and feasting he had known every other year of his life.

D.R. slapped him on the back hard enough to raise his ire. "Cheer up, Dabney. You can at least spare a smile for this holy day."

The boy's enthusiasm scoured Zander's nerves like a whetstone, honing his heartache to a piercing misery he had never known. Nothing mattered. Not here. Not back home. And *he* didn't matter. He had bought a bottle of whiskey from another private and intended to get acquainted with the vile drink just as soon as he could get back to his hut. A first time for everything, he figured. Why not now?

Another verse of *Hark the Herald Angels Sing* erupted from the cluster of celebrating souls, too blind to notice that this day was just like all the rest. A Savior was born. In Bethlehem. To save the world. His head knew the story, but his heart grasped at the Good News with fingers as numb and frozen as the icy rain that pelted the window.

Light and Life to all He brings, risen with healing in His wings.

He used to understand. At least, he thought he did. It was such a long, long time ago. The ignorance of youth. But what about James, Gus, Fin? Hadn't his whole family seen the worst of this storm? Recollection of Ol' Izzy drew him further down that path. The best man he'd ever known, aside from Pap. And he could still see the rope that took him from them.

Leach rose from the hard bench, stretching his thick arms. "Ready to head back? I haven't seen Bass since they first started serving."

"I reckon."

"Can't help but think about my folks. Wondering if they cut a tree without me there to do it for them." Leach buttoned his wool coat and pulled up the collar. "What about you? Thinking of your family?"

"Yeah. I thought about them. I suppose they're pretty sad, missing both me and Fin this year." He smiled to himself. "Another Christmas with Bertie trying to talk my sister into letting Coot sit up to the table with the rest of the family."

"Wish I had a big family. Being an only child is like growing up before you're ready. Nobody to play with, so you just skip that part." D.R. pushed open the door. "Here we go!"

Striking out for the huts at a jog, they dodged frozen slabs of ice on the ground and leaned into the bitter wind. They grabbed firewood from the pile, ran into the hut, and dropped it by the small stove.

"Well, well, well. If it is not the *West* Virginians, come to celebrate the birf of our Lord." Bass sat on his bed, his arms propped on his knees and one hand around a bottle of whiskey.

"Where'd you get that?" Zander pulled a shallow crate out from under his cot.

"I borrowed it, General Dabney. I did not belief for one minute that you pre...pin...intended it for your own self." His red-rimmed eyes drooped more than usual and supper potato remnants beaded his beard.

"Give it back, Bass! You're drunk!" Zander grabbed the bottle, but Bass jerked it back.

"You don't need that stuff. It'll make you look as pathetic as him," D.R. said to Zander, dropping to his cot. "Makes a man stupid. You're not stupid, Zander." He drilled him with a dare.

"Don't tell me what I need. Besides, a man has a right to be stupid now and then." He snatched the bottle from Bass and tipped it back the way he had seen so many others do. His throat constricted with the burn and he coughed it raw, to Bass's great amusement.

"Suit yourself then." Leach stretched out and yanked the pillow from under his head to cover his face.

Zander took another drink. This time he was prepared for the burn that seared all the way to his belly and took his breath.

"I need it worz dan you do." Bass lunged for the bottle, but Zander held it aloft.

"How do you figure? Did you get gut-kicked by the woman you planned on being the mother of your children?" Zander turned and gulped another couple of drinks.

Bass reached around him, capturing the bottle. "Never mind." He tipped it again, emptying it. "There. I leaf you da rest."

Zander dropped to his bed and stared at the empty bottle. The floor wavered like a river in the sunlight and he decided he best lie back. He closed his eyes to the spinning room and heaved a sigh. Some Christmas this was.

"I'll get the light." D.R.'s bed creaked as he rose to add more wood to the fire and douse the lantern.

In the pitchy blackness, Zander's mind played tricks on him. Those couldn't be sobs coming from Bass's bed.

Twenty-Eight

KANAWHA VALLEY

January, 1865

The telegraph office buzzed with activity as men waited in line to send messages to loved ones. Fin fisted and opened his hands, impatience getting the better of him for a change. Couldn't they have more than one telegrapher? This was maddening.

He turned to a tug at his sleeve. "How many times do I have to tell you? Melinda Jane will understand, and I won't be more than a couple of weeks."

Noah flinched, raising his hands like he was calming a spooked horse. "Now, now. I'm just trying to keep you from aggravatin' that purty little wife of yourn. She's waited three whole years for you to finish your service, and you expect her to be understanding about not coming home now that you're out of bondage? That's just expectin' too, too much from any woman."

"She's concerned about my brother, too. I just got a feeling about this. I need to see for myself." Fin shuffled forward. One step closer to getting that telegram off to Melinda Jane. "I say it's no coincidence that he's saving up money somehow and I'm hearing about some horseman making a name and money for himself at New Creek. Besides, it'll give me a chance to meet that girl he mentioned to the family. How many *Lolas* can there be around there. Huh?"

"Well, I'm coming with you. I don't much look forward to going home just yet."

Fin spun around. "You'd do that?"

"Not like I got a gal waitin' for me. With Bubba in a Federal prison, I don't feel all that welcome to home." Noah twisted his lips with a look of consternation. "Heck, Fin. Your family is more a family to me than my own."

Fin slapped him on the back and stepped forward again. "You're always welcome to come with me, Second Lieutenant Hicks." He chuckled. "Just trying it on ya."

Noah grinned, standing a little taller. Both had received brevet promotions just before Blazer's scouts disbanded last week. It had been one wild ride, that was for sure. And costly. The unit had started out two years ago with almost a hundred men, and only thirty-two remained.

"Next." The clerk waved him over and took the paper from his hand. "Charleston?" He counted out the words. "That'll be four dollars, Captain."

Captain. Fin liked the sound of that. He dug into his pocket and produced the money. "I'm not waiting for a reply."

"As you wish." The clerk handed the message off to the telegraph operator. "Godspeed, Captain," he said, sliding the receipt under the bars above the counter.

"Thank you, Corporal." Fin shoved his hat back on his head and followed Noah out the door.

Fort Fuller

"I wonder what Sarge wants with us?" Zander mused as he traipsed toward the command building with Leach and two others from his unit.

"He said the five of us were supposed to meet him outside the colonel's office." Leach tugged on his gloves. "I couldn't find Bass anywhere."

"Did you check the stables?"

"Sure did."

"What about the Quarter Master's?"

"Checked there too. I must've looked for him for more than twenty minutes before I came and got the rest of you."

Gleason, a powerful, bushy-bearded man from Greenbrier, kept pace with them. "He couldn't have gone to town. None of us got leave today."

They clustered on the porch of the command building, waiting for Sergeant McNeer as snowflakes sifted from the heavy clouds.

"Looky here. Issued by the governor," Gleason said, motioning to the broadside nailed to the news board. "And here I thought things were starting to settle down."

"What's it say? Read it, D.R."

Leach stepped up to the board. "'For months past, bands of armed men have infested the state, stealing, robbing and murdering, and within a short time, their numbers and the frequency of their outrages have alarmingly increased. Some of them claim to be Rebel soldiers. But whatever they profess, they neither observe the rules of civilized warfare, nor regard the civilities of common thieves and robbers or the decencies of ordinary murderers.'"

"Yeah, yeah. We already knew all that," Zander said.

After trailing a finger along, moving his lips in silence, Leach began reading again. "'In view of this anomalous and alarming state of things, I earnestly recommend the loyal people of the state to organize themselves into companies of such numbers as may be practicable and expedient for the hunting down and capturing or killing these outlaws wherever they may be found—executing summary justice where found in the act or where they cannot otherwise be captured—and thus aid the authorities of the state in restoring and preserving peace, order, and security.'"

Pegs, a private from Calhoun County, shook his head. "Why, that's nothing more than condoning vigilantism."

"Sounds like the governor is pretty desperate," Leach said.

"Attention!"

Zander snapped a salute as Sergeant McNeer and Captain Giles stepped onto the porch.

"At ease, men. Sergeant McNeer will be delivering these important documents to Beverly and you men will accompany him." He handed a courier pouch to the sergeant. "I'd like you back as soon as possible as it seems likely we may be in for some ugly weather."

Sergeant McNeer frowned. "Where is Private Bassom?"

D.R. glanced at Zander. "Nowhere to be found, Sergeant."

The sergeant grumbled and exchanged looks with the captain.

"I'll check into Private Bassoom's whereabouts. You better get going." Captain Giles returned salutes and stepped back into the office.

"You heard him." The sarge led the way to the stables, and within fifteen minutes, they were on the road as snow swirled across the ground, covering their tracks.

Zander scrubbed Rampart's withers. "Not going to be a very pleasant trip, I'm afraid, boy." Especially if they meet up with any of those bushwhackers the governor seemed so concerned about. And what of Bass? A nagging feeling ate at him and he just couldn't shake it. For some reason, this little trip felt as threatening as the sky looked just now.

The ninety-mile trek would take two just days, but the weather would make those some miserable miles to cover. Just how much they skirted Brier Patch depended on the sergeant's leading. Zander tucked his chin against the cutting wind as they dipped into a lowland without the cover of trees, so mercifully present for much of their trip.

After crossing the Cheat River on the second day, a shot rent the frozen silence. The five of them settled behind trees just off the trace, waiting for uninvited company. Rampart's ears perked up at the sound of horses.

"How many, you think, Sarge?" Gleason whispered, petting his long beard like a barn cat.

"Two or three, I'd guess." Sergeant McNeer answered, checking his revolver.

"Two," Zander said. "Definitely two riders."

The sergeant lifted an eyebrow. "You're sure of that, Dabney?"

"No doubt about it. You want us to split up?"

"You and Pegs stay here and come behind them. The rest of us will move farther up the way and stop them in their tracks."

Zander crouched behind cover as two horses passed. "It's just Ford and Stille." He relaxed and holstered his Colt.

"Wonder what they're doing out here? Pegs mounted and waited until Zander joined him.

They'd follow along behind for several yards until Sarge stopped the men. Seemed harmless enough, but orders were orders.

Zander topped the crest of the rise and Sergeant McNeer's solemn eyes flashed. "You sure the captain gave you this, Ford?"

"Not long after you left, Sergeant. Orders were to catch up to you and give it to you."

"There's got to be some kind of mistake." The sarge approached Zander. "I hate to do this, son, but I need to check your saddle bags.

"My saddle bags?"

The steely look in the sarge's eyes told him he was in trouble and he didn't have a clue as to the nature of it. Zander handed over his saddlebags and shifted uncomfortably in his saddle. The way everyone was looking at him gave him the mullygrubs. Rampart stomped a foot and tossed his head, sensing his master's predicament.

Sergeant McNeer dug through the contents of one bag, then repeated the action with the other before pulling out a folded piece of paper. He opened it, squinted, and after a few seconds, touched a hand to his pistol.

He threw Zander a look that punched his gut. "You are under arrest for aiding the enemy, Private Dabney. Turn your arms over to Private Ford."

"I . . . I don't understand. Arrest? Aiding the enemy? I've done no such thing." Panic told him to run. He could get away. But that would only make him seem even more guilty of whatever it was.

"This is a map of New Creek. Houses of citizens with Southern sympathies have been marked. There is also the outline of an attack plan for General Rosser's men for the November attack on Fort Fuller.

"But I had nothing to do with that. I don't know how that paper got in there! I've never seen it before." Zander's shock flamed to anger. It all fell together so swiftly in his mind that it left him dizzy. *Bass.* Bass had planted the map and now he was gone. He didn't know the connection between Carter and his *ex*-friend, but he was going to figure out this whole mess. And he would not go down without a fight, either.

"Tie his hands," the sergeant barked.

"You can't think for a minute I did this, Sarge."

"It don't matter what I think, son." Regret sagged his weary eyes. "What matters is what is determined by a military trial. You will be held at Beverly tonight, then we are to escort you to Wheeling to await trial."

Ford sneered as he tucked the two Colts into his belt. "Don't expect that even that brother of yours is gonna get you out of this, Dabney." He spat on the ground, pulling a thong of leather from his saddle.

Zander searched his comrades. Skepticism colored the eyes of all but Leach. D.R.'s eyes brimmed with concern and he seemed to communicate without words—*just hold fast*. No doubt the boy was praying for Zander's soul at this very minute.

Twenty-Nine

FORT FULLER

January 1865

F in rode into Fort Fuller, scrutinizing every soldier in view, hoping to find Zander before engaging the garrison commander's help. He even trotted over to the paddock for a glimpse of Rampart.

"Looks like you're out of options." Noah pulled up beside him. "What'd Zander say his sergeant's name is?"

"McNeer, I think."

Noah waved over a private wheeling straw and manure out of the stables. Seeming uncertain at first, the private dropped the handles, strode over, and saluted.

"Yes, sir?"

"You know of a Sergeant McNeer, son?" Noah frowned, all business and intimidation.

"Yes, sir. He's out on a dispatch at the minute, though, sir."

Noah turned to Fin. "Well, Captain Dabney. That leaves us with just one option, I 'spect."

"Captain Dabney?" The boy snapped to attention all over again, his eyes round.

Fin puzzled over the way the private said his name. "Yes." He looked the boy up and down. "Do I know you?"

"Oh, no, sir. You're with the Blazer Scouts, ain't you? B . . . both of you, uh, sirs?"

Fin chuckled. "At ease, Private. The Scouts have disbanded."

The young private seemed disappointed, then he snapped to again. "I haven't seen your brother today, sir. He tries for stable duty more often than most."

Fin chuckled. "Not surprising. Who's your commander?"

"That'd be Colonel Fleming, sir."

"Thank you, Private." Fin angled Duke toward the command office. "With any luck, we'll find Captain Giles before we have to bother the colonel."

Fin sipped strong coffee as Captain Giles settled into the chair on the other side of the desk. "Nice of the major to let us use his office." He passed a concerned look to Noah, wondering why the captain hadn't just pointed him toward Zander's quarters.

"It's an honor to meet two of the famed Blazer Scouts. I hadn't realized they disbanded." Captain Giles set his cup down and leaned forward, focused on Fin.

"Just last week, actually."

"And you are here looking for your brother, I assume?"

"Yes. He's not expecting me. I haven't seen him in some time, and I figured this was as good a time as any before I head back to Charleston."

Captain Giles tapped his fingers on the edge of the desk, his lips pressed in a firm line.

"Is there a problem, Captain?" Fin set his coffee on the desk. Noah gulped his, flinching as he swallowed before setting it down.

"I'm afraid something unexpected has happened."

"I knew it. Zander's the one doing all that racing, isn't he?" Fin clenched his fist.

"He does race, though not as often as he did the first several months of his enlistment. But that's not the problem."

"Then what is?" All this small talk was wearing mighty thin.

The captain raked a hand through his hair and let out a long breath. "Your brother left on a dispatch with Sergeant McNeer three days ago. When certain information came to light, I sent two of my men to intercept them and arrest Private Dabney."

Noah sprang to his feet. "Arrest him? What for?"

Fin stayed him with a raised hand and stood. "I'm gonna need more information than that, Captain."

Captain Giles took a deliberate gulp of his coffee. He steepled his hands and glanced at the papers on the desk. "We were informed that he provided the enemy with information relating to the attack on this garrison and the town of New Creek back in November. We searched his quarters and found no evidence, so I sent my men to search his person."

Fin's mind whirled, absorbing the information in a haze of anger and doubt. Zander would never do anything so despicable.

Noah threw back his shoulders and jutted out his chin. "I'd like permission to talk to this informant, Captain."

"The information came by way of a letter, I'm afraid. The only thing we could do was follow-up on it. We are hoping the letter is a ruse."

Fin nodded, grinding his teeth. The whole story reeked of foul play, all right. If they find evidence, whoever wrote that letter must've planted it on Zander.

"I'm sorry. I've already told you more than I should." The captain glanced at the door, lowering his voice. "If evidence was found, he was to be imprisoned in Beverly overnight, then transported directly to Wheeling for military trial."

"Thank you for your time, Captain." Fin pivoted and followed Noah out the door.

"Captain Dabney."

Fin turned, not sure he wanted to hear more.

"Your brother received a commendation for rescuing prisoners and horses after the Confederates' November attack. That doesn't sound like the actions of a traitor to me."

"No it does not." He stormed out of the office and down the front steps. Zander? A traitor? Never. And Fin was going to prove it.

"Where to now?" Noah asked, yanking his reins from the rail.

"Beverly."

Beverly, West Virginia
January 11, 1865

The attachment arrived at the garrison late evening, so Sergeant McNeer had to track down the commanding officer. He found him at the local hotel—at a party, where it seemed every officer was dancing and making merry. Zander waited in misery atop a stomping Rampart, disgruntled to be tethered to another horse. At last a lieutenant led the Fort Fuller contingent back towards the garrison.

After meandering through a series of log huts strewn all the way from the edge of town to the foot of Mt. Iser, the lieutenant dismounted and barged into one dwelling. Five minutes later, a drowsy sergeant shoved Zander into a dark cell, slammed the door, and turned the key.

Zander stared at the floor until all sounds of humanity faded away. At last, he dropped to the cold, splintery surface and sat cross-legged. Wind whistled through cracks in the wall, undulating and accusing, taunting him over and over—*You're alone. You're alone.* And alone he was, for no one believed his pleas of innocence.

Journeying to Beverly, the convicting glances of his fellows had pressed heavier with each passing hour. And try as he might, somehow, he felt guiltier and guiltier. He had not even faced a trial, yet the fight inside him had evaporated, leaving only defeat behind.

Zander stood, wrapped fingers around the icy bars of the door, and shook them with bound hands for the hundredth time. How was it that a single lock so thoroughly robbed a man of all he took for granted, all he considered for his future, all he'd ever hoped for?

How would he ever prove his innocence? Anyone could have planted that paper in his saddlebag. Grief knifed his heart for the loss before him. What if they hanged him? Isn't that what they did for people convicted of treason?

A forgotten voice, familiar since his youth, whispered comfort. *Lo, I am with you always, even unto the end of the world.* Somehow, in his mind, he knew he was not completely alone. But his soul screamed in anguished argument.

Zander sat on the singular cot, allotted but one dry blanket to accompany his damp coat. He sat with his elbows on his knees for hours, his eyes straining to see in the darkness and his body refusing to sleep. He replayed his last conversation with Lola over and over again. He just didn't measure up . . . again. He squeezed his eyes closed, imagining her standing there all perfect in sweetness and sass. The way her spectacles slipped down her nose when she wasn't paying attention, and then she'd be all self-conscious as she nudged them back up. The way one look from her could—

A ruckus of sorts drew his attention. He paced the small cell, listening to angry voices beyond the walls. In a few minutes, chaos erupted outside as his guard strode back and forth in a panic.

Zander grasped the bars. "What do you s'pose is going on out there?" he asked, wishing the man would stop his pacing.

"Can't talk to the prisoners. Can't abandon my post." The soldier blinked wide eyes, rapid as Morse code. He appeared younger than Zander as he repeated himself, "Can't talk to the prisoners. Can't abandon my post." The guard's hands flexed on his weapon, his eyes flashed wild like a stallion about to bolt.

Walls shuddered. The outside door crashed open. A confederate soldier stepped into the dim light. "We're gonna take a walk to Richmond, boys!" He motioned with a pistol. "Open that cell door!"

The young private fumbled with the key ring, dropping it on the floor before unlocking the cell door. Zander stepped back, his fingers itching for his Colt or the new knife he'd only recently bought.

The Rebel charged into the cell. "You ain't no Confederate!"

"Sorry to disappoint." Zander's gaze touched on the musket his guard had been quick to set aside.

"Don't even think it!" The Rebel ushered him and the guard out of the building.

Union soldiers funneled into the garrison yard, many still throwing on boots and coats. As the mounted Confederates herded them together like cattle, a Rebel musket prodded Zander onward to join the bedlam. How would he ever find Leach or the others?

The enemy loaded stores into wagons as their prisoners watched. Despite being clearly outnumbered, they'd had the element of surprise as the entire garrison slept. And what of the officers housed in the town? Had they escaped the attack? Or had a swarm of Rebels come down on those homes also?

Sounds of resistance popped from the streets of town and eventually died away. The enemy loaded supplies into wagons until pink washed the horizon. At last, mounted Rebels prodded the prisoners forward. Like a slow elk herd at first, the mass of humanity moved out of Beverly. In a short time, the captives marched off at a brisk clip, straight toward the mountains and the heart of the Confederacy—and away from all Zander had ever known. And farther from Lola, who still possessed his shattered heart.

Thirty

Eastern West Virginia

The Rebels nudged the captives forward only when necessary, and as long as their prisoners cooperated, they seemed content to plod along on their horses. But who said everyone was going to cooperate? These Confederates were like a snake swallowing a squirrel—just too much to handle all at once. And given just the right opportunity, Zander figured there was a more than fair chance of escape.

Lt. Colonel Youart, the Beverly Garrison commander, marched just ahead of Zander, one of the few officers he had noticed. Surely, he would try to escape if given the chance.

Zander watched the trail ahead, his mind imagining a variety of escape opportunities that might present themselves. He had counted about sixty prisoners between Rebs. If he could set up some sort of distraction and find a good place to leave the trail, maybe a few Federals could make it away unnoticed.

He sidled up beside D.R. to share his plan. "Worse that could happen, I end up dead now instead of in a Rebel prison. I'll do it," Leach said.

Next, Zander picked up his pace until he squeezed in beside the colonel. "Excuse me, Colonel, sir, but do you see the top half of that fir tree up there to the left?"

His brow furrowed in question. "Yes."

"I figure there's a ridge there that several men can jump over and stay hid until the Confederates pass by."

"But they'll see where we leave the trail and come after us."

"You just let me take care of that, Colonel."

"What's your name, Private?"

"Dabney, sir." He half saluted with his bound hands, then slowed his pace as the rest passed him.

When he was ten yards in back of the colonel and right behind the guard, he feigned a trip and grabbed his knee. "Ahhh!" He howled until the Rebel halted his horse and spun around.

He winced at the slap of a saber across his back. Hopefully the colonel was skittering down the other side of that rise and Leach was covering the telltale trace of escape with his own dramatic misadventures.

Zander struggled to his feet and hobbled along with the throng. Another soldier was pulling Leach to a standing position as the guard rode by, shaking his head. "Clumsy Yankees! Get back in line!"

Colonel Youart was nowhere in sight. And when Zander got close enough to D.R., he whispered, "How many did he take with him?"

"Eight or ten, I think. That was quite the calabalou you let go back there."

"And I've got a few more ideas in my saddle bags, too." Zander smiled, feeling for once like he had done something right.

Beverly, West Virginia

Fin and Noah arrived on Saturday only to find the supply depot in shambles. Just three log structures still stood, and mere remnants of the enlisted men's quarters remained.

"This nightmare just keeps getting worse and worse." Desperation dogged Fin as they pulled up in front of a clapboard building. A lop-sided sign above the door read BLACK-MAN-BOSWORTH in faded letters, and a painted sign below it, COMMISSARY.

"Good a place as any to start, dontcha think?" Noah swung down, groaning in pain as his legs hit the ground. "Molded to that saddle, I was."

"I got a feeling we're not gonna like any answers we get," Fin said, holding the door for Noah.

A private behind the counter briefed them on what had transpired, and before they could make sense of it, a major walked in.

Fin seized the chance for some answers and saluted. "Excuse me, Major. I'm Captain Dabney and this is Lieutenant Hicks."

"Guthrie," the major said. "What can I do for you?"

"We are looking for a detachment from Fort Fuller. They likely would have arrived sometime Tuesday evening."

The man was Fin's height, and his red beard reminded him of his old friend, Seamus McLaughlin. "Not a good time for visitors, I'm afraid. We were attacked early on Wednesday morning. As you can see, there is much to deal with around here." He scrubbed his beard in thought. "From Fort Fuller, you say?"

"Yes, sir. A small detachment, only a few men."

"I'm not familiar, but let's go check with some other officers. There was a dance in town that evening and nearly all the officers were there." He took off walking toward the Leonard Hotel. A hand-painted sign in the window marked the building as a temporary command.

Fin followed, noting the boarded windows and sounds of hammering from the nearby garrison. "How many did you lose?" he asked, keeping pace with the major.

"Ten dead, twenty-three wounded." He paused and his jaw clenched. "And eight hundred taken prisoner. About a hundred and fifty of us managed to evade the Rebels and escape to Buckhannon by fighting our way through town and crossing over the bridge." He motioned toward the far end of town.

"About fifty prisoners have straggled in, though. The Confederates—under General Rosser, we now know—couldn't have been more than a few hundred strong. We just got caught with our pants down, Captain." He shook his head. "Shameful, if you ask me."

"Didn't your pickets report anything?" Fin asked, shooting an incredulous look at Noah.

Major Guthrie laughed bitterly. "Too few, too close in, I'm afraid. Ah, here we are." He kicked frozen mud from his boots and led them into the hotel-turned-command center.

Fin and Noah stood in a corner warming themselves at the stove while Major Guthrie made several inquiries. In a few minutes, he returned, escorting a tall, blond lieutenant. "I believe this man can answer your questions. I'll leave you to it."

"Thank you, Major. I appreciate your help." Fin nodded his thanks.

"I hope you find the answers you are looking for." He touched off a salute and left them standing there.

"I understand you are looking for a detachment from New Creek, Captain," the lieutenant said.

"Yes. What can you tell me?"

"I remember a sergeant. Ah . . . McNeil? McNulty? . . ."

"McNeer?"

"Yes. That's right. He said they had arrived from Fort Fuller and needed to lock up a prisoner for the night. A Union soldier prisoner."

"Can you describe that prisoner, Lieutenant?" Fin held his breath. An ache climbed the back of his neck, wrapping its fingers around his jaws.

"About your height, I guess. Real light hair, straight. It was night and I'd had a few drinks, I'm afraid." The man's eyes grew wide. "Oh, I wasn't on duty, sir. I was just doing a favor for the colonel."

Noah blew air through the side of his mouth. "Well, go on."

"I escorted them to a cell at the garrison and assigned a guard. Then I assigned the sergeant and his men to quarters and returned to the hotel."

"And that cell is burned to the ground now, ain't it?" Noah asked, stepping closer.

"Yes, it is."

"Did any of the Fort Fuller men escape that you are aware of?" Fin asked, hoping against what his heart was already telling him.

"I don't think so. We've accounted for everyone left behind and even the escaped prisoners so far, sir."

"You have been very helpful. Thank you, Lieutenant." Fin's head swam, imagining his little brother in enemy hands. He clenched his fists and bolted for the door.

"We're going after them?" Noah asked as they strode down the steps.

"Yep. Right now—after I send a telegram to Charleston."

"That's what I thought. We'll catch up to them in no time."

He squinted at the threatening sky. Leaden clouds rode a malevolent current, dark and foreboding. His hard-fought optimism was floundering. "If only this weather doesn't stop us."

How he hated to think of the girls' faces as they read his message. The news would devastate them, but it would also drive them to their knees, and a miracle is what they all needed. Especially Zander.

Tracking a thousand men was not a problem. The weather presented Fin's greatest challenge now as the heavens opened. He and Noah pushed on through pelting hail as pouring rain froze on the ground. Miserable and numb, they tucked into their gum blankets and drove hard to narrow the three-day advantage gained by General Rosser's troops.

Fin was far too familiar with the ways of Rebels on a mission. He couldn't help but think of Zander marching all this time, feeling defeated and alone—and now critically cold and tired. Regardless of what he saw with his eyes, he continued to assail his Maker, swallowing the gutting emotion. He could not lose his brother. Not like this.

Noah held out a hand. "Hold up a minute. Are you seeing what I'm seeing?"

Several figures lumbered toward them, bent against the elements. One stumbled, and another braced him up again.

"They could be escaped prisoners." Fin pulled his carbine and advanced cautiously.

"Those are Union uniforms!" Noah said, kicking up his pace.

The soldiers trudged, eyes to the ground. They looked up, startled to see Fin and Noah on top of them.

A colonel! Fin dismounted as the man seemed to gain his stature. "Captain Dabney, sir. Are you escaped from General Rosser's troops?"

The colonel smiled, then winced as his lip cracked and blood appeared. He wiped it with the back of his bare hand. "We are, Captain. Where are you headed?"

"We are going after them, sir."

The colonel squinted down the path behind them. "Just the two of you?"

"Yes, sir. My brother is with them."

"Dabney, huh? You're with Blazer's men, aren't you?"

"Disbanded this month." Fin eyed the men behind the colonel. "Do you know if my brother and the men from Fort Fuller are among the prisoners, sir?" Hundreds of prisoners and he was asking the colonel about one young private.

The man nodded. "Young Private, light hair, about your height?"

Fin's heart leaped. "That sounds like Zander. Is he a prisoner, then?"

"Your brother made our escape possible, Captain. Private Dabney is innovative and shrewd, and I'm putting him in for a commendation. I just hope he sees his own way to escape."

Noah passed his canteen to the colonel. "Well, what do you know?"

"We plan to continue on, Colonel, but there's a farm just north of the trace about half a mile back. You'll be able to see the smoke. I hope you and your men will find shelter there for the night." Fin mounted, hoping the colonel would not force his hand and request an escort.

"Thank you, Captain. We'll make our way there. You go find that brother of yours."

Fin struck out, not waiting on Noah, who was heeding the call of nature. There was no doubt now. Zander was with Rosser's men, and by thunder, Fin was not about to let his brother end up in some Rebel prison.

Thirty-One

Prisoners clustered around small fires, feet hobbled like horses. Each man was tethered to the man next to him by his bound hands, making escape nearly impossible. The bit of warmth from the fire coerced Zander's heavy eyes closed. He slept fitfully for a few hours before his captors rousted the prisoners and went about untying their ankles and tethers.

"I say we leave 'em tied," a Rebel growled to another, picking at knots with his knife.

"And they'd be falling all over themselves. Besides, where they gonna go?"

One by one, the fires blinked out and smoke ascended into the darkness. As the prisoners shuffled into position, two of the Rebels huddled together, their backs to the wind as they lit cigarettes.

Zander glanced about wildly. "No one's looking. Now's the chance if you boys want to get, but not too many now," he whispered into the cluster of men close by.

"You heard Dabney. What are you waiting for?" Leach led the way into the darkness, followed by a dozen others. Zander motioned for others to fill the gap, and for the first time in a long time he asked God for a favor. To see these boys to home unmolested.

Even if God wasn't so keen to have Zander address Him after all this time. What could it hurt, though? Right?

"Prepare to head out!" The order echoed down the long train of captive humanity.

Prisoners crowded together and soon found a cadence to another day of marching.

"Miss me?" Zander startled at D.R.'s voice.

"What are you doing here, you fool. Why didn't you escape? Of all the stupid—"

"I wasn't gonna leave *you*. I think we make a pretty good team. Maybe we can get more of these boys away from here." He jarred Zander's shoulder. "Besides. You'd miss me."

Zander shook his head. D.R. Leach was one of a kind, that was for sure. "And the others?"

"They got off all right. I told them to lay low until daylight."

"How many?"

"Not sure, it being so dark. I grabbed a couple more on the way out of camp. Maybe twenty total."

Twenty! Satisfaction settled on him and it spurred his thinking. In the next hour, he collected every kind of opportunity for escape he could think of and quietly shared them with the men around him, hoping they would take advantage of the call of nature and the absence of daylight.

Dawn had come and gone and so had the sun. A blister on Zander's big toe burned through his entire foot as they trekked on, meandering through the mountains, hedged about by thick stands of spruce and cedar. Darkness would be upon them in another two hours and with it, the dropping temperatures. Lazy snowflakes floated down from heavy clouds that seemed to settle just above their heads.

The farther from the garrison they traveled, the worse the chances would be for escaped prisoners to survive, unless they could make it to a Union-friendly home. But with bushwhackers populating these eastern counties, it would not be easy.

Zander began limping heavily, stumbling into the soldier ahead of him and tossing boisterous accusations. At his cue, Leach hustled several prisoners into the woods and returned unnoticed. When a civilian dropped to his knees and began weeping, Zander signaled another escape as he tried to console him before the guard prodded him away with a rifle. Not long after, the Rebels stopped for another brief night, oblivious to the shrinking number among their captives.

To maintain better control, their captors kept the prisoners from huddling together in large numbers. And it seemed that the more prisoners escaped, the more vigilant the guards became.

Sergeant McNeer pressed in next to Zander, coughing violently as the Confederates tied their ankles. "I see what you're doing, Private," the sarge whispered. "You're taking a mighty big chance, you know."

"Why haven't you escaped with any of the others, Sarge? Surely, you've had the chance."

"With this cough, I'd be a detriment to anyone trying to escape. Besides, how far do you think I'd get?"

"You'd make it. You're strong."

The firelight reflected in the man's hollow eyes and beads of sweat dotted his forehead.

"I'll not make it to Richmond; you can be sure of that. And for what it's worth, I never figured you for a traitor, Dabney."

"Thank you, Sarge. That means a lot coming from you."

Zander flinched as the side of a sword whipped his back. "Quiet. No talking!" The Rebel edged his way around the circle of prisoners. "Here's a ration pack for you to share." He tossed the paper-wrapped square at the sergeant's feet. The first food they had received.

"Ahh. So, their plan is not to starve us then." The sergeant chuckled sardonically. "You boys take it. I'm on my way out anyway."

"Don't talk like that."

The soldier next to Zander tore open the pack. "These are ours."

"Stolen from *our* depot," a voice said from the darkness.

"Looks like we get about a bite each." The first soldier worked together with another to break apart the hard tack. "We'll have to pass the salt pork and chew off a portion."

A guard tossed a canteen on the ground at Zander's feet. "Drink up, Billy Yank. It's still a long way to Staunton."

Zander whispered to Sergeant McNeer, "What's in Staunton?"

"The railroad. We'll probably be transferred from there to Richmond by rail."

There'd be no chance for escape once they loaded on at Staunton. Zander grasped the sow belly and brought it to his mouth. He'd have to work that much harder to take advantage of the Rebel's numbers.

Snow collected under his feet as Zander traipsed on. His stomach roiled as it folded in on itself from hunger. The frozen mud and slippery snow hampered their progress, causing men to stumble frequently. Already the Rebels had grown short on patience. Loud talk bounced between them of using the stolen ammunition from the depot to deal with the *Federal chattel* now—instead of dragging them all to Richmond.

The sun hid behind thick clouds, heavy with snow. Soon snow flakes swirled around them and puffed from the tree branches on either side of the trace. Before long, the human train slowed as prisoners bent their heads into blinding snow as they inched ahead.

"Sit down where you are!" shouted the guards, moving about on snorting, pawing horses. "Sit down where you are!"

Zander huddled, tucking his head inside of his coat and sitting back on his haunches. No telling how long this white-out would last, but until it ended, only a fool would try to make a run for it. The Rebels on horses vanished in the stinging, white stuff as the wind howled around them.

He thought of his fellows without coats. How would they survive this? He'd grown accustomed to numb limbs and the deep cold that penetrated to marrow. Marching was the only thing keeping them all alive. The music of the tempest somehow lulled him to sleep, and he woke to Rebels barking orders to move forward again.

"Time to move on, Sarge." Zander tugged at the man's coat to rouse him.

"Come on, Sarge." The white figure sat cross-legged, head bowed to the ground. Zander gasped as he realized Sergeant McNeer would not continue with this nightmare.

He heard, rather than felt, the slap of the saber on his back. "He's dead. Move along!"

Zander stumbled forward on wooden legs, trying desperately to keep his balance until the blood returned to his limbs. What of Leach? He looked behind him, then craned his neck to see up ahead. Three more huddled figures, white in death, parted the hellish sea of captives flowing onward.

Fin huddled beneath the shelter of a rock overhang with Noah and several strangers. They had come across two batches of escaped prisoners earlier in the day, but this last batch of escapees from Rosser's troops had stumbled through the heavy snow practically right up to their horses before realizing they had company. Finding this shelter from the blinding storm had been a God-send.

They had hobbled the horses right up to the entrance as a door of sorts. But with all of them tucked into the space, there was no room for a fire, and from the looks of these boys, they needed one desperately.

"How long since you left Rosser's men?" Fin asked, passing his canteen.

"Last night, sir."

"You know of a Private name of Dabney?" Noah asked, plucking some rations from his saddlebag to share.

"He's the reason we got away. Saw our chance and sent us off."

Fin shook his head and pulled off his gloves, handing them to the man next to him. "Seems that brother of mine can get just about everybody else out of there but himself."

"I can't take your gloves, Captain."

"Well then stick your fingers in your armpits now that you can, Private. They're blue!"

The private shrugged. "I guess I've had them tied so long, I forgot I could do that."

"You oughta be real proud of your brother, Captain. He's been responsible for a lot of men escaping. It's easy to lose your sense of fight when you're so cold and in the middle of nowhere. That Private . . . your brother . . . he finds us the opportunity—or creates it hisself—and makes us take it."

The other men grumbled their agreement. Fin had never been prouder of Zander. The boy was too compassionate for his own good and probably going to *do unto others* himself right into a Confederate prison!

Hours later, the wind slacked, and Noah ventured out of their shelter. After a moment, he stuck his head back inside. "You better take a look at this, Captain."

Fin eased away from the sleeping figure next to him, carefully shifting so as not to have him fall over. He patted Duke's rump and stepped around him, groaning at the sight. Hope took a dive and splatted on the ground. Heavy snowfall and drifting had erased all signs of the trail. More than a foot of new snow blanketed the woods and traces, erasing even the dips and brambles of the terrain.

He slapped his hat against his leg, frustrated beyond reason. He had no choice but to turn back. If he had a company of men, they could fan out across the mountains and find Rosser's troops. But he didn't have a company of men.

Noah frowned. "Sorry."

"We'll head back and try to find out what we can. Before we do, though, those men in there aren't going to make it very far on foot without warming up and something more substantial in the way of food."

"Say no more." Noah checked his Colt. "I will return totin' something with legs and fur. You get kitchen duty."

Fin kicked the snow aside, looking for branches near the shelter's entrance. Disappointment washed over and through him. Somehow, he felt like he wasn't just letting down Zander, but his whole family. He'd best get word to Gus the minute he got back, before she heard something from the Army.

Thirty-Two

The trace narrowed to three men wide, and the terrain climbed, funneling the prisoners higher into the mountains. A familiar nicker pulled Zander's attention to the Rebel moving along the side of the path.

Rampart's nostrils flared at the sight of his master, and he called to Zander again. As activity up ahead captured the rider's attention, Zander worked his way up next to Rampart.

"Good to see you, too, boy." If only he could take his horse and head west. Even if they were already in Virginia, the Rebels would be no match for the two of them.

He longed to lean his head against the muscled neck, to rub the velvet nose. Tears unexpectantly stung the backs of his eyes. Was it so wrong for a man to be closer to his horse than any human being?

He smiled as Lola's face came to mind. He had wanted to tell her how much she meant to him. How he fell asleep thinking of her. They could've been close. Husband and wife close, like Mama and Pap, whose love kept right on burning in Pap's heart until he breathed his last. He wanted that with Lola. Sorrow sluiced through him with a powerful ache.

It was his own fault, being so closed off with her. But she said maybe after the war, didn't she? Without thought, he reached over and brushed Rampart's mane with his bound hands.

WHACK! A leather strap seared his back. "What do you think you're doing there, Yank?"

Rampart tossed his head and sidestepped. The soldier jerked the reins.

"Easy," Zander said, holding up his hands to calm the gelding.

WHACK!

Zander's legs buckled, slamming his knees to the ground. Rampart reared, snorting a protest. His front feet crashed to the earth and his back feet kicked out, throwing his rider into a granite bolder. The Rebel crumpled to the ground, motionless.

Scrambling to his knees, Zander staggered over and grabbed the Rebel's pistol before leaping onto Rampart. No other guards were in sight as he guided Rampart off the trace and down a gentle incline—followed by dozens of men.

He blazed a trail through deep snow for the prisoners, following a deer trail's winding path down the mountain amid thick forest. Stopping twice, he waited for the bound captives as they stumbled through the brush. If only he had a knife to cut their hands free. But time was precious. Warm, fed, and armed Rebels would soon be on them. The prisoners would not stand a chance.

Shots rang out and echoed. A bullet whizzed. Zander turned in the saddle, trying to make out where they were coming from. "They've got us at a disadvantage, being on the high ground," he said, waiting for the stragglers. "We'll keep going. They can't afford to come after us for long or they'll find themselves losing a whole lot more of their booty."

Zander thumped the horse's rump. "Ol' Johnny Reb needs to practice his aim some, huh, boy." It felt so good to be back on Rampart. "That was a real smart thing you did back there, throwing that Reb. Why, I bet he never saw *that* coming."

The going was slow until they had gone another hundred yards and then the path widened. Zander managed to unknot his bindings as they advanced. Rampart stumbled, nearly catapulting Zander headlong. "Whoa there boy. You're all right."

Rampart coughed. His steps dogged.

"What's the matter, boy?" Zander dismounted and his gut clenched at the dark stain on the horse's flank. Why hadn't he noticed? All this way, without so much as a clue from Rampart.

The once bright eyes that had always shined with spirit and spunk looked to his master, now clouded and dull. Rampart coughed again and pressed his head against Zander's chest.

In a moment's span, all the grief he had known—Mama's death, Pap's death, and Izzy's meaningless death—came flooding back, and it was all he could do to not throw his head back and scream out the agony ripping through him.

"He's shot. The horse is shot," said a private with wide eyes. The news passed through the sullen group of runaways.

Zander couldn't let him suffer. He just couldn't. Already Rampart had suffered plenty, carrying him this far and leading these folks away from the Confederates. He took a deep breath and knew what he had to do.

"You all go off in that direction." He pointed with a nod and ran his fingers through Rampart's mane. "I'll walk him in a circle to cover your path and give you time to get away. When I fire off this gun, they'll be quick to find me."

"That's some horse you got there, Dabney."

Zander turned to find Ford standing alone, since the others had taken off already. "What you're doing to save us . . . won't none of us forget it." He thrust out his hand. Zander shook it, stunned at the man's sudden humility. Ford nodded and scurried off after the others.

Rampart chugged, and he faltered as his master led him along the trail, circling back on itself and back again. Somehow, in Zander's mind, it was fitting that with his last breath, Rampart was a hero in his own right—saving lives. Zander choked back a sob and blinked back the sheer anguish of the situation. Hurting for Rampart. Hurting for himself.

"This is far enough." He let the reins slide from his hands and motioned for Rampart to lie down. His beloved friend dropped to his knees, lowered his back end, and rolled to his side. Breaths heaved and snorted through flared nostrils as he seemed to relax.

Zander crouched, running his hand along the star between the beloved eyes. "You've been the best friend a boy could have, old son. I'm gonna miss you something fierce." He sat on the ground and pressed his face into the warm neck, breathing deep of the smell, and setting it to his memory. Biting down on his cheek, he sucked in, savoring a sensation other than the agony of his breaking heart.

He stroked the velvet nose as Rampart blinked long lashes, the brown pools of those eyes even duller now. Somehow, within those depths, Rampart communicated a devotion that Zander knew he would never experience again.

"I'm so, so sorry," he whispered. He stood on feeble legs, and with a trembling hand fired the shot that would seal the painful goodbye. Rampart relaxed, free of pain. "You rest now, boy."

Blinded by tears, Zander stumbled off through fresh snow in yet another direction. He clawed and clutched at the brush, calling on every bit of will and muscle he possessed to propel himself forward—until a force jerked him back. The pistol flew off and disappeared in the snow as he sprawled on the ground.

"Knew you was here somewhere." The Rebel wrenched Zander's shoulder, hoisting him upright. "You thought you had it bad before, Yankee, you ain't seen nothin'." The man stood a half-head taller than Zander and the smell of whisky floated down from his bearded face as he fixed a leather thong to Zander's wrists.

Were it up to me, I'd just kill you here and now. But I got orders." He shoved his prisoner forward. "Get on back up there."

Zander walked for what seemed like hours until sounds of the Rebel train reached his ears. By the time they rejoined General Rosser's men, he figured he would be closer to the rear of the train.

"Blanchard!"

The Rebel jerked up his head, his steel grip on Zander unwavering. "Yes, Sergeant."

"You get your sorry hide up with the horses. I'll take the prisoner."

The tall, smelly Blanchard growled out an expletive and handed Zander over to the sergeant, who shoved Zander back in with the mass of prisoners. Prisoners he did not recognize except for one stooped, bushy-bearded private—Gleason.

Zander slowed, waiting for Gleason to catch up.

"Dabney?" The man's lip twitched. "So, they got you too, huh?"

"Stole me right out of the lock-up. Thought I was a Reb at first. What of Pegs or the others from New Creek?"

"Pegs is dead . . . on the trail." He frowned. "Don't know about anybody else."

"The sarge is dead too. Same as Pegs. Ford escaped."

Drilling him with a serious look, Gleason said, "I gotta know, Dabney. Did you do it? Whatever it is you were accused of? Are you a traitor?"

"What do *you* think?" Zander met his gaze and held it.

Gleason shrugged. "Kinda hard to swallow."

"Somebody planted that paper in my saddlebag."

They walked in silence as the sun's faint glow found its way nearer the Alleghenies.

"You see that Rebel?" Zander tossed his chin toward the guard up ahead. He recognized the slumped posture and the way he swayed in the saddle. The man was asleep!

Glancing behind, he gauged the distance back to the other guard. The next curve in the trail would be his opportunity. He eyed the hip knife on the sleeping guard. He could do it. He could snag that knife and hide it until the time was right.

He moved his bound hands toward his own thigh, remembering the knife his pap had given him. Remembering it covered in blood. Suddenly his ears seemed to roar with the sounds of battle and blasting caps, of sabers clashing and human agony.

"You okay, Dabney?"

He breathed in the crisp air, shaking away the memories. "That Rebel is sleeping. If he stays that way, when we round the next bend, I'm gonna take his knife."

"Without him waking up?"

"It's our best chance. If we can keep hold of it until dark, we can cut our ropes. Imagine how many of us can get away."

"And if you get caught? *Then* what do you think they'll do?"

"Then I get caught. Already been down that road once. But when we round that bend, if he's still sleeping, it's also a good opening for more of us to hightail it out of here."

The trace rose and fell and finally switched back, providing the chance he had been looking for. Zander pressed in close to the Rebel's horse, checking to see if the man still slept. He and Gleason had warned ten men, telling them to wait for his signal. As they rounded the blind curve, he signaled with a nod and waited while more than a dozen men skittered into the trees. Sensing he could wait no longer; he reached up to slip the knife from its sheath on the Rebel's thigh. His breath caught when a hand slapped over his own.

"What do you think you're doing, Yankee Bill?" the rider snarled through yellow teeth. He cocked his pistol, gouging Zander's neck with the cold steel.

Zander flinched against the pain, grinding his teeth. He refused to give this Rebel the satisfaction.

"The name's Dabney. *Private* Dabney."

"Mmm . . . Dabney, eh? You wouldn't by any chance be related to that Blazer Scout Dabney?"

Pride surged inside Zander's vulnerable self. Beyond all reason, with his neck still at the mercy of a bullet, he heard himself say, "He's my brother."

The Rebel sneered. "He's my brother," he said, mocking in a girlish voice. "Well, little brother. I guess you deserve special treatment then."

Zander stilled, wondering if he would hear the shot or feel the bullet first.

PART THREE

And immediately Jesus stretched forth his hand,
and caught him, and said unto him,
O thou of little faith,
wherefore didst thou doubt?

Matthew 14:31

Thirty-Three

Virginia

Blood-crusted leather bit into Zander's wrists, jerking him forward at a merciless pace despite his stumbling feet. The pack of prisoners marched on, each man weak with hunger—some falling by the way, never to rise again. Every mile took Zander closer to the railroad and Richmond. He would rather die than live in a Confederate prison.

Time trudged with cruelty until it claimed so many days, he wasn't sure how long it had been since leaving Beverly. At last, they arrived at Staunton and sat on the ground awaiting cattle cars for transportation to the Rebel prison. Two hours passed before his captor cut the tether to Zander and prodded him into a livestock car. As beef heading to slaughter, more and more men crammed into the car until movement became impossible.

The heavy door scraped shut, plunging them into darkness.

His hollow belly was full now—full of hopelessness. Every sinew vibrated with it. Who hadn't heard stories of Rebel prisons? Despite the press of humanity, he was utterly alone in his own complete misery. Had Leach even made it this far, or did he fall by the way?

A quivering voice lifted above the chaotic noise within the cold steel walls. Song sliced the fetid blackness like a sword as others joined in, lifting words to the Creator and the only One who saw this helpless, miserable clutch of fighting men.

Abide with me: fast falls the eventide;
the darkness deepens; Lord, with me abide.
When other helpers fail and comforts flee,
Help of the helpless, O abide with me.

Zander mouthed the familiar words—words that had found scarce time for his lips or heart within just a few short months. He couldn't deny the comfort that seeped into his soul—like winter rain that soaks the ground in early spring. But within him were no sprouts to spring up and reach for the sun, for the sun had hidden its face from him. Or had he blocked the sun somehow?

Hold thou thy cross before my closing eyes.
Shine through the gloom and point me to the skies.
Heaven's morning breaks and earth's vain shadows flee;
in life, in death, O Lord, abide with me.

He let the words caress his troubled spirit until little by little the singing ceased and men slept, held aright by the press of their comrades.

Richmond, Virginia

Swaying bodies jerked to a stop as steam hissed. Brakes screeched against iron wheels, setting Zander's teeth on edge as he blinked away his stupor. Silence hung an eerie black curtain over every soul in the car. For the first time since leaving Fort Fuller, he was not cold. He had no feeling below his knees, but at last the bone chill had abated. He breathed in the thick air that reeked of humanity and cattle dung.

"I do believe we've arrived to our accommodations, boys." The voice spouted from somewhere behind him, ending abruptly in a hacking cough.

The door scraped open and light seared Zander's eyes. Groans erupted throughout the car as he blinked against the stab of pain.

"You have arrived!" a voice announced, as if this was some grand occasion.

A dozen armed Confederates poked and prodded men as they clambered from the car on wooden limbs.

Zander craned his neck, hoping to glimpse Leach as prisoners poured from more cars. He waited in line, feeling as if he still swayed with the train instead of standing on solid ground. Soon the line crept forward as one-by-one men passed from view through a gate, like cattle through a branding chute. And D.R. Leach was nowhere to be seen. Something akin to panic dogged him. He had to find that boy. He just had to.

Caustic letters wrought in black iron above the gate shot a chill down his spine: LIBBY PRISON OF THE CONFEDERACY.

After giving his name, hometown, rank, and unit, he ended up standing in another press of men awaiting a cruel march to an even crueler new home—Belle Isle Prison Camp.

Zander had turned off his emotions back in that cattle car. Judging by the surrounding faces, so had the others, marching in complete silence. As the cadence of feet against the Virginia earth pounded in his ears, he lifted his chin and stared straight ahead.

After crossing a bridge, the line of prisoners mashed to a stop inside a gate. Zander looked across the fetid mass of souls, desperate to find D.R. At long last, he presented his numb wrists to the guard with the knife. The leather thong dropped and he gasped, biting his cheek to keep from crying out. Pain knifed his chest, shoulders, and back. Hugging his arms, he shuffled into the sea of prisoners, knowing he would not see freedom again until this whole ugly rebellion found its end. If he survived.

Charleston, West Virginia

Augusta blew her nose a third time and patted her damp face. Why, oh why, hadn't she stopped him? She should have forbidden Zander to join-up. Maybe if he had waited for the draft, he would be somewhere safe at this minute.

"And you are certain he didn't escape?" James paced the floor with uneven steps. "Could he still be out there somewhere? Perhaps he found shelter in a civilian's home."

Fin hugged Will and Melinda Jane to his sides. "I waited as long as I dare before bringing you the news. More than a hundred escapees have been accounted for and none of them Zander. But I've sent a telegram to Captain Giles at Fort Fuller, asking to be notified here if there's any information whatsoever. Union authorities are petitioning the Confederacy for the names of prisoners recently admitted to any of the Virginia prisons."

Augusta sat down, lifting Addie onto her lap. "Will? Would you please take Bertie into the kitchen for a snack?"

"I'm not a child, Gus. I want to hear what you all have to say."

"So do I." Bertie sat on the floor, his arms draped around Coot.

Augusta tossed Fin a look, her eyes pleading for his help.

"Will, I reckon you can stay, but Bertie . . . you take Coot into the kitchen and see what you can find for a treat."

Bertie puckered his frown. "I hate being the youngest! Come on, boy." He slapped his leg and Coot followed him into the kitchen.

"What's to be done about this other business?" James asked, sitting next to Gus and allowing Addie to crawl into his arms.

"I sent a telegram of inquiry about that, too. Now I have to wait and see if I get any response." Fin gulped the last of his coffee. "I also discovered that Colonel Youart has been dismissed from the Army, but that doesn't help us with the accusations against Zander."

Noah piped up from the parlor corner, where he had sat in brooding silence until now. "We don't even have the evidence that was supposedly planted on him to make him look guilty."

"I appreciate your helping Fin with all this, Noah." Augusta smiled at him, wondering why he was commiserating with them instead of enjoying a homecoming. She'd have to ask Fin about that later.

Melinda Jane crossed the room to add more coffee to Noah's cup. "And I am surely grateful that Fin didn't wander off into those mountains all by himself."

Noah nodded his appreciation for the coffee. "Thank you. There's nothing I wouldn't do for Fin or his family." One side of his mouth hitched up. "He's saved my sorry hide more times than I can count."

"Goes both ways," Fin said, lifting his empty cup for more.

"What about prisoner exchanges? There's a chance Zander will be traded, isn't there?" Will asked, her damp eyes bright with hope.

"That's not happening much anymore, I'm afraid. Shame too, because the situation in some of those prisons is downright deplorable." James's words were soft, but they fell like a hammer blow to Augusta. His sullen eyes shuttered as his chin rested atop Addie's head, whose eyes drooped with sleep while a wet finger slid in and out of her mouth.

The idea of her brother in one of those awful places sickened her. She may feel helpless, but she refused to be hopeless. "What about the girl, Fin? The one Zander seemed sweet on. He talked about her in his letter. Lola, I think her name is. Her father runs the mercantile in New Creek. Maybe she can answer some questions."

"I thought of that and asked about her in the telegram to Captain Giles."

"Oh." Augusta bit her bottom lip. There just had to be someone who could help. "General Lightburn. Surely, he could be of some assistance."

Fin passed a look to Noah. "I'll contact him, but until this war winds down—"

"And it's fixin' to do just that. I can feel it in my bones, I tell you. It won't be long now," Noah said.

Will glared at him. "Folks been saying that since it started."

"But now *I'm* sayin' it, Miss Willamina." He winked, drawing a gaping look from Will. "And you can tickle my ears in just a few months, reminding me how right I was for sayin' it."

Will huffed and opened her mouth to speak, but Augusta intervened. "Will, Noah is our guest."

The girl smiled sweetly and batted her eyes. "My apologies, Lieutenant Hicks. I am not accustomed to having myself enlightened by *know-it-alls*."

"Will!" Augusta scolded.

"*What*?" Will fired back feigning innocence.

Fin snickered, then flinched from his wife's jab.

"It's all right ma'am. I'm accustomed to insults of every kind, living among rough men these last few years." Noah's shoulders rose and fell with a sigh. A hang-dog expression pulled his chin low.

"There. You see? I didn't even insult him." Will stood and smoothed her skirt. "I think I'll check on Bertie."

Augusta shook her head. "I am sorry, Noah. I guess that makes you part of the family—being able to take the ribbing."

Will was hurting like the rest of them. Gus had to remember that. She looked at Melinda Jane, whose eyes still glistened, her mouth sunken in a sad smile.

Lord, we need a miracle.

Thirty-Four

BELLE ISLE PRISON CAMP

March, 1865

Weeks crept as years, hours as days, in this purgatory of death. Zander had found Leach, only to watch his friend fade before his eyes along with so many others. Anywhere else, the sun's brilliant display announcing spring would have been welcomed. Anywhere else, farmers would break ground for planting, and ladies would shop for store-bought Easter bonnets. But here, bedraggled men huddled in small groups, sharing stories of days past, when they were still men, strong and fierce—men with courage and hope and a will to survive.

Zander handed Leach a cup of water and settled down to scratch in the hard earth with a rock pried from the base of the camp's inner fence. Leach nodded his thanks and let his head fall back so the make-shift shelter blocked the brightness. He hacked a long, ragged cough, then sucked in a fragile breath. Zander adjusted his own rolled winter coat for a pillow, taking care to prop his friend's head higher.

So many memories of Mama's, then Pap's death—and the fight for survival a body faced as it withered, succumbing to a frailty God had allowed. Funny how his thoughts moved more swiftly to God. It was Leach's fault. The boy was dying, yet he found cause to smile, pulled from the deepest part of his upbringing and a preserved respect for the Almighty. Zander envied that.

"You need medicine, D.R."

"I'm not going to the medical tent. Save it for the boys who are scared of dying. That wouldn't be me, my friend." Leach squeezed his eyes shut with another racking spasm.

"I know your faith is strong, brother. And I admire the way you look death in the eye. But don't you get at least a little riled at the unfairness of it all? I mean, what good did we do for this cause, anyway? We're barely men now, wasting away—and what do we have to show for it?"

Leach opened one eye. "You serious?"

"Serious as a wasper nest."

"Pain ain't no respecter of persons, Zander—mighty or small. The Word says rain falls on the just and the unjust. This war. Cloyd's Mountain." He opened his other eye. "Gettin' taken at Beverly. This place. All of it is just a show of wind and rain from life's storms."

A voice inside cried out, defeated and desperate—*hadn't his family suffered enough*? Now the war would likely siphon his lifeblood away, just like it was doing to his friend.

Zander shrugged. "It don't seem fair is all."

"Yeah. Makes me wonder why, too."

"But it doesn't seem to bother you. Least not like it does me."

"I'm no fool. I'm not about to second guess God's plan, Zander." D.R. gasped, blinking pain-carved eyes, only to paint a sliver of a smile back across his wan face. "I guess I've just always been the trusting kind."

"Yeah."

"What I'm saying is this—down here, I may not understand. But I'll be doggoned if I'm gonna let go of . . . of that unseen hand that *does* hold the answers."

If only he could trust like his friend. If only he could see his way around feeling that God had abandoned him on that battlefield at Cloyd's Mountain. D.R. was the only thing making this corner of hell bearable.

"Don't let your anger keep you from God. He's just a prayer away, and His hand is stretching out to you, brother."

"Prayer." Zander huffed out the word. When was the last time he *did* pray for real?

"When He knows you want to trust Him, God doesn't mind the questions. Heck. Sometimes He even answers them this side of heaven." D.R.'s indomitable smile told him what the ol' boy had was genuine—and that he had never let go of that unseen hand.

Zander tipped the cup, urging his friend to empty it. "Finish this and rest." He adjusted the shade covering. "I'll bring you something to eat."

Zander lumbered across to the other side of the enclosure, eyeing the wire fence surrounded by a second wall of vertical logs. His mind spun, rehashing stories he had heard about attempted escapes and the few successful ones. His captors had culled some prisoners to man the hot ovens that baked the bread for the thousands of men at this prison and another. *Large* ovens, he'd heard. Large enough to hold a man. If only he could get on one of those details.

Men trailed toward the mess wagon like ants toward a mound of slop.

Ants.

He squeezed one eye shut and looked up at the sun. What if God looked down from his throne and saw them all—all of humanity as not much more than a bunch of ants, busily making their way from one meal to the next, thinking only of their own selves?

But he knew better than that. To believe such a thing would be to call his upbringing a lie. He may have lost touch with Mama's and Pap's God, but he couldn't accept for a minute that they had lied to him all his life.

Shuffling forward with the others in line, at last, he reached a weary, apron-clad man ladling gray soup from a tall kettle. Zander held up his cup and watched as the unidentifiable hot liquid filled it to the brim. Immediately he poured half into Leach's cup so as not to lose even a sip due to the hungry prisoners bustling all around him.

He moved down the line, where a Rebel's filthy fingers slapped a thick slice of bread atop one cup before digging at a scab on the side of a scarred nose.

For the last couple of weeks, he had assisted Leach to the chow wagon, because if a prisoner didn't claim his ration, he would get nothing. For the third day now, his friend had lain too weak to walk.

If only Zander could find a way out of here before it was too late for his friend.

Thirty-Five

REMOUNT CAMP, PLEASANT VALLEY, MARYLAND

"What do you mean, he's gone? When will he be back?" Lola ceased her nervous tapping, as her hopes plunged. She had traveled from Wheeling to Fort Fuller only to discover the Sixth Regiment was in winter quarters in Maryland! Her simple overnight train ride to surprise Zander had become a distressful ordeal.

"I'm sorry, miss. I am not at liberty to offer that information." The private behind the desk glanced at the door to his right. "If you'd like to wait, Captain Giles is in a meeting with Colonel Fleming at the moment. He'd be the one to talk to."

Lola set her carpet bag beside one of several chairs lining one wall. She paced the small entry for several minutes, but after a look of irritation from the clerk, took a seat. She needed to see Zander. And she had braved the trip from Wheeling alone to talk with him.

How she had tried to be strong, but every night as she lay in bed, it was his face she saw. It was his voice her mind heard, telling her again and again that he loved her. What if she were to never love again? What if she had pushed him away too soon? Perhaps he needed time—time to work things out with God in his own way.

She needed him now more than ever, for once again her heart had broken into pieces with the death of dear Papa. He had been ill when they left New Creek, but not even *he* knew just how serious it was. Even now, looking back, the signs were there—and they'd both missed them.

Blotting her wet cheeks, she prayed for the hundredth time, *please, God, please help me find Zander.* What if he had been called to Virginia, or South? But the newspaper said it was just a matter of time. It stated that the Confederacy was not much more than a walking skeleton of intention, soon to be buried and forgotten.

The door opened, and Captain Giles stepped out of the room and headed for the door.

Lola crossed the floor to intercept him. "Might I have a word with you, Captain?"

Recognition lit his face. "You're from the mercantile, aren't you? But it burned." He scowled. "I'm sorry."

"Thank you, sir. My father owned the store, but we left a short time after the attack and moved to Wheeling to be with family."

"And what brings you to Maryland now, Miss . . . Wade, isn't it?"

"Lola Wade, sir. I'm here to talk with Private Dabney. Zander Dabney." She nodded toward the man at the desk. "I am told he is not here. Might you tell me where I will find him? Has he been . . . transferred?" *Please no.* She yearned to see him so.

"It's a beautiful day, Miss Wade. Let's take a walk." He pointed to her bag. "You can leave that here."

Lola pulled her shawl across her shoulders as he opened the door, taking his arm as they descended the steps. "Is . . . is there a problem, Captain?" Why could he not just tell her in the command building?

"I am not at liberty to discuss some of the details, but I regret to inform you that Private Dabney, along with several others from the Sixth, was taken prisoner back in January."

As if a crack opened in the earth, she was falling. She gripped his arm again, pressing on her chest to still the sudden pounding of her heart. "Prisoner? How? Where?" This could not be happening.

Not Zander. Her stomach roiled as tears coursed down her cheeks. The ground seemed to heave. She frantically dug out her hanky, attempting to salvage some decorum.

The captain patted her hand, seeming oblivious to her distress. He was searching his surroundings as if to find the answer in the wagons and men that meandered through the yard. "Private Dabney was on a detachment to Beverly when General Rosser's troops attacked the supply depot there. They took hundreds of prisoners." He frowned. "I'm sorry to be the bearer of such awful news. I'm afraid you've come all this way for nothing."

General Rosser? Wasn't it his men who attacked New Creek? She fought back tears, dragging her mind from the dark place it had flown at the mere mention of the word *prisoner*. "Where are they now?"

She reeled as he explained about the trek over the mountains to Staunton, then the Railroad transfer to a prison in Virginia, which one, he was not sure.

The truth seized her. "The mountain passes . . . in *January*?" She groaned, remembering the vicious storms of January, wondering if the captives had missed them.

"I have one small bit of news that may bring you some measure of comfort."

She gaped at him. *Comfort*? "Please." She trembled all over now, needing desperately to sit.

"His brother, Captain Dabney, and another officer went after General Rosser's men. Although they were initially three days behind the train of captives, Captain Dabney came upon escaped prisoners. Many gave credit to Private Dabney for their escape. Even reports that Private Dabney sacrificed his own freedom for theirs were confirmed."

A quivery smile parted her sorrow as tears cascaded. She hastily wiped them away. "That's my Zander."

"I am truly sorry I cannot give you more information."

"I understand."

"I've been asked to relay any information to his family in Charleston. Captain Dabney inquired as to your whereabouts, but I could not offer information. If you will leave your address with me—in Wheeling, did you say? I will forward it to him."

"Yes, of course, Captain! Thank you. "

He escorted her back to record her aunt's address. It was hours before another train would come through to take her back. The thought of sitting and doing nothing was unbearable.

"Could you tell me where I might find Private Henry Bassoom? He is a friend of Zander's."

He slowed his pace. "Private Bassoom is AWOL, I'm afraid."

"So, he wasn't with Zander at Beverly, then?" From what she knew, Bass could end up in a prison himself—a Federal prison.

"He was to be a part of that detachment, but disappeared just before." His eyebrows mashed together for an instant, as if he wanted to say something, but couldn't.

She bid him farewell and climbed into the buggy she had rented at the B & O depot. A silly part of her wanted to wait right here instead of in her stodgy aunt's tiny home without her dear papa. But she would wait for Zander's return no matter what. And her prayers would keep him alive. A new wash of tears dampened her neck before she could dig a fresh hanky from her reticule.

Come back to me, Zander. It was as if her heart had cracked, spilling forth an agony that seeped through every part of her.

Searching the sky and blinking away tears that blurred the wispy clouds, she offered up her shattered heart. "Please, God. Bring him back to me."

Charleston

"I'm coming, I'm coming!" Fin handed Duke over to Noah and jogged to the house. Whatever was all the excitement about? You'd think Lee had surrendered already. But he couldn't help holding onto his skepticism. The Confederacy was a shrunken little man, just waiting for a safe bed to breathe his last. Some folks said the war had already ended. But it hadn't. And until that time came, there would be no cause for Fin to celebrate.

"A letter came from Zander's friend, Lola." Melinda Jane ushered him into the house.

Maybe this girl would have some information to offer that would make all these charges against his brother make sense. Gus handed Fin the letter to read the moment he stepped into the kitchen.

To the Dabney Family,

My name is Lola Wade, and Zander is a very special friend of mine. I feel I know you all from the many stories he has shared with me. In November, our store burned and my father, young brother, and I moved from New Creek to Wheeling.

Having suffered the death of my beloved father this past month, I recently returned to New Creek hoping to speak with Zander. But in finding the Sixth Regiment had moved to winter quarters in Maryland, I continued on to Pleasant Valley, Maryland, where I was soon sorrowed to learn of his capture by the Confederates.

I share with you the grief you must all surely be suffering at this time. I understand the war may soon be at a close, and I pray with all my heart that your dear Zander will find his way home to you in good health. He is a wonderful man, kind-hearted and given to a keen wit, and I know he is dearly missed. Please know that it is on his behalf I intercede to the Almighty most every hour of the day.

Respectfully, Lola Wade

Melinda Jane passed baby Izzy to Fin. "He's been wanting his pap."

Fin looked down at the tiny face as an O-shaped yawn wrinkled his brow. "And just what makes you think he's been a-wantin' his pap?" He pressed a kiss to smooth out his son's forehead.

"Because all children are hoping their pap will hold them tight and tell them they're loved." Melinda Jane smiled and winked at Gus.

"You best listen to that wife of yours, Fin." Noah stepped into the house and tossed his hat, hooking a peg on the wall. "Words of wisdom there."

Will grunted, rolling her eyes before wringing out a rag to wipe Addie's crumb covered face.

"Noah is right, as usual." Melinda Jane laced her fingers around Fin's arm.

"What'd I miss exactly?" Noah noticed the letter. "Good news or bad?"

Fin waved the missive.   "Got a letter from that *friend* of Zander's. Remember, Lola? Captain Giles mentioned her."

"And now I have to share my room again." Will said, lifting Addie from the high chair.

Noah wrinkled his brow. "You have to share your room because she wrote a letter?"

"We are inviting her and her brother to join us here while we wait for Zander to come home," Gus offered. "Will's just getting ahead of herself."

"She'll accept your offer, you'll see. I'm just already working at adjusting to the idea. I've had my room to myself now for too long, anyway. A person could get used to all that privacy." Will let Addie squirm from her arms to the floor. "It won't be so bad, I guess, having another sister around. That'll make it even then."

"Even until you marry." Melinda Jane added with a chuckle.

"Will? Marry?" Noah's eyes grew big as saucers. "Did I miss something else?"

Laughter rumbled around the room from everyone but Will.

"What's so funny about that?" she said, her lips in a pout.

"I . . .just . . . meant . . .uh." Noah stepped backwards and grabbed the doorknob. "I'll just go check on the horses." He catapulted out the door, chased by more laughter.

Melinda Jane wagged her head. "There's something about that man some girl will find irresistible someday."

Will coughed and turned for a glass beside the sink. She pumped it full of water and drank it down in two big gulps with her back to her family.

Fin remembered when the girl was the size of his son. Even with all her vinegar and spice, she'd always held a special place in his heart. And for the first time, realization settled in— she would be finding a special place in some man's heart, too. And maybe not so far off.

Thirty-Six

BELLE ISLE PRISON CAMP

Zander wiped sweat from his eyes with his stiff shirt sleeve as he set another dozen loaves of bread into the brick oven. He drew the peel board toward him, gauging its weight in his hands. He could take out at least one guard before another's bayonet pierced him through. *Such wild thoughts*!

The monotony of his tasks—mixing, kneading, and baking the bread in the cavernous ovens—called his mind to drift to all kinds of places. Some old and familiar. Some dark and regretful.

After his shift, he trudged back to the gate, lifting his arms as the guard searched him.

"Move on," the Rebel growled with an expression bland as the soup served most days.

Zander entered the camp, wrinkling his nose as the stench of human waste and dying humanity replaced the hot coals and baking bread. He wove through clusters of prisoners and around the dead cart, an assignment detested even more than cleaning out latrines. Pushing around a cart all day collecting your dead comrades had driven many a man over the edge.

He closed his ears to the refrain of suffering and sickness, angling off to where he had left Leach. He and several others had claimed a section next to the fence. Worn clothing, no longer needed for protection from the elements, served as their tent of sorts.

D.R. was sleeping, his breathing shallow and face red with fever. A cup sat with a bit of water still in the bottom and Zander dipped the ragged kerchief in it to lay across his friend's brow. He glanced at Haney, a corporal from New York, and pointed to his empty cup.

"Take it," he said, tossing his chin toward Leach. "He needs it more than I do."

Zander nodded his thanks, took the three cups, and returned with them full. He dribbled water over the kerchief, and when a drop landed in Leach's eye, his cracked lips parted.

"Here. Drink." Lifting his friend's head, Zander held a cup to his mouth. "Easy."

"Thank you," Leach whispered.

Zander leaned on one hand, sheltering their conversation from the others. "I think I found us a way to make it out of here."

D.R. chuckled weakly. "Us?"

"Yeah. *Us.*" Hadn't the boy been hounding him to have faith? Well, wasn't having hope the same as having faith?

"I'm not leaving here, brother. You just gotta accept that."

"No!" Zander squeezed his eyes to pricks of pain. "You can't leave me alone in this place!"

"You haven't noticed a few thousand other souls here?" The attempt at humor only turned the knife deeper in Zander's soul.

"You know what I mean."

"Yeah." His sunken eyes closed.

Zander watched the rise and fall of his chest, recalling the same vigil with his pap. Strange, the journey life takes leaving the body.

"D.R.?"

"Yeah?" His eyes remained shut. "I'm just so tired."

"I know." They sat in silence for a time.

D.R.'s eyes fluttered open, and he groped for Zander's hand. "The Lord's never been afraid of honest prayers."

"So you said. 'Sides, the Lord'll know if they aren't honest any way, right?" He forced a smile. "I'll think on it."

"And . . . and you remember what I said about that unseen hand. About how it holds the reasons why."

Zander re-wetted the kerchief and swabbed the fevered neck and chest. He dipped the cloth again and laid it across his brow. If only he had a cool crick to lower him into or some aspen bark for the fever. All his years watching his sister heal others and learning—and here he was with nothing but a couple of tin cups and tepid water.

He scooted around and lifted D.R.'s head onto his lap. He remembered Gus talking about how important it was for those in the throes of death to be surrounded by loved ones. For all parties. And as pathetic as he was, Zander was the only loved one Leach had here.

He thought of D.R.'s folks and how they were losing their only child. He would write a letter just as soon as the war allowed. *No.* He would *visit* D.R.'s folks. That's what he would do.

"Zander?" His friend squinted through watery slits.

"I'm here."

"The sun is still there. It's been hiding behind those cantankerous storm clouds, but it's there." He gazed up with clouded eyes. "Can you see it?"

"No. I'm sorry, D.R., I can't see it."

"But you know it's there, right?"

"Yeah. I know." He swallowed hard, realizing he truly did know God was still there.

Leach smiled and his eyes closed. "Good," he whispered. "Just making sure you know it's there." Long, silent seconds passed. "Zander?"

"I'm here."

"Once I've crossed over"—he pulled in a ragged breath—"pr . . . promise . . . Psalm 139." His face relaxed as he once again escaped into a peaceful sleep.

Zander held D.R. through the night until the shallow rattle in his chest grew sporadic and halted altogether.

He was alone. *So very alone.* A single sob stole his breath, but he denied another.

The darkness gave way to a rose-hued blush and birdsong bantered about beyond the walls. He didn't remember ever hearing birdsong in this place before. Or had he just ignored it? What else had he ignored? Maybe Leach really knew just what he was talking about—about that unseen hand.

If that hand *did* hold the answers to his questions, then why couldn't he see it? And if the sun was really up there behind those storm clouds, why had he pretended it wasn't? Why had he acted like there wasn't a sun when he had seen it every day of his life before . . . ?

He shook his head, shoving back hot tears with the heels of his hands. He had been every kind of a fool. Only a fool decides the sun just up and disappears just because he doesn't see it. And only a fool chooses to ignore a hand that has the answers.

He sniffed and buried his face in his elbow. *I'm so sorry, Lord. Forgive me. You didn't leave me—I left you.*

If only he could be alone instead of surrounded by such as this. He squeezed his eyes shut, pretending he rode the hills of Fayette County on the back of Rampart—his hair blowing in the breeze, feeling the sleek muscles pulse beneath him. He poured out his pain and his regret in silence, knowing for the first time in many months that his words did not go unheard.

When the others arose and prepared to collect rations, he stood and gently gathered his friend into his arms and headed for the front gate.

Thirty-Seven

CHARLESTON, WEST VIRGINIA

April 1865

Black smoke belched from the large steam ship next to the smaller one garnering Augusta's attention. A long whistle split the chaos of passengers and carriages bustling about with trunks, bags, and cargo. A bespectacled young blond woman with a carpetbag made her way down the plank, clutching the hand of a boy about Bertie's age. His mop of dark hair peeked beneath a brown cap above wide, curious eye as he toted his own bag, which appeared much too heavy for comfort.

"Surely that must be them." Augusta said, waving. The girl smiled, waved back, and strode forward, swinging her carpet bag with purpose and tugging the boy along behind her.

Stepping forward, Augusta folded her hands, smiling from the girl to the boy. "Please tell me you are Lola." She touched the boy on the arm. "And this must be Felix?"

"And you are definitely Gus . . . Augusta. I remember Zander tellling me your given name. He described you perfectly." She set down the bag and extended her hand.

Augusta pulled her into a hug, feeling her wilt against the embrace. "You poor dear. That brother of mine surely did not mean for us to meet under such trying circumstances. But as of this moment, you will be a part of the Dabney clan, and we have a room waiting for you."

Fin stepped up behind them, a grin on his face as his gaze flitted between her and Lola.

"This is my brother—"

"Fin." Lola finished. "Or shall I call you Lieutenant Dabney."

He pulled back his shoulders, which Augusta found amusing. "It's Captain Dabney now, Miss Wade. Pleasure to meet you. My brother sure knows how to pick the pretty ones." He reached for the bags. "I'll take these. The wagon is just up this way."

They followed Fin and settled into the buckboard. Felix climbed into the back as Fin hoisted the bags up to the bed. "What do you have in this bag, books?"

Felix nodded and shrugged.

"It was just an expression, but I reckon you're a book man. That true?"

The boy nodded again.

"He's a quiet one, your brother," Augusta whispered, leaning closer to Lola.

Lola pushed her glasses up her nose with a delicate finger. "Felix?" She chuckled. "Heavens, no. He's not quiet at all. I think he may be just a bit overwhelmed after the steam ship ride and meeting you folks."

"Well, I think he'll get along wonderfully with Bertie."

"I hope so. They are only two months apart in age." Her face sobered. "Zander enjoyed Felix's company because he said he reminded him a little of his own brother."

Augusta squeezed her hand. "I can tell you care deeply for our Zander. We'll all get through this together." She nodded, hoping to bridge the gap between their grief. "Together, because we all love him."

Lola lifted her chin, revealing a trembling bottom lip. "Is it so obvious?"

Augusta sighed. "We women who love our soldiers have to stick together. You'll meet Melinda Jane up at the house."

"Fin's wife."

"Yes. And you'll be sharing a room with Will . . . Willamina."

Lola chuckled. "Oh, I feel like I know her already. Zander missed his family so."

Augusta swallowed the sadness that threatened to bring her own tears to the surface. "And his family misses him."

Fin sat on a kitchen chair in the parlor, glancing at the wall clock every two minutes. Noah just stared at the floor as the women chatted amicably as women do. James stood and stretched his bad leg, passing an impatient look to Fin.

Enough of this. Fin stood and then sat again. "Please excuse the interruption, ladies. Now that you've got a little chance to get acquainted, I'd like to ask Miss Wade a few questions of my own."

Miss Wade adjusted her glasses and sat forward in the stuffed chair. "Of course."

"For starters, Miss Wade—"

"Please, call me Lola." Her gaze flitted around the room. "All of you."

"Lola," he continued, "my brother wrote that he'd seen our cousin, Carter Dabney, in New Creek. Do you know if he spoke with him?"

"I know Zander was upset because he'd seen your cousin talking with Bass—that's Private Bassoom. I don't know why, but he seemed to think Bass could be in trouble."

"What kind of trouble?" James asked, turning from his position at the window.

"I don't know. But he sure had hard feelings toward his cousin. Zander . . ." Her fingers pressed a new pleat into her skirt, then she folded her hands. "Zander had trouble talking about some things. He was a little closed off at times."

"It's all right, honey." Melinda Jane leaned forward, shifting little Izzy to her other shoulder. "It's just the way of our Dabney men—at times."

Fin cleared his throat. "You were saying?"

"I'm pretty certain that Zander came to blows with Bass over talking to your cousin. Their friendship was pretty strained after that. And when I was talking with Captain Giles, he told me Bass deserted when he was ordered to Beverly along with Zander." She frowned. "It just doesn't make sense." Her eyes pled with Fin. "Why would Bass do that? He wasn't that type. Why, he felt a strong conviction about the Rebellion. His family lived in Winchester, in the Old Dominion, and here he was fighting with the Union."

"Winchester, huh?" Noah scrubbed his beard. "I think we have us a little trip coming up."

"I agree. But it'd be fool hardy to go before the surrender. It won't be long now," Fin said.

Melinda Jane's eyes fired darts at her husband. "And after all we have been through, you are not chancing a Rebel bullet on account of some fact-finding mission."

Fin nodded. "Like my wife says."

"There are just too many coincidences here, and it reeks of Carter's involvement," James said, sitting down next to Gus.

Lola's brows knit as she looked from James to Fin and then to Gus. "Is there something you aren't telling me?"

Fin decided he had better be forthcoming. Maybe she could shed more light on this whole ugly affair. When he finished explaining the planted evidence and Zander's arrest, Lola's eyes were blazing through tears.

She dabbed her face, shaking her head. "Zander had some sort of issue with God and some things he didn't want to talk about with me, but he's not a traitor." She looked at Fin. "He idolized you, his big brother, Lieutenant Dabney of Blazer's Scouts. He lived in your shadow and he took a lot of ribbing for it, but I know he loved and respected you fiercely."

She regarded each of them. "Your Zander would never, ever do anything to hurt this family or bring shame upon you. My papa wasn't a Union man, but even *he* saw something special in your brother."

James leaned forward and clasped his hands. "We couldn't agree more, Lola, and that's why we are going to get to the bottom of this. And clear his name so when he does get home, *he* will know just what happened."

"We will leave just as soon as the surrender is official," Fin said, lifting his sleeping son from his wife's arms and planting a soft kiss on her cheek. With a sad smile, she nodded and squeezed his arm.

He walked upstairs and laid Izzy in bed. If his son was in Zander's fix, he would give his life just to root out the truth and clear his name. But Melinda Jane was right. After these long four years, his fledgling family needed him—alive.

Thirty-Eight

BELLE ISLE PRISON CAMP

April 7, 1865

Zander raked cooled, charred fragments and ash from the oven's firebox, mindful to leave none behind. Every other day, they left one oven to cool with a clean firebox lest soot build-up and burst into flames, rendering the entire oven unusable. He had waited for a moonless night and thick cloud cover, and it had arrived. Tonight, this oven would hold the key to his freedom, and it had to be cool enough for his plan to work.

Only yesterday he had worked at the trough, mixing the flour, salt, and water. Today, he scooped gobs of sticky, bubbling dough onto floured peel boards for several other prisoners to place in the deep ovens. Already, men mixed tomorrow's bread. The job was tedious, but far better than huddling inside the confines of the prison, waiting for disease or dysentery to take him. He pinched off mouthfuls of dough when no one was looking, and although stealing food meant death, it was a risk he must take to gain enough strength for what lay ahead.

Leach had been gone only a couple of weeks, but Zander found himself talking to him in his mind. And just as often, he spoke to God now. The conversations came haltingly at first, but now, it was downright surprising how all around him, even amid such suffering, he found things to talk to the Almighty about.

He thanked God every day that the guards generally allowed prisoners to hang on to Bibles and prayer books. D.R. had always carried his Bible in his pocket, so it had survived the trip, and it was now Zander's only possession. And just as he had seen his friend do before he took ill, Zander devoured the Scriptures. It was the kind of food that filled him up but made him hungry for more. Now he understood Pap's late night reading of the Word when he thought the young'uns were asleep. And Zander had memorized Psalm 139, knowing it would've pleased the ol' boy.

Of course, he would deliver D.R's Bible to his parents, along with knowledge of the legacy the stocky little towhead had left—namely himself and others in the unit willing to listen to what D.R. had to say about life.

He and the other workers finished washing troughs and pulled the last of tomorrow's bread from the ovens. Earlier he had hung a towel to dry, blocking all but a direct view into the cooling oven. He casually checked the bricks, pretending to wipe down the inside walls with a damp rag. Cool enough.

After making preparations to do it all over again tomorrow, the prisoners doused lanterns and lined up for their nightly trip from the courtyard under heavy guard. Just as the gate cracked open, blocked by the other prisoners, Zander climbed into the oven and scooted to the back, balling up his body as small as possible.

Zander focused on the sounds of the sleeping camp as the cramping in his legs told him at least an hour had passed since he climbed into the oven. He could not chance repositioning himself and drawing attention. Never, ever, before now, had he wished to trade in his long legs for shorter ones. Time crawled as he fought to keep his eyes open.

He hadn't slowed his petitions to the Almighty to aid his escape. Gus told him once to never try to make a deal with God. He'd had to withdraw a few promises tonight in his desperation, knowing deep inside that God was not looking to bargain—He was looking for a trusting heart.

He smiled, thinking of D.R. Zander was reaching out to that unseen hand, all right. For this darkness was so thoroughly complete, and he could only take it on faith that he still had two legs, since he'd long since lost the feeling in both of them.

Sucking in a long breath of courage and drinking up all the trust he could muster, with nothing to grab and useless legs, he scooted. He inched out of the oven far enough to see his surroundings. Not a guard in sight. He slithered down the wall on his belly like a snake, clawing at bricks and reaching for the surface below. With great difficulty, he kept his legs from crashing to the ground. Lying there in the stillness, he stretched his legs and flexed his muscles. Straining to hear any sign of trouble, he gritted his teeth against the needles of sensation returning to his limbs.

They had doused the courtyard lights, but the light seeping over the wall gave him just enough guidance to cross to the gate. He stood awkwardly, and with careful intention, strode to the exit. Pausing at the gate, he listened for sentries.

The guard tower oversaw the general population, but here, in the courtyard, he could slip out and past unsuspecting guards without notice. And just as if the Lord Himself went before him, Zander did just that. His heart pounded as he hugged the walls, creeping mere feet behind a guard. He rounded the corner and charged across the dark clearing.

Only God could bring in the thick cloud cover, making the blackness of this night so complete. And the four times he tripped headlong, wedging his face into the mud like steak into flour—did not dampen his giddiness one bit.

He'd have to put as much distance as possible between him and the prison before daybreak because come tomorrow morning, he would be missed. And the only thing to keep the dogs from following him was the river.

"I need Your help, Lord. Now would be a good time for some light to help me find that river." He leaned against an ancient tree, feeling the thick trunk, surprised the Confederates had not used it for building projects.

As he stood there, allowing his breath to slow and his heart to ease, the moon made itself known as a dim glow pressed through the night sky. In moments, clouds parted and he could make out the outlines of trees, brush, and fallen branches.

"Thank You!" he whispered a gleeful shout, which he promptly stifled before it gave him away. "Thank You."

Charleston, West Virginia
April 9, 1865

Augusta clung to James's arm and shouted above the festive voices. "Surely this is the most celebrated Palm Sunday since the first one when the Savior rode through the streets!"

She squeezed her daughter's foot as the little one squirmed in her pap's arms. "Look, Addie. See the horses?"

Dozens of Federal Officers, decked out in ribbons and medals, paraded their mounts, waving to the onlookers. Scores of infantrymen marched behind with rifles to their shoulders.

"Look there. It's Colonel Oley." James pointed out the man standing in his stirrups, waving jubilantly. Behind him followed a hearse drawn by four handsome black horses. A sign on the hearse announced SECESSION.

Melinda Jane laughed and clapped, raising her hands to the sky. "Hallelujah!"

Fin hugged her to his side, cradling little Izzy in his other arm. "I'll second that."

Women cried for joy and men slapped one another on the back in celebration as the parade advanced past the house and right up Cox's hill.

"What's that supposed to be?" Felix asked, pointing to the last wagon that lumbered by. A stuffed dummy hung from a propped-up tree branch labeled SOUR APPLE, and a sign around its neck identified the poor effigy as Jefferson Davis.

"That's just showing us that the Confederacy is no longer," Lola answered, beaming.

"Did they kill Jefferson Davis?"

"No, Felix. That's just a pretend hanging. They're not going to kill the man."

"Oh." The boy scratched his head. "Then what good is it?"

Will roughed up his hair. "It'll make sense someday."

The crowds trailed the last wagon, and James turned to the family. "Let's follow, shall we? We have waited for this day for four long years, might as well celebrate to the full."

"Let me keep the wee ones here." Mrs. O'Donell took Izzy from Fin and clasped Addie's hand. "You all whoop it up for me, now." She smiled and retreated into the house.

The family walked with the crowd, holding hands to stay together. They halted at the top of the hill, milling into a gathering of spectators. Citizens plugged their ears as cannons fired several volleys.

Augusta leaned close to James. "I pray that's the last I ever hear from a cannon!"

James nodded, his face taut, no doubt warring with memories. They all had memories to bear—only a few of which were good ones. The births of the two precious babes. And hadn't the war brought James to her? She squeezed his arm, and he bounced back from his reverie, kissing her cheek.

"Who is that?" Will asked, indicating a young soldier on the wagon bed used as a platform so the crowd could see. "He is quite handsome." She pressed a hand against her cheek.

"*That* man?" Noah's eyebrows shot up and Augusta swallowed a giggle. "Why, that's Chaplain Gregg."

"O-oh." Will strung out the word in wondrous discovery.

Noah frowned. "You think *he's* handsome?"

"Uh-huh."

Melinda Jane leaned forward, catching Augusta's eye, her own eyes twinkling with merriment.

"He ain't handsome." Noah huffed under his breath, pulling off his hat for the prayer the Chaplain read from a piece of paper.

Fin maneuvered himself to stand beside Augusta. "Soon as Colonel Ferguson is done with his speech, Noah and I are gonna head out. The sooner we get to Winchester the sooner we get some answers."

"Do you think it's safe to go home to Gauley?" Augusta had thought of little else besides Zander and the farm. "We'd talked about leaving just as soon as the surrender was announced."

"There's always a chance of some hold-out bushwhackers. I'd rather you wait until we get back from Virginia. We'll take the train. Shouldn't be more than a week. Besides, we'll need all the man power we can get to set everything aright and start rebuilding."

She sighed with disappointment. Another week. She had been away from home for years now. Surely, she could wait one more week.

She tugged on Fin's sleeve. "I hope you'll be back in time for Easter."

He smiled. "No promises, but I'd like that too."

Her heart leapt within her, chanting a rhythm all its own. "*It's over. It's over. It's over.*"

Thirty-Nine

Fort Fuller

April 14, 1865

"Go ahead." Fin urged, hoping to encourage Henry Bassoom as he stood at attention before the colonel's desk. "Tell Captain Giles and Colonel Fleming exactly what you told us."

"I am ashamed of what I did, sirs, but I did not see any way through it." Bassoom swallowed and continued. "A man came up to me, smooth talking, like a salesman. I did not mind talking with him until he started speaking of *meine Familie,* my family. The stranger talked like he was at my home, described my sister, my house—even Mutter's dishes, sirs."

"To be clear here, Mr. Bassoom, your home is in Winchester, Virginia, isn't it?" Fin asked, noting the Colonel's pen scratching on a pad of paper.

"Yes, sir. And this man told me if I did not do exactly as he said, he would see to it that my parents met with . . . 'with an ungodly awful lot of pain upon their deaths' were his words to me.

"I admit. I was scared. I have no care for my own life, but meine Familie did nothing wrong. It was Virginia that left the Union, not them. The man said he had connections and there was nothing the entire Federal Government could do to stop him."

"Continue Mr. Bassoom," Captain Giles prodded.

"He made me steal thirty uniforms from the quarter master. After I did that, I did not hear anymore from him until after the attack." Bassoom hung his head, his voice trembling as he continued. "It was all my fault—the attack on New Creek and the fort. The prisoners taken. All my fault." He lifted his chin and faced forward, staring.

"But Zander—Private Dabney—warned me. Somehow, he saw me and the man together. He said the man was his cousin, Carter, and that he was up to no good. But it was too late. I was at the man's mercy and had no choice."

"When did you hear from Carter again?" Fin asked.

"He gave me a folded paper and told me to put it in Private Dabney's saddlebag before his next call out. Then he showed me my sister's journal—the one she has written in every day since she could write. I took the paper and did as he said." His gaze dropped to the floor.

"I was consumed with the need to see if my family was safe, and I could not stomach the thought that my friend would be arrested for something *I* was guilty of. So, I deserted just before the detachment was to leave."

The colonel set the pen in its holder and tented his fingers. "Were you aware of what was on that paper, Mr. Bassoom?"

"Yes, sir. It was a map and information intended to frame Private Dabney for aiding the enemy in the attack on New Creek and the garrison."

"And was your family safe when you arrived at Winchester?"

"Yes, sir."

"Is there anything you wish to add?"

"Just that I am full of regret, sirs. And that I understand I am under arrest."

Captain Giles broke the pencil he had been toying with. He stood and approached the prisoner. "I understand that you were in a difficult position, but our men never would've laid over in Beverly had it not been for that blasted piece of paper. And they wouldn't be dead or imprisoned now."

He addressed Fin. "Do you know where this Carter, your cousin is now?"

Fin shook his head. "We are not a close family, Captain. Carter's home is in King William County, but I wouldn't count on him being there for a while."

Colonel Fleming stood. "The prisoner will be remanded to the military court for due process. And Captain Dabney, I hope your family will be reunited very soon."

"Thank you, Colonel."

The colonel motioned to the two guards flanking the door. "Lock this man up." He dismissed Fin and Noah and dropped into his chair, looking weary and spent.

Captain Giles followed them out. "I hope you'll let me know when Private Dabney returns home. I will do the same if he shows up here."

Fin nodded his agreement and trailed Noah toward the horses. He checked his watch. "We better hurry if we want to catch that train." He was determined to make it back for Easter, even if they had to ride through the night once they got off the train.

Only a few hours into their train ride home, a distraction arose, followed by a steward quieting the passengers. "Please, settle down. I have official word that—" He grasped the seat next to him, seeming to steady his own breathing. "President Lincoln has been shot."

Gasps and murmurs were quickly followed by the sounds of sobbing as the atmosphere in the car dimmed with grief. A passenger's snide comment sparked a brief altercation, leaving one man with a bloody nose. A thick fog of silence settled over the car's inhabitants.

Fin looked at his hands, remembering them covered in blood, both his own and the blood of others. How he had respected President Lincoln. Were it not for him, so many things would be different right now. Maybe there never would've been a war. Maybe the slaves would still be enslaved. Maybe there would be no United States. It was all too much to sort through, so he prayed for the Lincoln family and wondered what his own family was doing at this moment. Had they heard the news yet?

Charleston
Easter Sunday 1865

Road weary and in need of a bath, Fin burst into the house. He regarded the familiar faces around the table for the Easter meal. If only he had been home when they got the news.

Melinda Jane rushed at him, throwing her arms around his middle. "Whew! You're sure needing a bath this Resurrection Day, but no matter—you're home!"

"I hope I get a homecoming like that of my own someday," Noah said, smoothing back his hair and hanging his hat on a peg.

Fin lifted his wife off the ground, letting her legs dangle. "You just wait long enough and mayhap you'll find a plain looking woman who doesn't mind seeing your ugly mug every day." He lowered Melinda Jane and kissed her again. "But this beautiful young thing is all mine."

Melinda Jane slapped at his arm. "You two be nice, now." She motioned toward the table. "Wash up and have a seat. We're nearly done, but there's plenty left."

Minutes later, chairs scraped against the floor as Fin and Noah joined the family and filled their plates.

"I take it you've all heard about President Lincoln," Fin said, trying to gauge their mood.

"Yes," James answered. "Today is the first we've attempted some normalcy around here. He squeezed Gus's hand, his lips tipped in an unsure smile. "And we're anxious to hear your report."

"Well?" Will leaned forward, her expectant look drilling into her oldest brother. "Tell us. What'd you find out?"

"Let's let the men eat a bit first now, Will." Gus shifted the bowls and platters of food closer to the hungry men. "We're all anxious, but they've had a long trip home."

Noah downed an entire glass of water and poured another from the pewter pitcher. "Delicious meal, ladies." He passed his gaze between the women and paused when he got to Will, a smile on his face. "And a beautiful table fit for this most holy day."

A blush traveled up Will's neck and colored her cheeks before she stared into her lap.

Fin chuckled to himself. Had he ever in his entire life seen his little sister blush? This was a first, that's for sure. But when he considered the source of that reaction, mixed feelings bubbled to the surface. "How about passing those potatoes, Lieutenant."

Noah, startled as if awakened from a dream, and reached for the bowl. "Certainly, *Captain*." He caught Fin's questioning gaze and stabbed a piece of ham, sliding it off the fork with a grin.

Fin would need to have a talk with that boy.

Over the next several minutes, he shared what he had learned from Bassoom to a scowling audience. It was a wonder they held off their comments until he was done.

"I can't help but feel somehow responsible in all this," James said, scrubbing his beard. "But at the same time, I'm remembering all the convoluted events that have led up to this moment—how Carter's jealousy is what really started off this long string of miserable trials."

Gus patted his hand. "You're not to blame for any of this. Carter is the one who will have to answer to the Almighty one day. I just hope he finds God's love and forgiveness before it's too late."

"There's no telling how many more lives he could ruin with his want for vengeance." Fin shook his head. "I've been trying not to hate the man. He's kin, after all."

"But he deserves our hate for what he's done," Will said. She met the gaze of each of her family members. "But Pap would say we all deserve to be hated, death even, for what we've done." Her eyes misted.

"And Izzy would say that 'hatin' makes a man ugly as sin on the inside'," Melinda Jane reminded them.

James grasped Gus's hand and then Bertie's, waiting until the rest of the family did likewise. "I know we've all been praying for Zander, but this is a day we celebrate the miracle of resurrection and what Jesus did for us. And what Jesus has done for each of us, He can do for Carter, and He can bring our Zander back home."

James bowed his head and prayed for exactly that.

When they finished, Lola, who had sat in silence until now, sniffled, dabbing her eyes with her napkin.

"Are you all right, honey?" Gus asked, touching her arm.

Lola smiled timidly. "I'm overcome by God's goodness is all, and I'm bursting with thanksgiving that you are allowing me to stay with you. My heart has been so full of ache for Zander that I forgot to look around me and be thankful for"—her eyes floated over each of them—"for all of you." Moisture brightened her eyes as she breathed out a bashful chuckle.

Fin squeezed his wife's fingers, drawing her gaze. They'd had their own journey to each other and the happiness he felt just thinking about her and little Izzy brought his heart to near bursting. Lola could do that for Zander, too. But it would take time.

Augusta stared at the paper on the table, knowing it would either sting like a snakebite or bring salve to her desperate heart.

"Well? Do you want me to read it?" James tapped the paper. "If his name isn't here, it just means we need more information."

President Lincoln had required all prisons, both Federal and Confederate, release the names of prisoners within their confines at the time of the surrender. The Wheeling Intelligencer was extra thick with the names of fathers, sons, and brothers who would soon be home.

She unfolded the paper and began reading through the Virginia prison lists, running a trembling finger down column after column.

"He's not here. If not here, then where?" Her mind hovered over dark thoughts, and the tears fell like a waterfall.

James pulled spectacles from his pocket and reached for the paper. "I'll double check," he said, spreading the paper before him. "And then I'll check all the prisons. They could've transferred him for some reason. Maybe."

She stood, wiping her eyes. "We are still leaving for Gauley tomorrow, are we not?"

His eyes soothed with compassion as he took her hand. "Of course we are. It will be good to occupy ourselves with the task of recovering the farm. And I'm going to see Colonel Oley. Perhaps he can help us figure what to do next."

The war was over, and it was time to pick up their lives and start living again. But how could they go on without Zander?

Forty

THE VIRGINIA WILDERNESS

Zander secured a fresh piece of bark to the bottom of his foot with a strip of kerchief since the soles of his boots had long since stopped protecting his calloused feet. It sure looked peculiar, but it served its purpose.

A sharpened stone served as his only knife. He'd used it to carve a notch into the peel board-turned-spear to keep track of the days. He had trekked nine days, maintaining a short distance between himself and the James River to assure a fresh water supply. Following rivers would mean extra days, but he had no choice.

He just had to keep aiming for those familiar Allegheny mountains. The same mountains he had looked at all his life. He didn't have a map, so all he could do was head west, in a snaking river sort of way, watching for other rivers to spring off going the right direction. Skirting cities had stolen days from him since he had to search for the river to follow again.

The Alleghenies looked different from the east, and he didn't know exactly where he was, just that he would be in West Virginia when he crossed over those welcoming ridges. He had hunted that area some and marched right through there on the way to that wretched field of blood. *It felt like years ago now.* He reeled in his thoughts and traipsed forward, stopping only when necessary, amazed at the strength carrying him.

Several times he had heard horses, and even voices, but he couldn't chance a Rebel patrol. Nor could he chance someone looking for a chicken or egg thief, so patience had earned him a certain skill at spearing fish and although it slowed his journey considerably, his ability to snare a rabbit had kept him strong enough to keep moving. Pap and Fin had taught him well.

He chewed on a strip of bark as he plodded onward, keenly aware of the pike not far to his left, beyond the dense woods and brambles that offered him protection from discovery. He stopped at the sound of hooves pounding against the road's hard surface. Dozens of horses. They galloped at a fast pace and his curiosity wanted to close in on the pike for a look. But his better judgement won out, and he sat on the ground until the troops passed.

He had not seen a single person since leaving the prison, traversing open ground only at night. Even when he watered from the lazy James River, he chanced being seen by someone, but it was as if an invisible hand went before him, clearing a safe path. And he knew Whose hand it was.

He thought of heading to New Creek, or Charleston, even, but in the end, it was his home in Gauley Bridge that won out. He knew the area, and it was closer. But he would need to keep a keen eye out for bushwhackers. He could report to the Federal garrison in Gauley. Looking down at what remained of his tattered, mud-caked uniform, he frowned. At least, his Cavalry insignia was recognizable—barely.

He wanted home more than breath and his heart ached to see Lola. The homeplace would be empty, but he yearned to see it. Would he be able to get leave right away to travel to Wheeling to see her? He would tell her everything that had transpired.

An uninvited thought invaded, and dread washed over him. What if they stuck him in the stockade for treason? His head spun, trying to sort out the right thing to do. He had to prove his innocence, but how? Since home just seemed so very far away, he had stuffed these worries away for a long time now.

He carved another notch on the peel board the next morning, and the next. In the prison camp, the din of suffering and contrary attitudes kept him to himself after Leach died. But here in the woods, where he had found solace so many times in his life, he could almost hear God speaking to him, urging him on. He missed Rampart's company, and he traveled with no one, but of this he was certain—he was not alone.

Gauley Bridge, Fayette County, West Virginia

Fin paced the room, eyeing Gus as James shared his news. He should've gone with his brother-in-law in search of news about Zander.

"General Lightburn has done all he can for now. He has an army of assistants weeding through mountains of paperwork to piece together the whereabouts of more than two thousand of our men—men who have disappeared entirely or fallen between the cracks of paper trails and prison reports. The sheer number of unmarked graves that need to line up with regimental reports is astounding." James accepted another cup of coffee from Gus, drew a paper from his pocket and unfolded it.

"Zander's unit has been out on assignment. Following the assassination, Colonel Fleming took the Sixth to Washington to pursue Booth and his accomplices."

"That was the day after I met with him," Fin said.

James shook his head. "A day later and you would've had to cart Bassoom off to Wheeling or back to Charleston with you."

"Yeah. Good timing, I guess." More like divine providence.

James continued, "Fleming arrested Dr. Mudd in Surrattsville, Maryland and pursued Booth from Maryland into Virginia. Evidently, the regiment provided escort duty during the trial of the assassination conspirators. The bulk of the regiment is on guard duty on Pennsylvania Avenue between the capitol and Georgetown during the Grand Review."

Fin shrugged. "So that's what Zander is missing, huh? He'd probably be all right with that."

"You seem sure he's alive."

"James!" Gus lowered herself into the chair. "We have to believe he's alive. Somewhere."

"It has been almost four weeks since the surrender," James said, reaching for her hand.

Fin glared at James. "Zander is alive. I feel it"—he thumped his chest—"in *here!*"

Forty-One

April 28, 1865

Fin deposited the last of the charred remains of the Dabney barn into the wagon and leaned on the shovel. "That'll do it," he called to Noah. His friend led the gelding to the field, where Fin intended to till in the finer bits and pile the rest.

It felt so right to be back home. The family had worked hard this last week. The men kept busy mostly outside, but the women had the hardest job. They labored tirelessly to recover their beloved home from violations perpetrated by bushwhackers—who cared nothing for the property of others.

Melinda Jane strolled toward him, a bucket swinging from one hand and a tied bundle in the other. Her smile never failed to warm his insides. How did he get so lucky?

"I brought you a snack, and some water to douse yourself." She chuckled as she drew near. "Is that my handsome husband under all that soot?"

He laughed as she pulled a hanky from inside her cuff and wiped his cheeks and forehead. "Oh, hold still." She dabbed his lips, then stood on her tiptoes to plant a kiss on them.

He grinned and pulled her to him. "Why, Mrs. Dabney, people will talk."

"Let them. We can handle such chin-wag."

"We sure can." He kissed her deeply until she pulled back.

"I don't ever want to leave here again, Fin. I want to raise our family here and turn this back into a thriving farm. That's all I want, really. It's safe here . . . now."

That last word pierced his heart, reaching places he had not considered. How much had she endured these last four years? Surely, she had her secrets, as did he, about all that had transpired. She needed more than the farm. She needed security. *God, show me how to give her what she needs.*

Coot's abrupt bark drew his gaze to the field where Noah worked, raking charcoal into the freshly turned soil. Movement caught Fin's attention as a lone figure emerged from the trees on the far side of the field. He set Melinda Jane aside and fingered the gun strapped to his leg that he'd found hard to give up just yet.

Melinda Jane followed his gaze. "Who do you think that could be?"

Coot flew by like he was chasing a rabbit through the field—making a beeline for the stranger. The hound barked as he raced past Noah, who spun around with a drawn revolver, facing the stranger. He promptly holstered it, dropped the rake, and jogged toward the man.

Coot knocked the stranger down, and Noah pulled him back up, clapping the man on the shoulder like an old friend.

Fin squinted at the scene. *Could it be?* He charged for the field, heart pumping harder with every stride closer. As he ran, hope blossomed into truth and tears clouded his vision.

He stopped just five feet in front of Zander, looking him over, making sure he was all there. A ratty band of fabric held back his scraggly shoulder-length hair. His faded uniform hung loose on his lean frame. More grungy strips of cloth secured a pointed contraption to his side. When his gaze landed on Zander's feet, he smiled at the boy's innovation of bark for shoes. He searched the eyes that had held so much anger when last they met. Gratefulness flooded him, rushing from his depths. Unsure of his voice, he just stood there.

Tears squeezed from his brother's eyes and trembling lips gave way to a familiar lopsided smile. "I'm home."

Fin shook his head. "And a mightier miracle I've not seen in my lifetime."

"B . . .but what are you doing here?" Zander's eyes narrowed as he took in his surroundings.

Fin wrapped his brother in a bear hug, reluctant to let go. "We've had a heck of a time trying to find you since the surrender, brother."

"Surrender?" Zander's eyes rounded, darting from Fin to Noah and back again. "Who surrendered?"

"Lee surrendered first. Johnston just day before yesterday," Noah said, eyeing Fin. "You didn't know the war's over?"

Fresh tears trailed down Zander's cheeks and he looked off in the distance. "It's over?" The whispered words seemed drenched in wonder. "It's over." He slipped a sharp wooden stick from a sort of holder and counted notches. "How long's it been over?"

"Well, let's see now. The surrender was the ninth of April and today's the twenty-eighth."

Zander stared at the spear. "I escaped from Belle Isle twenty-one days ago." He shook his head. "If I had waited just two more days, the war would've been over."

Fin hugged him to his side and started toward the house. "Well, little brother, you're home now and that's all that matters." He looked up to see the family running toward them, Bertie in the lead. "And you're about to make a lot of people real happy."

Home. He had truly made it all the way home. Victory surged through Zander as his family welcomed him. Had it not been for the very real wetness of everyone's tears, he would think it was a dream. He'd thought of little else but the farm as he made his way back, scrounging for food and living in fear of being discovered. But never had he imagined a welcoming party.

Zander traipsed toward the house with Will under one arm and Gus under the other. Coot's excited barking added to the clamor of questions and concerns. Holding Addie, James met him part way and looked him up and down before pulling him into a hug.

They were all here. Everyone who mattered.

But not everyone. Remorse kicked against the thanksgiving inside him. Lola's face had filled his dreams by night and thoughts by day. If only he could talk to her. He had been a complete dolt. But she had seen something else in him. He'd tend to Leach's folks, then head to Wheeling. If only he could talk to her—tell her things were different with him now.

Lola stood on the well platform, clutching the front of her dress and watching the joyful reunion, not even trying to stop the tears. She had mentally nailed down her shoes to keep from running out there herself. Everything in her cried, shouted, danced—but she did not want to intrude on their special homecoming, and there would be time for the two of them later. *Them.* What if Zander no longer loved her? She had hurt him so. Even if they had no future together, she just had to see him. He would want to know about Papa.

"I still don't understand why we have to stay back here while everybody's out there welcoming him." Felix scowled, his arms across his chest while he watched the merriment.

"Just let him have this time with his family, first. Then you can say hello."

Would he be angry she was here?

She longed to touch his face, to look into those blue eyes, to see if the longing she remembered was still there, for in her heart still burned the desire to be with him. She had prayed and prayed, knowing only God could do a miracle in *his* heart while hers waited.

Oh, Zander.

Voices merged into jubilant chaos as they neared the yard. Zander jolted to a stop when he realized the barn was gone. He had watched it burn to the ground, but they had left for Charleston so soon afterwards. For some reason, the barn had always been a part of his thoughts about the farm.

"Zander!" *Oomph*. A dark, curly head plowed into him.

"Felix?" He crouched down, and the boy threw spindly arms around his neck. "Well, this is a surprise!" *If Felix was here*? Zander searched the yard, craning his neck to see past Will, who stepped aside.

"Lola." His breath caught in his chest. He politely moved Felix aside and walked toward her, his strides quickening until he was jogging.

Tears streaked her lovely cheeks and her lips mouthed his name. He seized her by the waist and spun her around to the music of her laughter as she held tight to his shoulders.

"You're here," he rasped, setting her down, keeping her close. The storm clouds had parted and yes, D.R., he could see the sun now and it shone with a brilliance nothing could ever dim.

"Zander, I . . ."

He captured her lips with his own, savoring the feel of her in his arms as he enveloped her. She wilted in his embrace, then after a moment, pushed back, suddenly self-conscious.

Her eyes, like a frightened doe, flitted to his family. "Zander."

"It's all right. It's kind of hard to hide anything from them."

She pressed her hands to his chest. Turning her head away from their audience, she whispered, "We need to talk."

Zander grabbed her hand, leading her away from the curious onlookers. "If you will excuse us a moment, please." He pulled her behind him as she trotted to keep up.

"Well. Will you look at that little brother of mine," he heard Fin say.

Zander winked at Lola and tossed a rebuttal back over his shoulder, "I ain't so little any more, brother."

Laughter floated through the air as they rounded the corner of the house, and Zander grasped her hands. "I need to say something first." He wiped his face with one hand, and grabbed hers again. "I've been an idiot. I blamed God for deserting me. You see, I . . ." He dropped her hands and turned, striding several steps, then stood in front of her again, slowing the breathing that had quickened just seconds ago.

She smiled sweetly and ran her hand down his arm. "I'm listening."

He held her hands again and stared at her chin. He didn't want to see his own reflection in those blue pools that looked back at him. "I had a hard time of it after Cloyd's Mountain . . . before I met you."

With sadness coloring her eyes, she dipped her chin in an encouraging nod.

"I felt so alone, Lola. I blamed God. And I harbored so much anger inside that . . . that sometimes I couldn't even think straight." He licked his chapped lips, feeling the roughness. "D.R. helped me see that God never left me—it was me that left Him."

He drew a breath, recognizing the sweet scent of Mama's jasmine, which bloomed each spring right outside the back door. What he had come to know as grace these past few weeks soared in his heart, and he looked into her eyes at last. "God has forgiven me, Lola, and now I'm asking you to forgive me."

She pressed her cheek to his and whispered. "I forgive you, my sweet, sweet Zander. And I love you so."

He drank in the joy in her eyes. It flowed over and through him as he tucked her head against his chest and held her. The blessing he'd been granted on the heels of such miracles was like nothing he had ever known. A hawk's screech pierced the air and faded away—assuredly proof that it soared on the wind higher and higher toward the sun's warm rays, even if he couldn't see it.

Forty-Two

Zander tightened Duke's cinch strap and turned to his brother. "You sure you won't be needing him for a couple of days?"

"Naw. I got too much to do around here to be going anywhere. You could wait another week or two. You only been home four days." Fin massaged the brim of his hat.

"I promised Leach, and I don't want his folks to have to wait any longer. He was their only child."

"You sure you don't want company to Grantsville?"

"I gotta do this by myself. Kinda seems like my last duty, ya know?" He mounted and Fin handed up the reins. "I'll be back day after next. You're sure about those charges being dropped, right?"

"That's right. Since I sent that telegram to Captain Giles to let him know you're home, he knows how to get in touch with you if they need any more information from you for the trial."

"It don't seem right that Bass has to suffer because of Carter." The whole affair still nettled him.

"Eventually, our cousin will get his comeuppance for all the grief he's caused. Maybe not this side of heaven, but he'll get it."

Zander leaned down. "Can ya keep a secret?"

"You know I can," Fin said, eyeing the doorway.

"I'm asking Lola to marry me just as soon I get back." He'd have a lot of hours in the saddled to dream about their life together over the next three days. He had yet to ask her what she thought about moving west, but it was just too soon to even think about leaving his family again.

∞

Fin waved his hat to the approaching buggy. He'd had second thoughts about letting Will go off with Noah to Gauley, but they had only been gone two hours. Hopefully, just enough time to get into some sort of fight, but not enough to make up.

Will waved a piece of paper. "Got a letter."

He wasn't expecting any mail so soon, given the post office had only opened back up a short time ago. He met the carriage and helped Will down. "Who's it for?"

"Zander." She pulled it from his reach. "But since he's not here, can I open it?"

"No, you cannot open it." Fin snatched it from her hand. He eyed Will, then Noah. "Everything go all right?"

"No!" Will huffed.

"What?" Fin growled, stepping closer to Noah.

"Jackson's was all out of licorice. Had to settle for horehound." Will snatched a wrapped bundle from the floorboards. "It was real nice to get out away from the farm for a while and see some people. Mamie is gonna come over later for a visit. We have ever so much to catch up on." She strode toward the house, her skirt swaying with each step.

Had that girl even donned her overalls since they got back to the farm? He turned back to Noah, whose mouth curved in a familiar grin as his gaze followed his sister. "Oh no you don't, Hicks. I know that look. You are not gonna court my little sister, ya hear?"

"Who said anything about *courtin'* her? She'd likely slap me silly at the mention of the word."

"Well, all right, then. Shove those eyes back into their sockets and come help me with felled trees."

Fin held the letter up to the sun, chewing his lip. Could be important. Too important to sit around for three days, waiting for Zander to return.

He pried the letter open and seconds later, wished he hadn't. Just when his family had gone through every kind of heartache possible, this news would slice their newfound peace like a knife.

Zander smiled as the willow at the end of their lane came into view. Almost home. He had considered returning by way of Charleston so he could find just the perfect engagement gift for Lola—until he realized he didn't have any money. He may have lost part of his winnings from racing, but what about the package he'd left with Will? Had she even told anyone about it? Maybe it was still in Charleston, at James's house. He should pay a visit to Mrs. O'Donell anyway. He could get it and buy Lola's ring then.

No welcoming bark from Coot. Maybe Bertie and Felix were off to the crick with the four-legged sentinel who seldom left Bertie's side. He had to smile. The way those two boys got on—you'd think they were brothers. Well, they very nearly will be someday. Someday soon, he hoped.

Zander brushed Duke down and turned him out into the pasture. Besides adding a lean-to onto the corncrib for the tack, one of the first things Fin said he did was secure the fence line. Couldn't chance the horses disappearing on them. With Zander and Noah to help, the barn would go up fast. Not the magnificent barn Pap and Izzy built, but it would do just fine, Fin said.

Mayhap Lola wouldn't mind living down in Izzy's cabin for a time. They could add on or fix it up easy enough. Used to be that thinking of Pap or Izzy brought nothing but sadness, but now a wave of sweetness followed right quick behind the bitter. He would see them again—of that he was certain. He lifted the saddle onto the rail in the lean-to and turned at a voice.

"You made good time." Fin took the bridle from his hand and slipped it over a nail. "I saw you come in."

"Yeah. Everything went fine. Mr. and Mrs. Leach were real glad I came. They'd already received the news, but what I had to tell them about D.R. brought them a measure of comfort, I think. Both of them cried when I handed them his Bible. They wanted me to stay, but I told them why I was in a hurry to get back. They asked me to invite them to the wedding." Zander knew they would be fine folks. It was clear where their son got his looks—and his faith.

Fin pulled a letter from his back pocket and slapped it against his hand. His brows knit together and he twisted his lips like he did when he didn't want to say something.

"I know that look. Spit it out." Zander pointed to the letter. "Bad news?"

Sadness colored Fin's eyes. "Yeah. It's from Colonel Fleming."

Zander read the letter, each line blurring more with angry tears. He blinked them away with the same fury that could rout the peace he'd found at last.

"It's all right to be mad, but you have a duty," Fin said.

He wanted to wad the letter into a ball and stomp it to pulp. *Duty*!

"You have this month to recuperate, and then you're expected to serve out your enlistment. I know it's hard." Pity shown in Fin's eyes.

Zander blew out a long breath, feeling the anger give way to resignation. God had not taken him this far just to leave him alone. He'd learned his lesson. He wasn't about to let go of that unseen hand. No sir. Not again. Life would have to wait. One more year.

His brother laid a hand on his shoulder. "She'll wait for you. Of that, I'm sure. And she can wait right here with us. She and Felix are part of this family now."

"That'd be real fine. Ya'll have been good to Lola. You would've liked her pap. He was a fine man."

"You don't have to report to Cloud's Mill until June 12th. You still got some time with your gal."

Zander followed his brother into the house. His sweet Lola. If she said no to the waiting, he just didn't know how he would survive another year.

∾

June 1865

Tears. Zander had grown up in a houseful of women and you would think it wouldn't bother him, but it did. Even Will had broken down and hung on his neck like she'd never let go.

He met every eye with a practiced smile and hugged each neck with trueness of heart. He would miss them more than he dare let on. He had put them through so much and now he was asking them to put the joy and relief on the shelf for another year. It was cruel.

"I packed you paper and stamps, and so help me, Alexander Dabney, if you don't write to your family more regular than you have over the last year and half, I'm gonna skin you alive when you get back here!" Melinda Jane crossed her arms over her chest. "There. I said my piece."

Fin hugged her to him. "Get it out of your system, wife. He'll have to wait a whole year to hear any of your sass again." He planted a kiss on her cheek as she dabbed at her red face.

"If ya don't mind, I'm gonna say goodbye to Lola outside." He lead her toward the door.

"Wait a minute. This is for you." Fin winked at Gus, and she handed him a small, worn Bible. "It belonged to Pap. Gus sent me off with it, and I'm passing it on to you, little brother."

Zander thought of Leach's Bible that had brought him through so much. He pressed Pap's Bible to his heart and the flood he had valiantly restrained threatened to break the levee. How had God ever seen fit to bless him with this family was beyond anything he could figure.

"Just a minute." James left and returned a few seconds later with his fancy officer's poncho. "You're gonna need this. It's raining out there, and it looks like it's going to for a while."

Zander removed his hat and his brother-in-law slipped the poncho over his head. "Thank you."

They prayed together one last time as a family. Gus hugged him tight, her body trembling with pent-up emotion. "We'll be right here when you get back," she assured him.

Noble words lodged in his throat, so he just smiled and nodded one last time, before he pulled Lola through the door with him. He held her in his arms on the porch, memorizing her face, even the way her glasses sat on her perky nose. His fingers combed the curly wisps of golden hair from her brow.

She rested her head on his chest as if listening to his heartbeat. "It's hard to imagine just where you'll be, so I asked Felix to show me in one of his books. Kansas is so far."

"I don't know how long we'll be in Kansas at Fort Leavenworth, but likely we'll move on to the Plains. Maybe Fort Kearney in Nebraska."

"But Felix says that's Indian Territory." A quiver touched her voice. She met his gaze.

"*Shhh*, I'll be fine. Besides, it'll give me a chance to see what the West is like. Mayhap I'll return there some day and build me that ranch I used to dream of."

"And raise horses to sell to the U.S. Army," she said, a faint smile brightening her face.

"But only if you are with me, Lola Wade."

"If that's your dream, it's mine too, Zander Dabney. And I will wait right here with my new family until I see your handsome face at this farm in one year."

Her eyes clouded. "You'll be all right, Zander. It won't be like before, will it?"

He pressed his cheek to the top of her head as thunder rumbled overhead. "It won't ever be like before, because I won't be alone. I'm never letting go of God's hand again." He kissed her thoroughly, memorizing her lips and the curves of her body. For this, he would return.

He trotted out to the lean-to where the new horse, Sentry, waited. He had used much of the money Will held to buy the gelding. No horse could ever replace Rampart, but Sentry was already nuzzling his way into Zander's heart. Snugging his cap down over his brow, he guided the young, spirited mount into the rain.

His poncho whipped against the torrent as charcoal storm clouds drifted with the wind, hiding the sun. But no matter, he knew it was up there—shining just like it had every day of his life.

And when they were come into
the ship, the wind ceased.
Then they that were in the ship
came and worshipped him, saying,
Of a truth thou art the Son of God.

Matthew 14:32–33

ACKNOWLEDGEMENTS

I am indebted to many people who deserve much credit. This series, "West Virginia: Born of Rebellion's Storm" has been a labor of love. Foremost, I am thankful to Jesus Christ, my Lord, and Savior, Who reminds me He chose me to bear fruit (John 15:16). For fifteen years, writing has been fruit-bearing for me. I want to thank the following people for helping me bear that fruit:

My hero husband who advised me on a variety of technical issues and sacrificed many a home-made meal while I worked away on this book. And to my four (now adult) children, whose tastes in entertainment spurred the viewing of a plethora of war movies over the years. (It's a guy thing.)

Present/past members of my critique group, the Encouragers, and Cascade Christian Writers, who have faithfully offered support and true encouragement over the last twelve years.

A special thank you to Melody Roberts, my ever-vigilant critique partner throughout four novels.

Kara Starcher of Mountain Creek Books LLC for her lovely book cover, expert recommendations, regional guidance, and patience with my unending questions.

Sarah Forster and Shelli Owen—proof-readers extraordinaire. Rachel Williams, Publicity Assistant extraordinaire.

West Virginia State Historic Preservation Office staff for answering a myriad of questions.

AUTHOR NOTES

I covered the American Civil War many times in my years of teaching school. Three thoughts caused me the most angst: 1) What would it be like to have my home, town, or county become a battlefield? 2) What would it be like to fight my neighbor, perhaps even a relative? 3) What would it be like to send my husband or sons to fight this kind of war; what would change forever? I address each of these considerations in the first three books of this series. I chose western Virginia because it was the most contested piece of real estate in the U.S. at that time.

When writing historical fiction, I first immerse myself in research for several months. After a time, ideas emerge for the foundation of a novel. I then weave fictional characters through a maze of factual events on a historical timeline. The characters undergo their various journeys inspired by accounts of people who lived during that period. I have taken some fictional liberties when portraying real historical figures.

Most of the Blazer Scouts' activities mentioned throughout these pages are a matter of historical record. This elite group shrank from 100 brave men to only 32 in a two-year period. Zander's Cavalry unit followed the historical timeline and activities of the 5th (later 6th) West Virginia Cavalry. Resources included newspapers (Wheeling Daily Intelligencer), regimental reports, records, letters, web sources, and non-fiction books. Discover more gems from my research and historical novels by signing up for my **newsletter** at **kendypearson.com**.

You will find numerous recounted historical events and genuine personalities within the pages of *In Tempest Winds*, and here are just a few of those facts:

- The timeline and details of the May 9 Battle of Cloyd's Mountain, southwestern Virginia's largest fight of the Civil War: Many Union soldiers died, screaming for help amidst the blaze caused by musket fire in the thick woods. I followed the action fairly closely. The battle duration was relatively short but contained some of the most severe and savage fighting of the war, much of it hand-to-hand combat. The purpose was to take out the Virginia & Tennessee Railroad, which President Lincoln called the "gut of the Confederacy" because it was vital to the Confederacy for food transportation. Two future U.S. Presidents fought in the battle (RB Hayes & Wlm. McKinley). (Ch 3, 10)

- Blazer's Scouts and the Fifth Infantry's band fooled the Confederates into thinking Lewisburg was under attack again by creating a ruckus. Union General Hunter's atrocities are all a matter of historical records: burning of the Virginia Military Institute, destruction of property, and mistreatment of civilians. (Ch 5, 10)

- In retaliation for Hunter's atrocities, CFS Gen McCausland burned and looted the town of Chambersburg when its citizens could not pay a ransom. He then headed to attack Fort Fuller, but changed his mind. (Ch 14)

- Indeed, farmhands with implements were mistaken for Rebels with weapons. (Ch 18)

- The too-late arrival of the 5th WV Cavalry to aid the Beverly Garrison and related details. (Ch 21)

- Most of the details mentioned here relating to the surprise attack on New Creek and Fort Fuller by an advance of

Rebels wearing Union Uniforms. Fort personnel thought these were Major Potts's returning detail until they let out a Rebel cry. Panic-stricken Federal soldiers abandoned Fort Fuller without firing a shot. The attacking force numbered one thousand strong and made off with: 2050 cattle, 800 horses, 3,000 pair of pantaloons and shirts, and other property. (Ch 23)

- With a volunteer force of 300, CFS General Rosser's 3:00 a.m. surprise attack on the Beverly garrison in January, 1865: Most details included here are a matter of record. Most of the 700 soldiers stationed at Beverly were taken captive, and about 200 escaped during the mountainous trek. (Ch 29, 30)

- A prisoner actually did escape from the Danville prison by hiding in a bake oven, and that was my inspiration for Zander's escape. The Charleston victory parade details are a matter of historical record. (Ch 38)

<u>End of the war</u>:

Word traveled slowly to those still fighting in the various armies of the Confederacy. Here is a brief timeline:

- **4/9**—Gen. Lee surrenders the largest Confederate force, the Army of Northern Virginia to Gen. Grant.

- **4/12**—Gen. Joseph E. Johnston's Army of Tennessee, the second largest Confederate force, receives news of the surrender. Pressed by Sherman's cavalry, Johnston sought peace talks. But Johnston is ordered to resume fighting by Confederate President Jefferson Davis after newly elected U.S. President Andrew Johnson and his cabinet reject an accord giving concessions to the South.

- **4/26**—Sherman and Johnston sign a new surrender agreement similar to Lee's and Grant's, giving up most all Confederate troops in Carolinas, Georgia, and Florida.

- **5/4**—Confederate General R. Taylor (son of President Zachary Taylor) surrenders 10,000 men.

- **5/9**—Confederate General Nathan Bedford Forrest (American slave trader and Grand Wizard/founding member of the Reconstruction-era KKK) surrenders his cavalry corps.

- Despite a Federal military presence, warring continued in Texas for five years as newly arrived white Southerners clashed with formerly enslaved people. By the end of that five year period, Black citizens comprised 30% of Texas's total population.

In Tempest Winds was quite difficult to write at times. As the mother of two war zone veterans (Iraq and Afghanistan), I often found myself in tears. Looking back at this series, it has been an emotional investment I didn't expect. Now, I will expand my vision to *Beyond the Storm* (of Rebellion) to watch Will, Bertie, and Felix live out their individual legacies.

I sincerely hope I have sparked your interest in this tumultuous, heart-wrenching era of our nation's history. Unfortunately, this subject is no longer commonly taught in public schools. At one time, I had this large sign on the wall of my classroom:

THOSE WHO CANNOT REMEMBER THE PAST ARE CONDEMNED TO REPEAT IT.
—George Santayana, 1905

Gifts
just for my readers!

Receive the Free
Extended Prologue
of
Fires of Injustice
(ebook or audio)

Receive the free
First Five Chapters
of
When the Mountains Wept
Book 1 of West Virginia: Born of
Rebellion's Storm
(ebook)

Visit
kendypearson.com
for your FREE ebook or audiobook!

AMERICA'S FORGOTTEN WAR

FIRES
OF
INJUSTICE

Heart
of
History
an imprint of
PEAR BLOSSOM BOOKS

FIRES OF INJUSTICE

San Francisco, California
November 1884

Yakira dropped the sweet potatoes into her market bag one by one, attempting to hold her tongue. The attempt failed. She squared her shoulders and skirted a row of tall rice baskets, to part the caustic space between Azalea and the awful woman, seeking to set things right. "Pardon me, madam—"

"Mrs. Hickman. Mrs. *Reginald* Hickman." A ridiculous feathered hat complemented the woman's beaked nose and chicken-necked pose.

"Well, Mrs. Hickman, you are gravely mistaken. My lovely cousin here is not now, nor has she ever been—"

"I know a Mongolian prostitute when I see one." The woman sniffed, scrutinizing Azalea from hat to shoe. "And dressing like a white woman doesn't change what you are. You . . . heathen!"

Yakira bristled at the venomous insult. God forgive her, she wanted to slap the woman. 'Twould not be the first time her temper dunked her in hot water.

Azalea tugged on her arm. "Yakira. It is all right. Let us leave." Brows pleated, her gaze jumped to the half dozen spectators gathered for a feminine row. Another tug.

Yakira ignored her cousin's warnings and plunged ahead. "Tread carefully, Mrs. Hickman, lest God judge you for your hateful attitude toward His children. Children who are simply different from yourself. I, for one, am thankful that Azalea is nothing like you—for she is kind to strangers, whereas you have proven sorely lacking."

"Well, I never!" The woman blustered, and crimson quickly mottled her cheeks.

Pulling on Yakira's arm again, Azalea gained a couple of inches for the effort.

"And furthermore, Mrs. Hickman, if you were to loosen your corset and lower your nose, you would see that people are people everywhere, regardless of how they look or what they do or from whence they've come." Yakira cringed as Azalea's fingernails knifed into her flesh. "There is none worthy, Mrs. Hickman."

The woman gaped like a carp on the fishmonger's cart.

Azalea squeezed between them, forcing Yakira to step back. "Good day, Mrs. Hickman." She donned a sweet smile and bowed before trotting away with Yakira in tow.

They'd gone a full block before Yakira unclenched her fists and panic set in. *What had she done?* She yanked Azalea to a stop. "Please don't tell Da what just happened. Or Aunt Lara."

Azalea smoothed her bustle and fingered the lace confection pinned atop her sable plaits. "And let them find out I nearly had to break up a fisticuffs? Why ever would I do that?"

"Women like her . . ." A very un-lady-like growl purled in her throat. With a slow breath, she banked the fire inside and took Azalea's hands. "I'd fight to the death for you. You know that."

"You are my *laotong*—we are sworn sisters for life. Of course, you would. And I for you." Azalea hooked her arm through Yakira's, and they turned down Dupont Street, the only other street in Chinatown where they were allowed to walk without an escort.

They sidestepped a huddle of older children tossing sticks while a young child dressed in the split pants of a toddler watched-on. Yakira knelt and smiled at him. *"Jóusàhn."* (Good morning.) She paused for a return grin before they continued walking. "I'd like one of those someday."

"A little Tang boy?" Azalea chuckled.

"Any little boy will do, actually." She hugged the familiar ache of paper dreams. "We are officially spinsters, you know."

A red-robed Taoist priest skittered past, wide sleeves swallowing his hands and snapping like sails in the breeze. The long hem flailed against black trousers with every clipped step.

Azalea urged her on. "Well, *I* prefer to think of myself as a lady in waiting—waiting for God's choice for me. Mother says God chose me. Then she and father chose me. Now God will choose a husband for me in His timing, not mine. For now, I am content." Azalea bumped her shoulder. "You are not?"

"You know me better than anyone. I am more than content in my work. And I can do without a husband if God will give me children." How ridiculous she sounded. But her cousin understood her heart. Did Yakira truly not care if she ever married? Unbidden, her traitorous mind flickered an image—a beardless face, a mischievous smile. It poked at a corner of her heart, still bruised even after all these years.

"God knows your desires, my sister." Azalea comforted, seeming to read her mind.

An eatery door opened and closed, wafting aromas of boiled rice and fish. On the corner, an enterprising young boy hawked his wares.

He rattled a basket of peanuts—a symbol of prosperity. "You buy? Good fortune to you."

She fished out a penny, and he dumped two handfuls of peanuts on top of her potatoes. *"Dōjeh"* (thank you), she said, amused by the way he bit the coin before tucking it deep into his pocket.

They halted at Jackson Street and turned around. Any farther would take them too near the gambling dens. And too near the cribs where the Chinese prostitutes hawked their services through barred windows or beckoned from guarded upstairs rooms. It was Da's rule, and she'd not give him cause to distrust her. They would return on Friday—but with Miss Culbertson. And a mission.

They crowded together to permit a man room to pass, but he kept pace beside them instead, uncomfortably close. "Please walk," said a female voice. She wore a man's quilted jacket and wide-brimmed hat. "You from Mission Home?"

"Yes. I am Yakira." A finger of warning drew down her spine. She scanned the sidewalks and streets, watchful for the black hat and coat of the *Tong*.

"I am Dong Ju. I go with you?"

"There." Azalea indicated two men just exiting the alley across the street. *Tong men.*

The girl had to come with them now, or she might not live through the beating she'd receive when those men caught her. In seconds, Dong Ju would have no choice. Not ever again.

Yakira shoved her bag into the girl's arms. "Cover your face," she said in Cantonese. She tossed a coin to a weaver, asking to borrow a large basket. He nodded, and she propped it onto Dong Ju's shoulder.

"Just keep walking," she told the girl. Two more blocks and they would be out of Chinatown and too near the police precinct for the Tong to trouble them.

"Jíng hái douh!" (Stay There.) One of the Tong men pointed straight at them; his face twisted with rage.

"Hurry." Azalea caught the girl's hand, and they all ran.

"Follow me." Yakira turned into a shoe shop and rushed straight out the back door. She cut across the alley, into another shop, and out through the front. Blood thumped in her ears as she strained to hear shouts or heavy footsteps.

"Wei Ming." Azalea's breath puffed behind her. "He will help."

Yakira darted into the herb store, her senses slammed by the sharp aroma of ginger and wormwood. Wei Ming sat behind the counter, pretending to read an American newspaper.

"Tong. Behind us." Yakira's frantic words spurred him into action.

He tossed the paper, ducked under a rack of hanging herbs, and locked the door before pulling down the shade. His long queue swung with a quick turn. "You wait here. They go."

Four sets of eyes stared at the door. Breaths heaved in the stillness. Yakira squelched a ripple of fear and reached for Azalea's free hand.

The doorknob rattled. A booted foot bashed the door, quaking a shelf of clay jars. One crashed to the floor, casting shards of crockery and dried seahorses across the floor. Curses. Fists pounded. Wood shuddered.

Soundless minutes ticked by before Wei Ming chanced a peek. "They gone. Think you go out back." He unlocked the door, and they thanked him. He turned to Dong Ju, tenderness softening his brown eyes. "*Síusām di*" (be extra careful).

Running now would only call attention, so they walked up Sacramento Street with a comfortable silence between them. The familiar brick building with its rounded windows and stately chimneys rose into view.

Yakira caught Azalea's gaze and smiled knowingly. Dong Ju's entire world was about to change.

Yakira wilted with relief as she opened the door to the Occidental Mission Home for Girls. "You'll like it here," she said, ushering in her newest student. They stepped onto a bright rectangle of sunlight painted across the floor.

Aunt Lara descended the stairs—dignity and sweetness gracing every inch of her tall frame. "And who have we here?" Her fingers grazed the few silver threads at her temple. "I am Mrs. Campbell," she told Dong Ju in Cantonese.

Azalea hugged her mother, and Dong Ju's eyes rounded at the sweet exchange. It was likely she had never seen such love between a white woman and a Chinese girl.

"This is Dong Ju, and she found *us* this time." Yakira set the borrowed basket beside the door. "Where is Miss Culbertson?"

"She is in the classroom." Aunt Lara dipped her head. Searching out the girl's gaze, she touched her hand. "You are most welcome here, Dong Ju."

The girl nodded, a quivery tilt of her lips adding to her striking beauty. She took in her surroundings with a hundred questions scribed across her face as she scratched one arm.

"Let's get you to your room, then I will show you around," Azalea told their guest, removing the man's hat from her head. "Do you speak English?"

"Little," she said, staring in wide-eyed wonder at the framed photos on the hall bookshelf. Dozens of Chinese girls, all wearing lovely Western dresses, smiled back at her.

"Every one of those girls lived here, or still do. You will meet some of them soon." Azalea motioned for her to follow and led her by the hand. "I will show you the Home."

Garlic and herbs permeated the house, taunting Yakira's stomach more with each step closer to the kitchen. She greeted Cook and deposited the sweet potatoes and peanuts on the counter before heading down the hall to the main classroom. Her fingers caressed the warm woodwork as she walked. How hard her father and Uncle Errol had worked to start the home—just a year after Azalea came into their lives.

Perhaps she would never leave this place. Perhaps she would die here—a happy spinster, content to impart God's grace to all who walked these halls. Or perhaps God would grant her fondest desire—a mission home of her own. She tussled with Him at times, racked between contentment and hope, between what was and what could be. If only she could build on her father and mother's legacy—blaze her own mission field with her own Home for Girls.

Miss Culbertson sat at the desk, hedged-in by stacks of papers. She looked up, and her drawn face brightened. "Well, you are a welcome sight. I can't seem to find the repair list." She sat back with a huff and smoothed a lock of pewter hair that had eluded her snood.

Yakira opened the desk drawer, dug for a moment, and withdrew the list. "Don't feel bad. I looked for it for ten minutes only yesterday."

Chagrin tilted Miss Culbertson's smile as she snatched it from her. "Your father is due from a meeting. I want to make sure he has it. The door hinges will not replace themselves. Oh, I do wish he would approve a new handyman."

"I brought home a new girl. She found us at the market."

"She *found* you?" Miss Culbertson stepped around the desk. "Were you followed?"

"At first, but Wei Ming took care of that."

"Bless that man. Well, she is safe now. What is her name?"

"Dong Ju. She is very young."

"Who is verra young?" Her father filled the doorway and tipped his head to clear the threshold. "Do we have a new resident?"

Yakira greeted him with a kiss to his bearded cheek. "We do, and she is thirteen at most." Hopefully, he wouldn't ask any questions about her outing today. She could only pray he didn't learn of her exchange with Mrs. Hickman. "How was your meeting with the Chinese Consul?"

He dropped into the nearest chair and tossed his derby onto the table. "It seems Six Companies is engaging the services of a fancy east coast lawyer. The Chinese Consul, Mr. Bee, isna particularly happy about it at this juncture, but says he will abide by the Federation on behalf of China's districts. I think he's expecting more trouble in some of the other Chinatowns across the west."

"There you are." Aunt Lara strolled into the room, a twinkle in her blue eyes. "What did I miss?"

Yakira excused herself, hoping for a bit of rest before the noon meal. She found Azalea stretched across their bed, holding her brother's picture.

Azalea looked up and brushed away tears. "Do not say it, Kira."

"Do not say what?"

"Do not say, 'Why do you do this to yourself?' That is what."

"Is that the way I sound?" The bedsprings complained when Yakira plopped down beside her. A worn-smooth, years-old weight pressed on her conscience. "I'm sorry."

Azalea sniffed and rolled onto her back, setting the frame back on the bedside table. "I know you miss him too. What if he never comes back?"

Yakira shared everything with her laotong—all but her deepest feelings about Grant. He'd been so much more than a cousin. He'd been her closest friend and confidant, her only playmate before Azalea. His presence tangled with all her best memories. And just when Aunt Lara needed him most, he left.

He left *her*. Her fourteen-year-old heart had missed him so fiercely that she had cried herself to sleep every night. Pierced anew, she drew in a quivery breath.

Her finger grazed the bronze frame. She had memorized every nuance of that sixteen-year-old face—the dark brows and firm jaw, the serious indigo eyes that had probed her deepest thoughts. Would she even recognize him today? Was he tall like Aunt Lara or shorter like Uncle Erroll?

"Kira?"

She swiped at her wet cheeks and squeezed Azalea's hand. "Just reminiscing."

RECOMMENDED READING – Fiction

Do you enjoy clean and Christian Historical fiction set during America's Civil War? Here are some books I'd like to recommend:

- *A River Between Us, and* "Heroines Behind the Lines" Series by Jocelyn Green, https://jocelyngreen.com

- "Refiner's Fire" Series by Lynn Austin, https://lynnaus tin.org

- The "Belmont Mansion", "Belle Meade Plantation", and "Carnton" series by Tamera Alexander, https://tamera alexander.com

- These three novels by Tara Johnson: *Engraved on the Heart, Where Dandelions Bloom,* and *All Through the Night,* https://tarajohnsontories.com

- The "Accidental Spy" and "Ironwood Plantation" Series by Stephenia H. McGee, https://stepheniamcgee.com

- The "Rescued Hearts of the Civil War" series by Susan Pope Sloan: *Rescuing Rose, Loving Lydia,* and *Managing Millie,* https://susanpsloan.com

RECOMMENDED READING – Non-Fiction

If you are interested in further reading, I recommend these books to learn more about the Civil War in West Virginia:

- *The Civil War in West Virginia*: A Pictorial History: Cohen, Stan

- *Bullets and Steel*: The Fight for the Great Kanawha Valley, 1861-1865: Andre, Richard, Cohen, Stan, Wintz, William D.

- *The Atlas of the Civil War*: McPherson, James M.

- *Civil War in Fayette County West Virginia*: McKinney, Tim

- *The Coal River Valley in the Civil War*: West Virginia Mountains, 1861 (Civil War Series): Graham, Michael B.

- *A Banner in the Hills*: West Virginia's Statehood: George Ellis Moore

Also by
Kendy Pearson

April 2026

A story of resilience, redemption, and love, **FIRES OF INJUSTICE** blazes with the courage of those who dared to stand against the darkness of America's Forgotton War.

About the Author

When Kendy Pearson discovers a pocket of American history omitted from the schoolbooks, she enjoys digging in and turning that pocket inside out. Her novels merge fictitious characters with historical events, timelines, and personalities—and she always includes a romantic thread to warm the heart. Every story is a journey through tragedy, secrets, regrets, and God's undeniable grace. Her books have received eight literary awards to date.

Kendy is a veteran high school teacher, worship leader, novice bluegrass fiddler, and Civil War reenactment enthusiast. She enjoys public speaking and teaching writing workshops. Her favorite things include ice cream, snowy days, fireplaces, and maple trees. Kendy is the mother of four grown children and five grands. She lives in the Pacific Northwest with her sweet hubby and two amusing miniature dachshunds.

Subscribe to her newsletter to learn more about upcoming books, freebies, and insider nuggets at **kendypearson.com**.

Follow Kendy:

bookbub.com/authors/kendy-pearson
goodreads.com/kendypearson
facebook.com/kendy.pearson.author
instagram.com/kendypearson
threads.net/@kendypearson
twitter.com/kendypearson